THE SEA TURTLE'S BACK

Walter Bazley

iUniverse, Inc.
Bloomington

The Sea Turtle's Back

iUniverse books may be ordered though booksellers or by contacting:

iUniverse
1663 Liberty Drive
Bloomington, IN 47403
www.iuniverse.com
1-800-AUTHORS (1-800-288-4677)

ISBN: 978-1-4502-7458-6 (pbk)
ISBN: 978-1-4502-7549-3 (ebk)

Printed in the United States of America

iUniverse rev. date: 2/16/2012

Editorial services by Stiff Sentences Inc.
Stewart Dudley, Senior Editor
9 Gurdwara Road, Suite 101
Ottawa, Canada K2E 7X6
www.stiffsentences.com
1-613-683-4100

Cover photograph © Copyright 2010 Kenny Coots. Used with kind permission.
Design and layout by Stewart Dudley and Simon Hanington.

For my grandchildren:

Alex, Claire, Philippa,
Rachel, Rebecca, Jennifer
and Michael

Acknowledgements

My thanks go out to all my brother officers, friends and even a few relatives who have combined, whether they know it or not, to make up this book. In most cases I have changed their names, just as I have changed the names of the ships. Most of the incidents involved occurred more than sixty years ago, and if my memory is faulty in some of the details, it does not diminish my respect for those about whom I write.

Walter Bazley
Ottawa, June 2010

Prologue

Another gigantic wave reared up from the depths and advanced on the stricken ship, rolling broadside across the sea with precision and fury, like a row of ghostly houses and seeming to hesitate before engulfing the gray bulwarks and sweeping over the hatches. Thirty-thousand tons of ship shook and groaned under the onslaught but despite the awful punishment the vessel slowly righted itself, if only to prepare for the next encounter. No ship that had been fashioned by the hand of man could sustain such punishment indefinitely. It might sink in water two miles deep unless the storm abated, the engines came to life and the bow of the ship could be steered into the oncoming waves. The ship had lost power, an almost fatal condition. Indeed, a vessel a quarter her size could have ridden out the storm as long as there was power on the shafts and the Captain knew his business. Without power, the greatest ship afloat was helpless. These were the simple calculations which occupied the mind of the lone figure who was hunched on the bridge, glancing first at the chart of the North Atlantic spread out in front of him, then through the dripping windows at the turbulent sea. The great steamship *Marquess*, two years from the fanfare and ceremony of its launching, lay in mortal danger.

Paul Henriques wore the four gold stripes of a captain on his epaulettes plus the oak leaves specified by the steamship company for officers in command. He was the only person on board, the crew and passengers having been taken off by helicopter. Their departure had been a relief; he had watched from his vantage point on the wing of the bridge as they were shuttled away in groups of six by a craft that resembled nothing so much as a frail dragonfly. He had bidden them farewell and then brusquely waved off the helicopter, which had returned for one last trip. He was alone with his ship.

In only one sense he was not alone because he had a battery-powered radiotelephone that had enabled him to summon help in the early hours. Five ships had answered his call. The largest, a passenger liner, stood off a mile distant and conducted a rescue that must have thrilled the passengers who crowded her decks. The other ships were thanked and informed that their help was no longer needed. An ordinary seagoing ship cannot pick up a tow, certainly not in foul weather, and all the captains involved knew that their presence was futile. They had done their seamanly duty by answering his distress call. Their engine room telegraphs clanked to 'half ahead' and they steered away through the storm to their various destinations. Only a deep-sea tug with its specialised equipment could save *Marquess*. Paul's final contact had been to request the passenger liner to make a lengthy signal on his behalf, knowing that his words would be heard all over the northwest Atlantic. He was equidistant from Boston and Halifax, some five hundred miles from both. It was the responsibility of authorities ashore to assign a vessel, a deep-sea or 'fleet' tug as they had been known in wartime, to come out and find him at the co-ordinates of latitude and longitude that he had given in his mayday signal.

His message was brief and to the point: "Steamship *Marquess* bound Cape Town to Montreal in sinking condition without power in position," he began, adding the co-ordinates. "Passengers and crew with exception of captain transferred by helicopter to Ocean Dancer first light 23rd. Rogue wave set ship over 65 degrees loosening heavy items of cargo in number-five hold. Ocean tug only hope. Henriques. Captain."

He knew what had gone amiss. In Cape Town they had loaded massive blocks of stone at the bottom of number-five hold. These had been secured with chains, but the chains were new and could have stretched, despite their being fastened with bottle screws. He had remonstrated with the foreman and had asked for more chains stretched fore, aft and athwartships, plus baulks of timber set between the stone blocks and ship's ribs. His first officer had only half-heartedly supported him. It would have taken an additional day to arrange, he was told; the expense could not be justified. Besides, other items of mixed cargo were accumulating on the jetty, timetables would be put out and passengers would complain. As they steamed into the North Atlantic the weather had been uniformly foul and a succession of small problems had bedevilled the ship.

Realisation washed over him that he was beyond the reach of help. The loneliness of command, the isolation that a captain normally feels aboard his ship was nothing compared with his present situation. Until a few hours ago he had been surrounded by his deck officers, engineers, purser and wireless officer. His decisions, so far as the ship was concerned, were his alone, but the officers were professional seamen like himself. He could call on their opinions and listen to what they had to say; but now he did not even have the familiar comfort of their voices.

His signal passed, he went in search of something to eat. There was a small captain's galley on the upper bridge, but because electric power had been lost he had to make do with bread and a slice of corned beef. He wondered what Rebecca and the children were doing. There was a four or five hour time difference; they'd be at home. Someone from head office could have phoned her by now. Perhaps, by the time she heard, it would all be over. He drew his scarf more tightly round his neck as his mind wandered. He had to put himself in the position of whatever tug or salvage ship was sent, assuming that *Marquess* remained afloat. 'Passing the tow' at sea was tricky and there were different ways of attempting it. The cable used would weigh many tons and hauling it inboard and securing it to the capstan of *Marquess*, without power, was out of the question. Perhaps, he reasoned, he could lower the anchors to the waterline and, by holding them with the capstan brake, a salvage vessel might grapple them. *Marquess* could then be towed by her own anchor cable. Difficult, he thought, even in a calm sea, and although the storm had abated, the swells were still long and hazardous. He estimated the ship to be three feet below her Plimsoll[1] line, which represented a huge amount of water in the holds. In a word, she could sink at any moment.

Paul returned to the chart table across the sloping deck and made his entries in the ship's log. He wrote slowly and carefully, first filling out the standard entries of wind direction and force, temperature, pressure and cloud conditions. For the ship's course and speed he simply put "Lying stopped. Engine room abandoned." Under the 'Remarks' column he used all the available space, then turned to a separate sheet and continued his account. He decided that if it became obvious that *Marquess* was sinking, he would stow the logbook in a canvas bag and preserve it as best he could. There was a Carley[2] raft abaft the wheelhouse, which he might launch and use for himself. He knew that if the logbook could be saved it would be scrutinised and its wording studied by the owners in London, their lawyers and insurance agents, and by marine experts on both sides of the Atlantic. It would be prime evidence in whatever legal proceedings there might be, and probably quoted for years to come. He made it simple and factual and when he was unsure, as for instance in estimating the height of the rogue wave, he described it in layman's terms: "It appeared to be twice the height of the foremast, but not part of the storm itself. The storm was generally from the west but this wave seemed to have reared up from the south. The ship's heading, as noted elsewhere, was north. She did a corkscrew, buried her bows and rolled to starboard." Then he

---

[1] A marking on a ship's hull to indicate the submersion limit when loaded with cargo.

[2] A form of life raft used mainly aboard warships during the First and Second World Wars.

added, "There were no lookouts on the wings of the bridge and, when the ship was more or less righted, the first officer reported injuries but no fatalities." A little later he wrote, "A list of crew and passengers is attached. The purser informed me that the two passengers travelling as Mr. and Mrs. Smith were travelling under false passports."

He put his cap on the chart table, lay down on the settee and tried to compose himself. At least he would not have to watch the final agony, the roll that would never be corrected, the wave that would come up from the deep and break the ship in two. If I'm lucky, he thought, she'll go without my waking, she'll sink without groan or sigh. He had switched off the radiotelephone to spare its battery while his thoughts took flight to the pleasures and perils of other days. Some people, he knew, had a love affair with their own infancy, a nostalgia for lost innocence, but Paul's childhood was in the nature of a thousand separate memories. He rested his head on a leather cushion and braced himself against the motion of the ship. Gratefully he closed his eyes and became conscious only of the agony of his ship and the sounds of the storm.

Chapter 1 — Broxbourne

Paul was born and grew up near the village of Broxbourne, which lay in the shallow valley of the river Lea. It was twenty miles north of London, a nondescript confusion of cottages with small charm or character; a thrown-together sort of village with railway station and church, a tedious collection of houses and a main street that was too narrow even by the modest standards of the 1920s. One night a lorry missed its turn in the centre of the village and went crashing through the wall of a house, killing two of the occupants. On another occasion, when Paul was four or five years old, he watched as an airship made its stately progress overhead. The villagers gathered on the street as the vast contraption appeared in the sky and seemingly lurched forward on its journey to distant lands. The grownups said that it was going to India, where Paul had lived briefly when he was very young. It was only a few hundred feet aloft and although he could not see the passengers, he could hear the engines and make out the propellers thrashing the morning air. He wondered why they were not larger, like the sails of a windmill.

If Broxbourne could be said to have had a centre it was the post office where people took letters and parcels to be stamped and sent to their destinations. Not far away, on a corner, was the Saracen's Head with its gruesome sign showing the severed head of a dark-skinned man apparently horrified by its own detachment. During public-house hours the drinking fraternity stood with glasses in their hands and in good weather a few sat on a bench that rested against the wall of the building. The ripe aroma of malt and hops was ever present and drifted into the roadway, a gratuitous advertisement of the satisfactions to be found within. The harness shop, a little further down, was filled with saddles, bridles and shiny brasses. It had an elegant smell in keeping with the skilled workmanship of the leather trade. Each

7

employee was a craftsman in his own right, which gave the place an unspoken seniority within the village. The bakery and cake shop was a little apart, its aromas a reminder of the homeliness and monotony of English life. The butcher shop, by comparison, reeked of animals and their insides. In those days, the line had not been drawn effectively between death and dinner, the butcher had not cleaned up his act and there were forlorn creatures tethered at the back of the shop awaiting the completion of their misery. Further on, the bookshop appeared neutral, having no distinctive or compelling odours beyond dust and oldness. An open Bible was displayed in the window but, as with most shops in Broxbourne in those days, the windows were not formed of wide expanses of plate glass but ordinary panes. The ironmonger was next with his shiny collection of hammers, saws and nails.

On Saturday mornings Paul would ask his mother if he could accompany Amy and Stubbington on the weekend shopping expedition. Paul's mother did not take part in these excursions but agreed, because it got him out of the way while leaving her secure in the knowledge that he was in trustworthy hands. Stubbington would back the car out of the garage, which had been a stable until the Henriques family had purchased the house, and Amy climbed into the back seat with her shopping basket. There was a glass partition between front and rear seats so that in more opulent circumstances such confidences as might be exchanged behind would be known only to those responsible for them. The car, an Armstrong Siddeley, had a square, dependable look and a roomy interior. Stubbington said that it had been designed so that a gentleman would not be obliged to remove his top hat, and a lady in court dress would not be inconvenienced.

On Saturdays it was the custom of the village shopkeepers to clear their shelves of perishable items. Refrigeration in those days was just another long word, and it was with reason, therefore, that the well-dressed customers would be served until midday at regular prices, after which the poor were offered leftovers at much reduced rates. In later years the practice might have been called 'dumping', but in those days it was known as charity. As the clock struck midday, the poor, sometimes whole families together, would wait to be beckoned inside and costs fell to levels that had not been seen in England for more than a century. A loaf of bread went down from two and a half pence to a halfpenny, cakes and pastries to a quarter of their normal price and meat scraps would be wrapped in newspaper and pushed across the counter without the ceremony of a weigh scale. Nor were local fish, such as pike and bream, as well as rabbits, milk, cheese and vegetables allowed to go bad or collect dust over the weekend. The drama lasted no more than half an hour and, as shelves were cleared, the conscience of the village was eased. The poor took their way homeward with sacks over the men's shoulders and baskets in the hands of women and children. Meanwhile, the more affluent stood back and chatted among themselves, seeming to take comfort from the shopkeepers' largesse. From his level no higher than the counter, Paul saw Stubbington take a shilling from his pocket and nod to the shopkeeper at the same time indicating a distressed little group.

"That lot's genuine," he said to Amy. "Thirteen children. Not like some here that dresses in old clothes of a Saturday morning."

"I wish they had done that in India," Paul's father said later. "I applaud this sort of charity because the recipients pay in some measure for what they receive. Government handouts are not the same." That afternoon Paul's father asked about the family with thirteen children and was told that they lived two miles out in the country in a village so small it didn't have a name.

"There's Romany blood there somewhere," Stubbington said. "I heard tell that the man could divine for water with two sticks. Good at it, he is. He works as a labourer and has a vegetable garden."

"They'd need to grow vegetables with thirteen children," Paul's mother said.

Paul's father was a judge, not senior in his profession, but fortunate to have been appointed to a judgeship in England after his career in Bengal had been cut short. Paul's mother could not tolerate life under the hot sun of India, was always ill with sunstroke and put on such a display of dissatisfaction that they felt compelled to pack and return to England. It was a move with which few of their friends could sympathise because it flew in the face of the assumption that the standard of living was higher on the sub-continent than it would be in a comparable position at home. A few years earlier he might have practiced law in England, but in his heart he wanted to do justly, to be seen doing it and possess the authority to make his decisions count for something. To embrace only one side of a dispute left him unsatisfied, and he had perplexed his contemporaries by announcing that a lawyer who had not at some stage of his career been called upon to sit and pass judgment had sidestepped the demands of his profession. Indeed, to be retained by one litigant or another, to be recompensed according to his performance in the courtroom, could never equal, in his eyes, the higher duty of determining where justice truly lay.

As a father, Justice Henriques was not so well defined. When Paul was born he was nearly fifty and, having been married several years, he had allowed the thought of children and the good intentions that he had manifested as a young man to slip silently away. His wife was younger, he reasoned, she did no work, had few hobbies or interests outside the home so she was likely to make a suitable mother. This was one of his few faulty judgments.

Paul's mother regarded her son as an intrusion in her life, an incident for which she had been unprepared, so she had handed him over to an Indian nursemaid, later to Amy and Stubbington. Only when a visitor, relative or neighbour came calling was Paul summoned to be ritually kissed and fussed over. Her only notable accomplishment was her facility with languages, but her harsher critics would say that she made little sense in any of them. To the quiet, uncomplicated people of Broxbourne she appeared breezy and theatrical. She had chosen, together with her studious husband, to live in a house on the edge of the village, although she might have fitted more naturally into the teeming metropolis of London. On first being introduced the natural reaction was that she was an actress, or should have been. She fitted the stereotype of no particular national identity, did not walk into a room but effected an entrance, did not contribute to a conversation but blew it asunder, did not smoke a cigarette but flourished it like a work of art. The words and phrases of other languages decorated her pronouncements and left her listeners baffled. It was hard to imagine a wider disparity than that which lay between herself and her serious husband, nor was it hard to see why Paul, in his early years, gravitated toward the plain normality of Stubbington and Amy.

All human societies, except the most primitive, share the characteristic of embodying wealth and poverty between the covers of the same book, luxury on one page and squalor on the next. England in the 1920s was no exception, and the first Great War, which had ended in 1918, had brought the disparity into sharp focus. The minds of the wealthy were rooted in the pious certainties of Victorian England, and the poor had been aroused by the war and experienced horrors that Dante himself could not have visualised. Returning servicemen who clamoured for change were greeted with brave rhetoric and pious sentiment. 'Houses for Heroes', yes, but who was to build and pay for them? 'A country fit for those who won the war', but they faced soaring unemployment, which was the more frightful because the wounded, mutilated and distressed had now joined their ranks. There were men who hobbled on ill-fitting crutches, who had empty sleeves, sightless eyes, and speech that was rambling and disconnected. They stood on street corners and in public parks, and the names of those who had not returned were carved on Broxbourne's war memorial. In the main, however, Broxbourne could absorb its wounded and give some succour to its poor, but a constant reminder of the plight of others were the beggars from the metropolis of London who slept in barns and begged from house to house. They left chalk marks on doors to communicate to their brethren the amount of generosity that might be found within.

The word 'empire' was much on the lips of public figures at that time, as though it excused the country's plight. Being an unplanned empire it was often assumed that lack of organisation was a component of British genius. The trophies of empire glimmered afar for few to enjoy, but while the sun never set on the empire beyond the seas, rarely did it rise over the dark tenements at home. A baleful side effect was the shortage of men. The war had claimed a higher proportion of men than women, and a further drain was created by the need to govern a quarter of the globe. A whole generation of men disappeared into the jungles, deserts and bazaars of countries that were painted red on the map. It was said that there were three million surplus women left in the British Isles, only a few of whom, the very rich, could afford to go on world tours and shamelessly hunt down husbands in the military messes and up-country stations of empire. Their accidents and adventures, particularly in places that had few amenities to offer visitors, were a source of constant humour.

The village of Broxbourne could boast a lord of the manor, or at least an approximation of one since he was not actually a lord, but whose magnificent house, tree-studded parkland and ample fields lay about a mile distant from the Henriques house. Paul remembered him in later years as a large, imposing person of commanding appearance and impeccable dress. He was a retired military man and master of foxhounds, and these two qualifications clung like ivy to his hyphenated name, Smith-Bosanquet. The fact that he was able to trace his lineage back to the Norman Conquest gave him a ready topic of conversation by which he could command the attention of people to whom he had just been introduced. Paul's father and mother lived in a much smaller house and kept only two servants, not twelve, and the uneasy truce between the two families rested on the unspoken acceptance that one had more money and the other more brains. Invitations to dinner parties tended, as Mrs. Henriques pointed out, to be last minute affairs that came in consequence of cancellations by more socially prominent guests.

The lady of the manor was also large and imposing, which was not surprising since six, seven and eight-course meals were served regularly at her table. She dressed, perhaps reluctantly, in the pitiful fashions of the 1920s, when dresses had suddenly become short and hats were like saucepans. She did not ride to hounds but was much in evidence at the 'meet' which preceded a hunt. Such an event, which took place on the broad gravel driveway in front of the great Bosanquet house, was regulated in fine degrees of class-consciousness. The apparent confusion created by forty or fifty mounted men, some of whom wore 'pinks', or full hunting regalia of red coats and white breeches, plus a large pack of hounds, was something of a delusion. The social niceties were all the while being observed. Footmen would serve liquor in what were called stirrup cups, containing a couple of ounces of whiskey or brandy. The cup itself was made of silver or some other metal with appendages on the sides making it easy to grasp by a man on horseback. Theoretically undroppable, they did occasionally fall to the ground and had to be retrieved from the driveway or grass. On one such occasion a lady on a restive horse dropped her cup and Stubbington retrieved it. Paul noticed that when he handed it back he was not thanked; indeed, the footman snarled at him with words that Paul was unfamiliar with. What Paul did understand, even at that early age, was that the employees of a wealthy man did not necessarily possess the same amiable sentiments which were to be found in the Henriques house.

At the lower end of the social scale was the Crismaru family, thought to be Romanians, with their thirteen children. It was known in the village that the government was operating a scheme whereby indigent families with numerous children could send those whom they chose to part with either to Canada or Australia. Proponents of the scheme said that the children would be adopted by farm people who were childless or would accept additions to their own families. The children would find themselves bathed in colonial affection, leading healthy lives and enjoying opportunities they could never expect if they remained in overcrowded Britain. It was made out to be a privilege, a golden opportunity, a sort of Rhodes scholarship for the poverty stricken. Opponents of the scheme were horrified. The government, they said, had no idea where the children would go or how they would be treated. It was little better than slavery and brought nothing but discredit on the British government and the colonial authorities who had done nothing by way of preparation. Most of all, it brought contempt on the parents who were gullible and did not know enough to limit their own reproductive processes. How, in this green and happy land, could people cast off their children for adoption beyond the seas?

At all events, the Crismaru family was swept up in these crosscurrents and, with misplaced faith in the government, the parents nominated two of their offspring for the honour of being deported. It was learned that Timmy, aged seven, and Annie, six, were to be the lucky ones. Looking back in later years Paul could make no sense of what had happened, and when his parents spoke about it Paul had become saddened, refused his supper and said he wanted to be sick.

His mother, however, assembled household items and some cast-off clothes, put them in a bag and sent Stubbington to deliver them. Paul went with him but did not go inside the cottage, which was small, smoky and crowded. There was no word of thanks from Mrs. Crismaru, merely a command, "Leave them there!" Stubbington was not within earshot but in the garden helping one of the little girls as she pumped water into a wooden bucket.

"Come and meet Miss Annie," he called out to Paul. "She's going all the way to Australia to live on a farm." Little was said between Paul and Annie, whom he had met a few times before. When he saw her again sixteen years later in Australia, he remembered the dark eyes and haunted look of her youth, a look that had been far beyond tears or expressions of self-pity.

It was at Broxbourne that Paul suffered his first migraine headache, as the condition was then called. The malaise would begin during the day —never at night—with a headache that developed into chronic nausea and a feeling of approaching doom. So long as he lived he would not forget those headaches: the pain, the perspiration and weakness accompanied by waking nightmares, distorted visions and dark mental ravings. The worst of it would last two or three hours after which his recovery was slow. From the age of six they ravaged his childhood by taking one day in every ten or twenty from the calendar. They hurt his school years and showed up the medical profession for what it was. One black-suited, stiff-collared practitioner thought it was something that "the child" had picked up in India—probably from "the natives". Another confessed himself at a loss, but recommended that he not eat oranges. An Indian friend of his father had suspicions that the condition had been carried forward from a previous incarnation. If there was one crumb of consolation it was that when an attack had passed, there would be an interlude during which the feeling of doom was reversed and Paul would be overcome by lightness and joy. It was as though nature was attempting to make amends for the suffering it had caused. Paul's migraines persisted throughout his school years and came to an end only when, at the age of eighteen, he went to sea.

The memory stirred him and he turned uneasily on the leather couch aboard *Marquess*. He was astonished that storm-lashed seas, and the dangers and miseries suffered by a junior officer in those prewar years, could have cured him of the affliction that had ravaged his childhood. He recalled how sunlight and shadow would follow each other across the landscape in bewildering succession and it was probably for this reason that Paul was seen as a strange and detached child living in a world of his own creation. He had been described as a good boy, almost unnaturally so, but people insisted that he could see things that they could not see, asked questions that were unanswerable and spoke of matters that were incomprehensible to ordinary mortals. As a man he was too practical to think much of these opinions although he knew he was different. In earlier and more superstitious times he would have been claimed by the church or else burned as a heretic. But even now, aboard *Marquess*, he was not able to banish the persistent vision of his childhood: a man on a distant shore, someone he knew, beckoning him to come in from the sea.

It was the hour of nautical twilight and Paul knew he must switch on an array of battery-powered masthead lights that would be visible to other ships. It would use up electricity that might be needed later for the transmitter, but he had no alternative. As long as there was power, the lights had to be on. He stood, as darkness fell, balancing himself against the motion of the ship. The sea was still rough and *Marquess* wallowed between giant waves. He was horrified to be without engines, to have no control of the forward progress of the ship. From being her master, he was a mere appendage, a captain in name only, his ship lying athwart the storm-tossed sea. Was this to be his last adventure, he wondered, the final page in a stormy life? There were some men who sought adventure, took deliberate risks, but he was not one of them. Paul saw himself as an ordinary man performing necessary tasks. He was not an egoist or a show off, he wanted to have an uncomplicated existence, to deliver cargoes and passengers to their proper destinations, retire from the sea and someday, perhaps, end his working days ashore.

He was unsure how he had come to a life at sea, especially when railways and railway travel had been his boyhood fascination and remained among the most vivid of his childhood recollections, a mysterious world of mighty machines, metallic noise and distinctive odours. From the moment of arrival at the railway station he felt caught up in jolting movement, passing scenery and fellow travellers. Later in life he would look back on ships and trains as a golden age that air travel could never equal. The characterless aircraft is entered through a tube-like device; the passengers go in like insects to find themselves staring at the back of other seats. Even with a window nearby, the scenery does not parade past for instruction or enjoyment, it merely disappears. By comparison with surface travel, one has the impression of being cheated, of departing from one place and arriving at the next without having benefitted from the journey.

In later years, Paul would look back in wonderment at the early years of his life, culminating in his first train journey to school. Up to that point his schooling had been in the village and had given him basic literacy. The predominant influence had not been his parents or his school, but the two employees in the house to whom his upbringing had been largely delegated. There was Amy, good-hearted and uncomplicated, whose husband had been killed in the war and who had never had children of her own. The lessons she taught remained with Paul for life. She insisted that the house be tidied last thing at night and the kitchen left spotless in case the Second Coming of the Lord should occur while the house slept. Think how embarrassing it would be and how much explaining would be needed if Jesus were to walk in the door and find the house in disorder and unwashed dishes in the sink! Another of her aphorisms was even more theologically profound: If you had said Grace before a meal and asked for God's blessing on food to sustain you while you did His work, then you should have eaten up all that was on your plate. It was ill-mannered to ask God's blessing on bread and butter and then throw it out, blessings and all.

Then there was Stubbington, ten years younger, who had served overseas, risen to the rank of sergeant and been invalided out of the army. He had first met Paul's father in India. He was a quick-witted man who kept himself busy, without working excessively hard, and who possessed the uncanny ability to supplement his income at the racetrack. Paul's father knew how Stubbington spent his off-duty afternoons but had little idea of the consistency of his winnings. He thought that Stubbington was lucky and that he won a few shillings more than he lost, and that Amy came up a winner more often than could be explained by chance. What he did not know was that Stubbington would not lay a bet until he had walked through the stables exchanging innocent chitchat with the stable hands and jockeys. "I think he also talks to the horses," his father had said, and Paul wondered if the horses replied.

The word 'important' figured largely in people's minds in those days, and was applied to a person's status in life. Words and phrases attain cachet at certain periods but then fall into disuse: "the divine right of kings", "transubstantiation", "laissez-faire", "manifest destiny" have all had their day and passed into oblivion. In the 1920s, when the old structures of society were breaking up, many people clung to the idea that some people were of more value to society than others, and many were obsessed with the exactitudes of who was slightly more important than whom. Paul discovered that his father was more important than his mother, and his mother more important than himself. The King, of course, came at the very top and the bad people whom his father sent to prison were at the bottom. As a child, Paul became accustomed to the idea that he was of no importance, to which he attributed the frequency of his headaches. Oscar Wilde had written a play, *A Woman of No Importance*, but it had contained humour and subtlety and was not a condemnation of the poor or ill-educated. In those socially unforgiving days, in answer to the question, "I saw you speaking to someone, who was it?", the answer might be, "Oh, a person of no importance", which seemed to be a sad way to dispose of someone with whom one was not particularly proud to have been seen in conversation.

In his short life, Paul had seen two sides of English life. On one side the Smith-Bosanquets with their roots in the feudal system and their expectations for lives of uninterrupted pleasure. They employed a staff of rather surly servants, had a beautiful house and gardens and their excursions into central London, 20 miles distant, were undertaken in a Rolls Royce complete with chauffeur and footman. At the other extreme was the Crismaru family in a small cottage crammed with children. Wealth and poverty were not disguised, there were no gated communities, no refuge taken behind barbed-wire entanglements. The Smith-Bosanquets and the Crismarus were in plain view.

The parish church was at no distance from the Henriques house and while neither of his parents were seen in church on a regular basis, both Amy and Stubbington attended every Sunday. Amy had duties as a lay assistant, responsible for the cleanliness and repair of the choir vestments. Stubbington was a sidesman who welcomed newcomers, helped the elderly to their pews and took up the collection. His erect bearing, strong physique and friendly manner were a comfort to frail parishioners.

When Paul was ten years old, a new incumbent was appointed to the parish, the Reverend Fortescue Farqueson, Doctor of Divinity, one of whose first decisions was to leave Amy's and Stubbington's responsibilities unchanged. The Reverend's wife, Bessie, took over as organist and Paul was summoned to try out for the choir. A few verses of *All Things Bright and Beautiful* convinced Bessie that Paul could sing in tune and it was thus that his connection with the church was established. A further attraction appeared in the person of Rebecca Farqueson who, being a girl, was barred from the choir in those unforgiving days, but sat near the organ and helped her mother with the sheet music. Paul could see her from his place in the choir stalls and his eye often wandered in her direction. She was about his age, and the prettiest girl he had ever seen. After church there were always a few minutes when they could walk and talk in the churchyard, and he soon discovered that, like himself, she was an only child. She spoke of family holidays in the south of France and wondered if her daddy would now be too busy to go again.

At the age of eight Paul had gone to boarding school, known as prep school, and from then his early childhood was in the past tense. He would wear a school uniform, sleep in a dormitory and attend chapel every day of the week and twice on Sundays. He would eat school food, obey rules and be under the supervision of masters during his waking hours. He would take part in school sports—cricket, football and rugger—depending on the time of year, and would write to his parents on Sundays. He would rarely venture beyond school boundaries and would receive sixpence a week to spend in the school shop, which contained pens, pencils, erasers and postage stamps. On Saturday evenings there would be a lecture on some work-related topic such as coal mines, missions overseas or the Royal Lifeboats Institution. His locker, which was actually a desk and could not be locked, was one of twenty in the classroom and held, in its box-like interior, his exercise and other books. This monastic and disciplined existence would ensure that his mind was not diverted from his schoolwork and that distractions were few. It gave him, theoretically, the best chance to develop good habits of study and secure a solid education. Latin was compulsory; in fact all subjects were compulsory. Most significant of all, school taught him to turn his back on family life, although holidays spent at home meant that Paul, like thousands of others, had to accustom himself to a double life: school and home.

There were times when Paul tried to remember why he had chosen a sea-going life. Was it to do with the migraines he had suffered as a child, the unhelpful influence of his mother, or a genuine desire to share the adventures of Jaime Henriques, the Portuguese ancestor who achieved mythic status in Paul's mind? Paul had not been compelled into his decision. His final exams at prep school when he was 13 had been good enough to get him accepted by any public school of his choosing—Eton, Harrow, Winchester—but he chose Pangbourne, the merchant navy school. It offered an education in academic subjects combined with the special instruction relevant to the merchant navy. It was the merchant navy's answer to Dartmouth, and his migraines had diminished in number and intensity during his four years there.

Both Paul's parents had been disappointed at his choice, but for different reasons. His mother thought the merchant navy was not quite *atcha jart*, borrowing the words from Hindustani (she might have said "good class", but that would have exposed her as a snob). Gradually, however, she came to accept the idea of him becoming an officer aboard some great ocean liner, which she presumed would be the outcome of his studies. A comfortable stateroom on the upper deck, she thought, attendance in uniform at the first-class passengers' dances... yes, it might be worse. In any event, he would probably tire of the seagoing life and decide to become head of his own shipping line. Her real preference as a career for her son would have involved the study of languages followed by appointment in the diplomatic corps. That would have been something she could talk to her friends about.

Paul's father had been disappointed that his son had not chosen to pursue classics and earn his degree in law with subsequent call to the bar. He was clever enough, had a good memory and could have succeeded if he had applied himself. A law degree was a steppingstone that could lead in many directions, but what Paul's father had not understood was that his son was running away, distancing himself from his mother. Subconsciously, Paul had attributed his migraines to her, had connected the miseries of his youth with her failure to give him the understanding he needed. Most of all, Paul wanted to escape the gabble of her languages, the cacophony of meaningless sounds, the wild gesturing of non-communication. Yes, Paul was in flight from this aspect of his home life, and his father, despite his legal skill, could not counter the final argument that his forebear had been a Portuguese seaman and his choice of a career at sea was legitimised by what people chose to call the salt in his blood.

In the event, Paul discovered that Pangbourne was a school much like others in England, only with a curriculum that emphasized seamanship, navigation and geography. He passed his final exams without difficulty and found himself applying for the berth of an apprentice in a number of steamship lines. Only one, however, could offer him something immediately: a Greek company with its head office in Thessaloniki. One of their vessels lay in the port of London and was due to sail in hours. If Paul wanted to accept their offer of a berth he would have to join the ship straight away. After a brief talk with Stubbington, Paul decided to go ahead.

His parents did not accompany him to the dockside. His father was in the midst of a difficult legal case and his mother had an appointment at a London beauty salon. As usual, it was Stubbington and Amy who fulfilled the parental duty, Amy by helping him pack his sea chest and Stubby by driving him to the ship and slipping him five pounds until he received his first pay. The SS *Canopus* had little to recommend it. The name, Paul knew, was taken from a bright star in the southern heavens, well known to navigators, but the vessel was old and travel worn. It had no passenger accommodation and no doctor, and to save money the purser's duties were shared between Captain and first officer. Paul soon discovered that he would be paid as an apprentice but would in fact perform the duties of third officer. Money was tight and Paul was told that ten shillings a week would be subtracted from his pay for 'washing'. The Captain, Paul soon learned, could be expected to pocket the money and his washing would be done by no one but himself.

Stubbington behaved stoically.

"I can drive you straight home if that's what you decide, but I don't advise it," he said. "You'll soon learn the duties of third officer; from what you say you had a good training at Pangbourne. I'd say this were an opportunity, but not one I'd wish your mother to know too much about."

"I'll stay," Paul replied. "If you'll help me to get settled in…"

Paul walked around the ship with the first officer, was introduced to the others and took an immediate liking to the chief engineer, a Scot. The crew, he discovered, were Lascars, a generic term for Indians. Stubbington, meanwhile, unpacked Paul's sea chest having first cleaned the small cabin that Paul had been allocated. The first officer put his head around the door and announced that he had coat hangers at half-a-crown each. Paul noticed that Stubby had brought half a dozen coat hangers.

"No thanks," Stubbington replied cheerfully. "You can get them in Woolworth's for threepence." He whispered to Paul, "You want to watch out for these rascals."

Finally, Paul had met the Captain and signed on. The man's English was not the best and Paul was informed that he would be expected to deal with correspondence that called for replies in English.

"You ever at sea?" the Captain asked Stubbington.

"No, not me. I was army," Stubby replied, and left it at that.

"You're lucky," the engineer said to Paul a bit later, "to have a dad who drives you to the ship in his handsome car."

Chapter 2 — HMS *Artemis*

Paul spent nearly two years in the Greek registered steamer *Canopus*. He kept watches on the bridge, took star sights at dawn and dusk and a sun sight at midday so that, despite his apprentice wage, he was performing the work of a regular officer. As Captain's secretary he wrote letters and made entries in the ship's log. He got along well enough with the other officers, although he learned to be cautious about going ashore in their company. There had been an event in Alexandria where he found himself with a small group on a visit to a notorious nightclub. What he saw was bestial and upset him deeply, particularly the exploitation of a girl who bore a disturbing resemblance to Rebecca Farqueson.

Despite this incident, Paul gained grudging respect for his brother officers and even a feeling of attachment to *Canopus*. The Captain, Simopoulos, was related to someone in head office, and was probably the person who had been in mind when the word 'skinflint' had been coined. The first officer had been a whaler in the Antarctic; the second officer had forfeited a year's pay to buy his way out of a smuggling conviction in Cuba. The food aboard *Canopus* was uniformly bad, the cook being a master of disguise more than a practitioner of the culinary arts. The only sane officer, so far as Paul was concerned, was the engineer, who had his hands full with auxiliary machinery, such as pumps and generators, that was in deplorable condition and always breaking down. Nonetheless, they did manage to load and unload cargoes, usually to about half the ship's capacity, ensuring a meagre profit for the owners. With the shipping industry going through the worst of hard times and hundreds of ships laid up, the crew gave thanks to what must have been a motley collection of gods and saints. The cook's standard ingredients of rice, chilies and horsemeat meant that all aboard had something to eat, and their wages—a few shillings, rupees or drachmas—gave the crew something to send home to their families. The very harshness of their existence was a bond and if Paul had been more perceptive he might have excused their apparent seduction by the vileness of Alexandria. These men, none too well educated, had persuaded themselves that bestiality was a manly diversion, merely a bit of sophisticated entertainment.

In the mid-summer of 1939, *Canopus* shaped course for Thessaloniki and a much-needed refit. Back in port, Paul collected his pay, packed his sea chest and said his goodbyes. He persuaded Captain Simopoulos to give him a written report that detailed his duties and indicated they had been performed to the Captain's satisfaction. With this in his pocket, Paul made arrangements to travel across Europe by train. By chance, he met up with a group of university students who were making the same journey. There were many advantages to travelling in a group. Out of ten or twelve, someone was bound to speak the local language, while the luggage could be watched over and protected from theft. Joining the students, Paul found himself passing from the level of a Greek tramp steamer to the rarified atmosphere of scholarly discussion. He had crisscrossed the Mediterranean and made a voyage down the coast of Africa, but in later years it was the train trip, the conversations, the glorious scenery and the overnight stops that he would remember as the journey of a lifetime.

On arrival home there was rejoicing in the Henriques house and excitement at the rectory. Paul's father was the same as ever, studious and questioning. His mother took the view that she had been right all along and that now Paul would come to his senses. He first saw Rebecca at the rectory and did no more than kiss her cheek in the presence of her parents. Later, they walked in the churchyard, following the footsteps of other lovers over the centuries, and then embraced for long minutes. She asked him if he had been in danger and he told her of an occurrence off the coast of Africa. The Admiralty chart gave clear warning of danger at certain times of year where the Agulhas current passed over an undersea range of mountains. The surface water was disturbed like a fast flowing river over an uneven bed of rocks. Paul had reviewed the chart with Captain Simopoulus, expecting him to order a course alteration to skirt the danger, but Simopoulus thought the precaution unnecessary and mumbled something about needless fuel consumption and loss of valuable time. In the event, *Canopus* was fearfully battered and lucky to survive. Unlike a normal Atlantic storm, the waves had been short, irregular and separated by deep troughs. Internal fittings had been smashed; the cargo fared little better. Rebecca listened with tears in her eyes.

During the next few days, Paul came to a decision that would change his life. Believing war to be inevitable, he volunteered for service in the Royal Naval Reserve and was accepted on the basis of his record at Pangbourne and the letter from Captain Simopoulos. It was assumed that he possessed the basic knowledge of seamanship and navigation and that he would become proficient in Morse code and semaphore. He would have to learn flag hoists, which were different and far more complicated in the navy, and he would have to master the elements of naval gunnery. It was this latter defect in his knowledge that the navy was first to address.

His uniform had become a straightforward officer rig with eight gold buttons and the blue collar patches of a midshipman in the reserves. His brothers-in-arms in the permanent navy wore white patches, while the Volunteer Reserve wore dark red, and it was these variations in colour that created humour, if not confusion. The red collar patches, in poor light, were mistaken for those of army generals and saluted vigorously. The blue ones seemed to put the public in mind of a bus conductor or railway official, the whites appeared to be the markings of a medical orderly.

In his new uniform, Paul reported for duty at Whale Island, the navy's gunnery school near Portsmouth. In his group there were six other midshipmen plus twenty or so sub-lieutenants, the distinction between them being solely that of age. At nineteen, a midshipman automatically gained a single, gold stripe—wavy for the RNVR, who were thought to be gentlemen, and crisscrossed for those who were presumed to be professional seamen. It was a relief to discover that all his classmates, predominantly yachtsmen—and many well into their thirties—knew as little about gunnery as he did. When asked by an aggressive chief petty officer whether he had any gunnery experience, Paul replied that he had shot a few rabbits, and was relieved to discover that this was an improvement over some of the others.

One of Paul's predominant recollections was of the gunnery school's dormitory, where the beds smelled of cheap disinfectant. Paul found himself chatting with a boy his own age who had been at Eton a few weeks before. He had somehow combined his schooling with attendance in the reserves because his father owned a yacht and he had gained experience during holidays cruising the coasts of Britain. He was the only member of the group to have a medal ribbon on his uniform and he explained that it had been won at the coronation of King George VI the year before. In a white silk suit, he had acted as page to his uncle who was a non-royal duke. With the horse guards and dozens of other horses defecating vigorously outside the abbey, he had to be careful when manoeuvring his elderly relative in ducal robes across the road after the ceremony; but not, he thought, to the point where he deserved a medal for it. It was called the Coronation medal. Paul discovered later that the award of any medal bearing the image of the sovereign must be worn when the recipient is in uniform. Failure to wear such medal, or at least the ribbon that belongs to it, could lead to the accusation of being improperly dressed.

The gunnery school at Whale Island had a reputation for strict and mindless discipline and from the commanding officer downwards the staff seemed to think that they had not done a satisfactory job until they had insulted and belittled the students. However, the class in which Paul found himself did not take the treatment lying down. A lawyer and a West End actor formed the backbone of the resistance movement, and at the end of every lesson they asked questions so penetrating and acute that the instructors were left floundering.

His three weeks at Whale Island taught Paul the elements of naval gunnery and qualified him to control either a single gun, such as was mounted on an escort vessel, or the multiple guns of, say, a destroyer. Aboard an escort, the gun was mounted on a reinforced platform on the vessel's forecastle. It was manned on the left side by the gunlayer, who controlled the up-and-down movements of the barrel, and thus the range. The gun trainer occupied the right side and controlled the left-and-right movements. Two or three men behind the gun were responsible for loading. If the officer on the bridge spotted a U-boat on the surface, he would shout his orders over the rail.

"Alarm, port. Bearing red five-oh,[3] enemy U-boat. Range four-thousand yards."

Reports would then flow back from the gun.

"Gunlayer sees target."

"Trainer sees target."

"Four thousand yards," from the sailor who fine-tuned their aim by applying the corresponding elevation.

"Fire!" the officer would shout, and the gunner, taking into account the roll and pitch of the ship, pulled the trigger when the crosshairs of

[3] Fifty degrees off the port bow.

his binoculars were on target. He would observe the fall of shot while the gun was being reloaded. The cardinal rule was to correct for 'line' first. If the first shot fell to the right, the officer might order, "Left eight, shoot!" This, he knew, would be too much. But it was considered better to bracket the target than make minuscule corrections toward it. Once correct 'line' was found, the officer adjusted for range, again by making large initial corrections up or down. To make matters more difficult, ranges were constantly changing due to the movements of the ship. The gunnery officer continued to correct by observing the fall of shot until he hit the target. When a hit was scored, the next order would be, "No correction. Shoot!"

Gunnery control, in other words, demanded patience, steadiness and a good eye.

Paul and his brother gunners continued to hone their skills as they were moved up to a destroyer, which had four guns of larger caliber. High on the bridge was a turret called the 'director', which afforded a good all-around view for its occupants: the gunnery officer; the director layer, who aimed and fired all of the destroyer's guns simultaneously; and the director trainer, who controlled the left-right movement. With guns controlled from one location, the four projectiles would, in theory, hit the sea in a tight cluster. This concentration of fire made targeting more accurate and enabled the gunnery officer to make corrections to all four guns at once.

There were other short courses available to junior officers in Paul's position. Navigation and pilotage, which was held at Greenwich, would have been a waste of his time. He had received a good grounding at Pangbourne and done most of the navigating aboard *Canopus*. No signal course was offered, which Paul regretted, and the torpedo course, a friend advised him, was of little use, unless he was interested in learning how to pull torpedoes apart and tinker with their insides.

"It's enough to remember," continued the friend, "that it's not so much the officer aiming the torpedoes, as the captain aiming the ship."

Anti-submarine training left Paul most unsure of himself. He knew that asdic,[4] as it was called, involved a sound being cast into the depths and, if it struck some object, carrying back information to the operators on board. Once identified, an enemy submarine was attacked with depth charges. At the time, Paul did not realise that he had a good ear, and was able to decipher more from the sound of a return echo than most of his brother officers—a skill that was invaluable in anti-submarine warfare.

On leaving Whale Island, Paul received his first sea appointment, which turned out to be the naval equivalent of a pleasure cruise. He was appointed to the cruiser HMS *Artemis* which was to spend four months 'showing the flag' in South America. He went aboard in Portsmouth and discovered that his mess, known as the gunroom, contained three other midshipmen, and two sub-lieutenants who obviously detested each other. This, he concluded, was an ideal situation because their constant bickering gave them less time to bully the midshipmen. Paul had never ceased to wonder at the behaviour of Dartmouth officers who, on being promoted sub-lieutenant and given some small authority over those who still wore the midshipman's white collar patches, became petty tyrants and bullies overnight. He had not been accepted for Dartmouth when he had applied some years before —had not even been called for interview—so he was inclined to believe that family connections were more important than talent.

Paul's duties in *Artemis* were those of navigator's assistant, and after his time in *Canopus* this was child's play. He supervised the charts, kept them clean and free of old pencil marks, looked after the chartroom and helped the navigator by noting down the time to the nearest

---

[1] Acronym for 'Allied Submarine Detection Investigation Committee', a form of sonar.

second of the observations of morning and evening stars. For morning stars, the navigator, a lieutenant, would come up on the bridge half an hour before dawn and take note of the stars he wanted to use. Paul would write down the name of each on a separate sheet of paper. When the sky was light enough to see the horizon, although most of the lesser stars had by then become invisible, the observation would begin with the navigator using his sextant to measure the angle between star and horizon. If observed a few minutes too early the horizon would be mushy and indistinct, if too late the star disappeared in the brightening sky. Only when conditions were perfect would the navigator measure the angle and say "now", at which point Paul would take the time and note the sextant reading. Using logarithm tables, Paul would then work out the ship's position on the surface of the earth.

Artemis shaped course for Georgetown, British Guyana, after which they turned eastward, putting in at every port that had a British consul. Ranchers, businessmen and expatriate British subjects were generous and thoughtful in the type of entertainment they offered. Sightseeing parties, race meetings and field sports occupied the afternoons; dances and suppers the evenings. Sometimes expatriates would open their doors to two or three officers and arrange a visit to the theatre followed by a sumptuous meal. The ship's company numbered just over five hundred, and while fully one third were required to stay on board in case of emergency, chartered buses would pull up at the dockside and carry off three hundred others. A favourite outing would consist of a drive to a cattle ranch where they would have displays of horsemanship. There would be an amateur band, girls in costume and plenty to eat and drink. Paul had no idea how he had landed such a plum assignment, although it was assumed that strings had been pulled on his behalf.

On a southerly course between Recife and Salvador the weather was blustery but, to keep up with the prearranged schedule, the Captain kept *Artemis* steaming at 22 knots, which produced much discomfort. The ship had been laid down in 1918, the last year of World War I, and with hesitations and false starts had been finished and commissioned in 1921. In early 1939 it emerged from refit, underwent two month's trials in which the six-inch guns had been fired, the torpedoes run, engines increased to full power and the ship provisioned. Two of the midshipmen succumbed to seasickness on the passage south, which gave Paul the opportunity to volunteer for watches on the bridge. The Captain had ordered that the officer of the watch would always be assisted by a midshipman, but it made no difference which midshipman was on duty at any particular time. It was a duty that Paul particularly enjoyed, the sheer power of *Artemis* being so much more thrilling than the blundering *Canopus*.

Salvador turned out to be a dull, hot little place with not much to recommend it. A few years earlier, it had exported wild rubber from the forests of the interior, but had fallen into decline when rubber was planted at the other side of the world in Malaya and Burma. Huge fortunes had been made in those early days, and there lingered the atmosphere of ill-gotten wealth and decadence. Paul found it rather disturbing, particularly when he learned of the treatment meted out to the local natives by merchants who profited from the trade.

During the next few weeks the ship settled down to a routine of sailing to each port in turn. Official visits were paid by the Captain to dignitaries on shore, receptions were held and football matches played, although the ship's team was always beaten because they had eaten too much supper and drunk too much beer the night before. On a brilliant, white southern day two months into their cruise they sailed into the broad estuary of Rio de la Plata, with Uruguay and the great city of Montevideo to starboard and Buenos Aires ahead and to port. Of all

South American countries, Argentina had the closest and most agreeable ties with Britain. There was a large expatriate population and a friendly relationship between the two countries. Everyone in England knew about Oxo from the pampas of Argentina. They were to have been there for three days, and the high point was to be a visit to an *estancia*, or ranch, which covered half a million acres and carried untold numbers of cattle. It was a two-hour bus ride, the road was good and the scenery magnificent along the Santa Fe River.

It was Paul's turn, however, to remain aboard together with another midshipman, Featherstone. The first lieutenant, Lieutenant-Commander Young, would also be on board together with the gunnery officer, Lieutenant Holgate, and an engineer. At 1000 hours the busses arrived, led by a car for the Captain. The second in command, Commander Preston, went ashore early, having received an invitation to spend the day with his distant cousins, so Paul found himself standing on the upper deck contemplating a day of peace and quiet in a very depleted ship. He inspected the lines that held *Artemis* alongside the jetty—the headrope, which was doubled, the backspring, breastropes and sternropes—and the positioning of the fenders along the ship's side. Next he went out on the jetty and surveyed the situation from ashore. All seemed well, except for a small surge that he couldn't account for. This meant he'd have to get some men on deck and ease up the breastropes, which were taking too much strain. He returned on board, called for the petty officer of the watch and began writing midday entries in the logbook. The log was on a table near the gangway, together with the chronometer and barometer. The sea was like glass—no wind, not even 'light airs'—the sky cloudless and the temperature... his eye passed to the barometer. Why, he asked himself, had it dropped five degrees in the last hour? He knew that a fast-falling barometer indicated changing weather. A few moments later, Featherstone appeared on deck for the afternoon watch and the two of them decided to alert Lieutenant-Commander Young, who was in temporary command. Paul made a notation under the remarks column: "Barometer fallen 5 degrees in past hour", then he went aft to the wardroom and found the Lieutenant-Commander reading a newspaper. He could have sent the boatswain's mate, a young seaman who stood watch at the gangway and whose duty was to pass orders, carry messages and be generally useful, but Paul decided to go himself.

"Sir," he said, "barometer falling fast. Five or six degrees in the past hour. And there seems to be a tide surge that has affected the breastropes, so I called out the duty watch. And one other thing sir—" Young cut him off, getting to his feet. "Steward," he called out, "cancel that gin." He reached for his cap and ran up the steel ladder with Paul on his heels. On the quarterdeck, Young, Featherstone and Paul stood for ten minutes watching the barometer drop another degree. Young broke the silence.

"Featherstone, write a signal. To: Naval Officer-in-Charge on shore, begins, 'Request you provide me forecast of weather this p/m. Stop. My barometer falling. Stop. HMS *Artemis* alongside.'"

The boatswain's mate took it, saluted and ran to the bridge to find the duty signalman.

"Here you are, mate. To the tower."

The signalman looked it over and switched on his four-inch lamp, aiming it at the signal tower a mile distant, then began tapping the preliminaries to get attention.

"The bastards is all asleep," he mumbled after a minute or two. He changed to a more powerful six-inch lamp and said over his shoulder, "Tell Mr. Young I can't immediately raise them. He might have more luck on WT."[5]

---

[5] Wireless telegraph

Young had been pacing up and down by the gangway. Suddenly he sent for the duty engineer and ordered him to raise steam.

"If it turns out to have been unnecessary," he said, "I'll have wasted fuel and made work for the engine room staff. But I shall argue that on the basis of the information I have in front of me it's a reasonable decision. If this turns out to be a full gale, or whatever weather they have in this part of the world, I'll have to take *Artemis* to sea. It's safer than a cluttered harbour."

He turned to Featherstone and told him to go to the wireless office and check whether there had been any reply to his signal. Next he ordered that the ship's log be entered every twenty minutes, not at hourly intervals as in normal circumstances.

"Wind, barometer, preparations made on the upper deck, get it all down," Young said. "The worst thing at a time like this is a blank page."

At 1530, the storm struck. Wisps of cold air, like knife blades, flew across the harbour, the sky filled with clouds and the ship began to surge, gently at first but with increasing violence. The wind seemed to be coming from all directions.

"I could bring up chain cable and make the ship doubly secure," Holgate suggested.

"No, we won't do that." Young turned to Paul. "Go and ask the engineer when I can expect power on the shafts."

"Full power, another half hour," replied the engineer, wiping his hands on some cotton waste. "I could give you a bit of power now, enough to turn the props. We weren't cold at midday when we began flashing up."

Paul ran back to the gangway. "From acting chief engineer, sir. He can give you a bit of power now. Enough to work the capstan and turn the shafts. Full power by 1600."

"Very well, these are my dispositions. You, Henriques, go to the bridge and take the logbook and barometer. Featherstone, stay here and take in the gangway. Holgate, clear lower deck and have every man standing by."

A sudden cold wind had begun to blow and the harbour became a mass of foam. The sea birds, plentiful a few moments before, had vanished. Small boats were tossed about like toys. A fishing vessel of a hundred tons was careening down the harbour, dragging its anchors until one of them fouled something on the bottom. The vessel hung there thrashing from side to side like a dog on a leash.

Young had given little thought to what the Captain's reactions would be when he returned later that evening. If the precaution of raising steam had proved unnecessary and neither main engines nor capstan were needed—if, that is to say, the weather moderated—no harm would have been done. He would probably be rebuked for being over-cautious, but he'd give the captain back his ship unharmed. "If I am in temporary command," he kept telling himself, "I shall conduct myself as though it were my ship." Commander Preston was supposedly at the opera, and Young smiled at the thought that the Commander was suffering vicariously for the woes and misadventures of a hero and heroine singing their hearts out when he might have been participating in an adventure of his own.

At 1545 there was a lull in the storm and the wind fell. The men on the upper deck who had taken shelter began to emerge. Their dress was haphazard and Holgate's first thought was to send them to their messes and get them back on deck looking like real sailors. At that moment, however, the wind hit them from a new direction and with renewed fury. In minutes the harbour was thrashed with squalls and the smaller craft were torn from their moorings. They crashed into each other, rose and fell wildly in the short, steep waves and, if their mooring lines didn't part, they were dragged or capsized.

Suddenly Paul heard shouting and men were pointing. Two miles distant, a large vessel in obvious distress was careening down the channel. On present course, it might collide with *Artemis*. Young studied it for a moment and ran up to the bridge.

"All hands to stations for leaving harbour. Obey engine room telegraphs," he called down to the wheelhouse, and the sailor who stood beside them grasped the two handles and held them at 'Stand By'.

"Midships," Young ordered.

"Midships it is," replied the seaman on the wheel.

"Singled up," came word from Holgate.

From his position on the wing of the bridge, Young could see the ship's side. He ordered slow astern on the outboard engine and the sailor on the backspring eased it away very gradually as the weight of the ship came on—a tricky manoeuvre made more difficult by the fluctuating wind. Young knew he had to get the bows into the stream and using his backspring was the accepted, and indeed, only method. After a few agonising seconds, the bows began to swing, and Young ordered "half ahead" on his starboard engine and twenty degrees of rudder. The ship swung faster and he made an upward gesture with his hands, which means 'let go'. The backspring was loosened and taken off the bollard and the sailor who had been on shore leaped across the gap. The bows were now twenty, thirty degrees away from the jetty and once *Artemis* was clear he ordered half ahead on both engines with full port rudder. The out-of-control merchant vessel was a mile distant, carried by the wind and bearing down on them stern first, towing its anchors. The danger was that it would collide with *Artemis* before she could turn.

"Full ahead both engines," Young called into the voice pipe, but there was little discernible change in the throb of the engines. A huge gust rolled over the sea towards them and struck *Artemis* broadside.

Young looked over his shoulder at the merchant vessel, which by then was little more than half a mile away, and seemingly determined to crush them.

"I don't see men on the upper deck," Paul said, lowering his binoculars. "They have a stern anchor they're not using."

The engine-room telephone sounded. "Bridge," said Paul as he snatched it off its housing. He listened a moment. "Yes, we're aware of that. Give us everything you've got. We must have power." He turned to Young. "You heard that, sir. They're doing their best."

"Thank you, Midshipman. Now I'm going to point to something that I have never seen before in my life and hope never to see again. That ship was alongside. She had a dozen lines out, headropes, sternropes and everything in between. The wind strikes her broadside. What happens? Either the lines part or, in the case of the headrope, the bollard is pulled out of the jetty together with about ten tons of concrete. I see it hanging down over her bows. You may ponder the quality of the cement that was used to connect that bollard with Argentina."

At its closest point the merchant ship came within a hundred yards of *Artemis*, but was then struck by another gust and mercifully driven ashore. Heavy rain began to fall, the raindrops seemingly the size of grapes, and *Artemis*, at reduced speed, turned in the channel and steered for open water. Young conned her out with Paul at his side reading relevant information from the chart. In an hour they were at sea.

"Close all scuttles and deadlights," Young ordered. "Secure for sea." His order was repeated throughout the ship.

Holgate appeared on the bridge.

"Upper deck under control?" Young asked.

"Yessir. I haven't stowed the gear. I assume we'll be back when this has died down."

Young nodded and turned to Paul. "I think we're in the clear. Plot me a course. We'll steam for two hours in open water and hope to be back by midnight. The engineer can work up steam as we go. Switch on navigation lights."

As it was getting dark, a call came from the wireless office. "Sir, I have a distress call. I'm here by myself and don't want to leave the set. Can you send someone?"

"Oh God," Young mumbled, then ordered Featherstone to fetch the message.

"International distress call," said Featherstone, who returned a minute later and handed the message to Young.

"Mark it on the chart," he said to Paul. Young studied the chart for a moment and wrote a signal in reply. "HMS *Artemis* coming on at full speed. Expect to sight you before midnight. Indicate your difficulty."

He called the engine room. "I must have full power," he said. "*Full power*."

Later, Paul's gunroom friends told him the story of their day ashore.

After a long afternoon of entertainment—horsemanship, music, dancing and singing—the ship's crew sat down to a meal of beef that had been roasting on spits for three days, plus sweet potatoes cooked in the local manner in hot sand, with salads, cream cakes and black coffee. But even as they seated themselves Captain Remington expressed concern at an apparent change in the weather.

"It's unusual," admitted his host, "but I don't think it's anything to be worried about."

Darkness was falling when Remington was called to an old-fashioned telephone and found himself speaking with the resident naval officer, Buenos Aires.

"Your ship," he was told, "has put to sea. There's a storm here and the harbour's a mess. Ships loose and out of control. You better get back. Your second-in-command is with me."

"My God. When did she sail?"

"Sixteen hundred or thereabouts... Went out slowly with no pilot. Last I saw, she was in safe water."

It took only a few minutes for the ship's company to be rounded up, counted and loaded aboard the buses, for the Captain and officers to thank their hosts for such memorable entertainment and finally for the bus drivers to be persuaded to drive in the darkness. Ten miles from the ranch the rain started, gently at first, then more heavily, which slowed down the little convoy and taxed the skill of the drivers on the wet road. It was ten o'clock when the Captain's car came to an abrupt stop. Through the rain, the headlights revealed a wall of mud and rocks that blocked the road. It was a mudslide for which the region was notorious.

"Officers gather round," Captain Remington called out, and sixteen officers spilled from the front seats of the buses and gathered in the headlights. Like the rest of the shore party, all were in white uniforms. There was not a raincoat among them.

"Navigator, how far to Buenos Aires?"

"Twenty miles, sir."

"Very well, we'll stay in the vehicles till daylight, then scramble across and march the rest of the way."

"May I suggest," said the engineer commander, "when we see this in daylight we may be able to clear a path. We have three hundred men..."

Meanwhile the lights had attracted the attention of some local people. In broken English they explained that the slide had covered their houses and some residents were thought to be buried.

"Leaves us no choice," Remington said. "All hands turn to."

During the hours that followed Captain Remington was tested in his powers of leadership and ingenuity as he had not been in many years of naval service. He had been a captain for ten years and had been in the navy for thirty. He had been informed by the Admiralty that his only chance of reaching flag rank depended on whether there would be another war, without which *Artemis* would be his final command. He had not wanted to be sent on this venture to South America, being a seaman of the old school with a deep love of his profession and its demands, but not socially inclined. Now he appointed the engineer to take charge of digging operations with the object of pushing tons of rubble from the roadway and lifting yet more mud and stones from the houses that had borne the brunt of the slide. He told the paymaster to find dry straw, tie it in bundles and, with the help of petrol from the busses' tanks, make torches that would give some light. The two sub-lieutenants were ordered to clamber round the whole area and estimate the extent of the task. Two lieutenants, navigation and torpedo, were told to make their way across the rubble and proceed to the city at their best speed. They were to stop at any police or National Guard post and attempt to telephone. If they could borrow, hire or steal a motor vehicle they would do so. Arrived in the city, they would alert the civil authorities and report to the Naval Officer-in-Charge.

Three hundred crewmembers, ashore with the object of enjoying themselves, worked throughout the night; on hands and knees they clawed to clear stones and mud as best they could. They were wet, tired and filthy as they stumbled and gasped in the dark, but somehow they made progress. By first light they had cleared a single lane of roadway and rescued a dozen people from the rubble of their houses. Wearily they climbed back aboard the buses and dozed in their seats. Captain Remington handed over his car to the surgeon-lieutenant as an ambulance and took a seat at the front of the leading bus. It was midday by the time they drew up at the quayside that they had left in such good spirits the day before. The Captain stood staring at the harbour. Merchantmen had run aground and there was a tangle of smaller ships, but no sign of *Artemis*. He could do nothing beyond stand and try to ignore the filthy uniforms of his men.

Commander Preston approached, his uniform noticeably clean.

"My dear Preston," said the engineer commander. "How did you enjoy the opera?"

Lieutenant-Commander Young and the men who had remained aboard *Artemis* also spent the night on an errand of mercy. The distress call they had picked up was identified as having been sent by the *Santos Trinidad*, a ferry that carried passengers from Buenos Aires to communities along the river. According to the Buenos Aires signal tower, the ferry had a capacity of four hundred passengers but often exceeded that number. It was now somewhere south of Sacramento. Paul marked its supposed position on the chart, then laid off a course almost due east. With full power restored, *Artemis* raced over the dark sea and an hour later the ferry was sighted. When half a mile distant, Young reduced speed, went astern on the engines and noted how deep the ferry lay in the water. The sea had moderated but, even so, he guessed the ship might sink at any moment.

"I wonder how long I have," he said when *Artemis* and the *Santos Trinidad* were about a ship's length apart.

"Get out every fender you've got," he shouted through a megaphone to the men on the upper deck. Two powerful Aldis lights were trained on the ferry from the bridge of *Artemis*. On the ferry's deck, passengers and crew were fighting among themselves, screaming and surging about as the ferry, despite its broad beam, rolled in the swell. Young had already made up his mind that stopping *Artemis* and lowering his own boats was out of the question. It would take hours to transfer all the passengers; meanwhile, the ferry would sink. It had to be the slam-bang approach and risk everything on a single attempt. He ordered Holgate to unlace the torpedo guardrails on the upper deck so that survivors could come over at that point.

"There must be a thousand of them," said Young as he gave the helm and engine orders to bring *Artemis* alongside. He thrust the megaphone into Paul's hand and said, "Do your best to settle them down. Tell them to step across in an orderly manner."

Paul took the megaphone, but his commands were lost in the elementary scream of humanity. He turned to Young. "You have about six feet, sir. Holgate is on the torpedo tubes…"

The rest was drowned out as the two ships scraped together and a wall of people jumped, fell or were pushed aboard *Artemis*. Paul saw an elderly man fall between the ships and get caught on a fender. As the two ships came together, the man was pressed to the thickness of a doormat. Two hundred passengers came across in the first wave, then stood embracing, crying and babbling, which prevented those behind from getting aboard.

"Move back! Go to the other side of the ship!" Paul shouted. "Move! Don't stand there! Move!"

A new noise was now adding to the cacophony of sound. The whole starboard wing of *Artemis'* bridge was being rammed against the ferry with a scream of twisting metal. The two seaboats on the starboard side, turned in as far as possible, were demolished. And still the survivors from the ferry jumped, fell, were carried or thrown from the ferry to *Artemis*. One hesitant passenger was decapitated as his head was caught between the ferry's deck going down and *Artemis* lifting up.

It took about five minutes to complete the transfer. Holgate ran up to the bridge but words died in his mouth. The ferry was sinking. It rolled, slowly at first, and the tall funnels and even taller masts crashed on *Artemis* and sent debris across her deck.

Paul picked himself up from a corner of the bridge where he had taken refuge.

"That was close," said Young as he retrieved his cap and got to his feet.

"Henriques, find Holgate and tell him to make an assessment of damage. I want to know if any of our fellows—"

"I'm here," said Holgate, who had chosen the far side of the bridge when he saw the ferry make its final roll.

An old-fashioned ventilator shaft had come down on the flag deck and blocked access to the bridge. Crewmembers lifted it to the ship's side and tossed it overboard.

"Wheelhouse, you alright?" Young called down the voice pipe.

"Yessir."

"Slow ahead both engines. All fenders in," Young ordered. "Lookouts, search the sea for swimmers." The ferry had sunk almost beneath *Artemis*, and her lights could be seen glowing green as she went down. An oil slick was spreading over the sea.

When they were clear, Young dictated a signal. "To Captain Remington, care of Naval Officer-in-Charge, Buenos Aires, from Lieutenant-Commander Young. Ferry *Santos Trinidad* sunk. Stop. Approximately 800 survivors aboard *Artemis*. I report with regret that *Artemis* has suffered damage to upper deck although seaworthy. Stop. It is being reported to me that looting is taking place which is difficult to control with depleted crew. Stop. Request shore authorities be prepared to search all survivors including women. Stop. My ETA 1400. Twelfth." He assumed that Captain Remington would receive it from the shore authorities.

Three hours later, at the harbour entrance, a pilot boat was waiting to guide *Artemis* to its berth where the shore party and police were mustered. Although the men who had remained aboard *Artemis* had no idea of the adventures of those on shore, there was no hint of mockery. Later, when the mud had been washed off, members of the shore party were found to be cut, bruised and horribly scraped. Their hands and knees, in particular, were in terrible condition.

The scene that remained fixed in Paul's mind was the quayside as *Artemis* approached. The shore party were bedraggled and filthy, some bleeding, others limping, all soaked by the rain. The Captain and a dozen officers stood in a group together, but appeared little better. Paul realised they would have seen one of the ferry's tall, dirty funnels lying grotesquely across *Artemis'* torpedo tubes. The cruiser's whole starboard side, from 'B' gun almost to the quarterdeck, was a shambles of torn metal. Ferry survivors crowded the upper deck of *Artemis*, but by this time were mercifully silent. Only one gangplank was put out so that they could be moved in single file to a building where they were searched by police.

It took two days for normality to return, for reports to be written and for the damage to be assessed. Two looters had been shot; others had been beaten by seamen who found them stealing their possessions. A stoker caught a man stealing his razor, an old-fashioned straight razor decoratively engraved with his name. When the thief attempted to slash him with his own razor, the stoker and a shipmate exacted full retribution. Theft on board ship was among the most serious of crimes, and the men of HMS *Artemis* were steeped in a tradition that demanded punishment. On shore, the women were led screaming to a shed and forcibly undressed by local police. One young woman was found to be wearing five sets of underclothing stolen from the petty officer's mess.

The damage to *Artemis* was serious, the starboard wing of the bridge being mangled and two seaboats demolished. The flag locker was gone, two Aldis lights missing and the navigation light swept away. She was still seaworthy, however, and the Admiralty ordered an immediate return to Portsmouth.

The incident as a whole received little attention. Locally, the politicians, ship owners and city authorities were blaming each other for the appalling condition of the ferry, the gross overcrowding and the absence of any control by officers and crew. There had not been a lifeboat drill for years and it was noted that the ropes that lowered the lifeboats, known to seamen as the 'falls', were so rotten they parted when the weight of the boats came on them. It was the davits, leaning over the ship's side, that had done the most damage to *Artemis*. Young estimated that some twenty passengers had been lost, but there was no record of how many had been on board at the outset, nor how many went down unseen in the ferry. The only thing known for sure was that 821 went ashore from *Artemis*.

Newspapers at home ignored the incident. War clouds were gathering in Europe and there were things of more importance than the fact that a navy ship had rescued survivors from an overcrowded ferry while other sailors were clawing their way through a mudslide. Captain Remington in *Artemis*, and the navy representative on shore were taciturn men and inclined to understatement. The looters with bullet holes, broken bones and bloody faces were accepted by the local authorities as a price which had to be paid.

The story did, of course, find its way through the messdecks of the navy. It was thought to be the only incident, on or off the record, where a Royal Navy ship had two totally different missions of mercy operating at one and the same time. While half the ship's company were struggling with their bare hands to clear debris and free victims on a mountain road, the other half were rescuing the survivors of a grossly overloaded ferry.

That evening Paul was again on duty at the gangway. The survivors had gone, but the upper deck was in shambles. He and Lieutenant Holgate had been detailed for the last dog watch because they were the only ones not plastered in mud. A car drove down the jetty and stopped at the gangway. A uniformed driver got out and handed Paul an envelope from the owner of the ranch. Remington read it to the whole ship's company on Sunday morning parade before sailing for home.

"Dear Captain: My driver has told me of your adventures on the road last night. I want to thank you from the bottom of my heart..." It continued in language that deeply touched the crew. As the Captain was not slow to point out, that letter was the only expression of thanks the ship ever received.

When Paul looked back at his brief service in *Artemis*, he could not be other than amazed at how much had happened. The worst moment was when the ferry sank with its tall funnels and masts crashing down on the upper deck of *Artemis*. It had been about twenty years old, possibly three hundred feet in length and stoutly constructed. It was low in the water and listing when *Artemis* came alongside, and it was probably the damage down its side that caused it to take in yet more water and sink. It had a lower deck for vehicles but these were awash when *Artemis* came on the scene. Most surprising was the fact that Paul had not been able to identify the Captain, officers or crew on the bridge, which spanned the full width of the ferry. There may have been a hundred or more people clinging to the bridge, but Paul could not recognise anyone who seemed to be in charge.

Apart from an old ferry, poorly maintained, grossly overloaded and without the authority of competent officers, what else, Paul asked himself, had contributed to the tragedy of lives lost aboard the *Santos Trinidad?* The answer seemed to lie in the country as a whole, its corrupt government and non-functioning public service, which allowed ferry boats to go to sea overloaded and in a deplorable state of repair. It lay in the people themselves, poor and ill-educated, a church that could not distinguish right from wrong, and the failure of a so-called people's government to spread the country's wealth. It was said that the economy of Argentina was the sixth largest in the world, but no one would have guessed it if they had witnessed the wholesale theft of clothing and personal possessions from those who had just saved their lives.

Chapter 3 — Iceland Trawler *Badger*

Paul's first wartime appointment was to HMS *Badger*, an Iceland trawler that was nearing completion on the Clyde. The term 'Iceland trawler' was applied loosely to this class of ship, indicating that it was capable of sailing in northern waters in all but the worst weather conditions. *Badger* had been requisitioned from the builders in early August 1939, and all available space below decks that might have held fish had been converted to additional fuel tanks, living quarters and an ammunition magazine. A four-inch gun was mounted forward on a strengthened platform, depth-charge racks aft. It had a displacement of 1,200 tons, a top speed of 18 knots and good sea-keeping qualities. For escorting coastal convoys it could never equal the speed and firepower of the Hunt-class destroyers, which were purpose-built for coastal work, but it would be more than welcome to the commodore of a wartime coastal convoy because it possessed three essentials: asdic to detect U-boats, depth charges to attack them and a four-inch gun in case of surface action.

When Paul stepped on board he was wearing the newly acquired gold stripes of a reserve sub-lieutenant. Each stripe was made up of two criss-crossed strips of gold lace, with a curl at the centre that gave it a rather dashing, exotic appearance. During a brief leave at Broxbourne he was mistaken for a wireless officer, but on the Clyde in western Scotland there were no such delusions, the reserves and their uniforms being well known there. As Paul rapidly discovered, no one was called 'Mac' in *Badger*, because almost everyone was Mac, the entire crew being from the west of Scotland. The full complement of officers was five and the rest of the crew ninety. They were accommodated temporarily in a small hotel a short distance from the dockside, the officers in a nearby house. They were to go aboard when the dockyard workers were finished and the engineer had satisfied himself that there was fresh water, electrical power and adequate cooking facilities. The first few days aboard would be spent provisioning with munitions, food rations and naval stores.

The flotilla to which *Badger* belonged was based in the Mersey and consisted of four ships—*Squirrel, Badger, Porcupine* and *Vixen*—with the promise that *Otter* would join later. They had been built in different shipyards and were not identical in appearance or capabilities. Their speed and armament, however, was sufficiently similar to allow them to work together as a flotilla. Their task was to guide convoys into the Irish Sea and get them into formation for the Atlantic crossing.

The simplest and most obvious way to organise a convoy would have been a long line of ships, as the battleships had sailed during the First World War. A line of battle enabled every ship to fire its broadsides at the enemy; indeed, the battle of Jutland had been fought on this principle. But for merchant ships whose enemy was the U-boat, a line would have been disastrous. A convoy of fifty or one hundred ships cannot be defended in line; a single U-boat in the right position had only to launch a torpedo at each ship as it passed. The way to protect a convoy was for the ships to be formed into a well concentrated square. The convoys that assembled in the Mersey often consisted of fifty or sixty ships in four lines, the lines being a thousand yards apart. Vessels from as far south as Milford Haven and as far north as the Clyde would join, either in the Irish Sea or to the north of Ireland, and all would be allocated their positions in the square according to a master plan. The organisation of the convoys was one of the successes of the Second World War, although in the early months not all were agreed that convoys were necessary. Many thought they had a better chance if they sailed alone and added a bit of zig-zag on their own initiative. Some captains believed that a concentration of ships would attract the U-boats, but the number of single ships sunk in the early weeks of the war showed how mistaken was this belief.

Where convoys were concerned, however, much could go wrong. Some of the older ships had difficulty maintaining a constant speed because they had no proper revolution counters, and the captains could not order precise increases or decreases of revolutions. In such cases, for a ship to keep its assigned place, orders from the bridge to the engine room had to be shouted down a voice pipe: "Eh, Bill, can ye go a bit faster?" Nor were captains pleased to be jostled into formation by escort-vessel commanding officers who were often much younger than they, and wore half the number of gold stripes on their uniforms. When the conditions of the Irish Sea were taken into account—sudden storms, tides, darkness—and the fact that ships were blacked out at sea, the convoy system worldwide, and the Atlantic convoys in particular, were a remarkable achievement.

It was in these difficult conditions that Paul served his wartime apprenticeship. He learned much from his captain, Lieutenant Laidlaw, a reservist with ten years experience as a fishing captain. The first lieutenant was a schoolmaster, Percival, who had skippered racing yachts. The ship's navigator, Sub-Lieutenant Forsyth-Thompson, had not been to sea until the war, but his mathematical knowledge, which had been intended to qualify him for a career in the insurance business, was now put to use in the chartroom. He discovered that wind, sea, tide and careless steering took the accuracy out of his most meticulous calculations. On one occasion, when the coast of Ireland was not where he thought it should have been and his pad was covered with jottings, the captain suggested that a good guess might be better than a bad calculation. A second sub-lieutenant, Ross, was the son of an agricultural scientist and cattle breeder in the border country between England and Scotland, and with him Paul shared a small cabin. Ross was a cheerful young man and a quick learner. The engineer was a failed Church of Scotland preacher. His brother officers made a dozen guesses as to why he faltered in his churchly duties, and all were probably right. However, he came from a family of engineers and had been well versed in steam engines before his meandering steps took him toward and then away from the pulpit.

Looking back on his time in *Badger*, Paul was amazed at what a hardworking and happy little ship it had been. Where the crew was concerned, the captain had noted that they were decent boys, all volunteers who knew how to behave themselves. "We don't need a defaulter's book because there won't be any defaulters," the captain had said. By the time Paul was transferred two years later, not a single man had been brought before the captain for misconduct. Minor instances of indiscipline were dealt with on the spot by the first lieutenant.

Forsyth-Thompson, the navigator, was one of those officers whose abilities were the object of admiration; he was out of his element at sea, but always the centre of wardroom conversation.

"When I was at university a couple of years ago," he said, "we had a fellow who could make the most difficult mathematical calculations in his head. What no one can understand is how the human mind prepared itself for mathematics; what kind of apprenticeship we received during our pre-human development. Put it like this: for a few thousand years, when my wife was picking mushrooms and I was making stone axes, and we were both wearing rather smelly animal skins, how did mathematics gain a foothold in the human brain?"

It occurred to Paul as he listened to the conversation in *Badger's* wardroom that all these reservists had lives outside the navy so that their ideas were more interesting than those of the junior officers in *Artemis*. The regular navy personnel trained in Dartmouth, Paul concluded, had been taught the standard lessons but their ideas did not range widely. The two sub-lieutenants in *Artemis* would have been too busy asserting their authority to have had any time for an interesting discussion.

Paul's duties were anti-submarine, in addition to which he controlled the four-inch gun and took his turn as officer of the watch. As a competent navigator Paul was also able to offer some advice to Forsyth-Thompson. "Make the stars your friends," he said. "Navigators spend too long trying to identify which star is which before they pick up their sextants. There are only about sixty first-magnitude stars of interest to a navigator and with a bit of study you can discover where they are in relation to each other. Learn them by heart, and you'll never regret the time spent. And another thing, the stars have different colours: Vega is ice-blue, Arcturus red, Spica is orange. Your eye will learn to distinguish them after a bit of practice." Paul himself would have been appointed navigator but for the fact that he had been at Whale Island and Laidlaw wanted him in charge of the gun.

When *Badger* dry-docked to have its boilers cleaned, its hull scraped to clear the marine growth, and other repairs carried out—a process that took place at six-month intervals—the ship's company was sent home on leave. Railway passes were issued from the ship's office, which was run by Sub-Lieutenant Ross. From being a hive of crowded activity, *Badger* became suddenly silent, waiting for an invasion of men in civilian clothes. A ship that had passed through dockyard hands was always dirty, but at least it was in better working order. Meanwhile, the sailors, with their kitbags and hammocks, were heading in various directions in overcrowded wartime trains. On arrival home, their mothers, wives and sisters would go to work to wash, darn, patch and repair their navy 'blues'. The navy was not generous in the issue of new uniforms, and 'making do' was one of many wartime virtues.

Paul noticed the changes that were taking place in English life. As the year 1940 passed into history, France lay at the feet of the German hordes and air battles were raging over southern England. The country prepared for invasion and there developed an intensity of purpose that was not ill-suited to the English character. Gas masks appeared over the shoulders of people in uniform, barrage balloons decorated the skyline to protect bridges, factories and military targets. A new species of uniformed official appeared on the streets, the air raid warden, and the wailing air raid sirens and crump of bombs became the signature tune of south and central England. With total blackout in force, the English night became darker than it had been since the Middle Ages. A carelessly drawn curtain would attract accusations, an out-of-control bonfire could provoke the neighbours to gather and put it out. Ration books appeared in women's handbags, cars disappeared from the streets as petrol rationing took hold, and bicycles were suddenly worth their weight in scarce commodities. New bicycles were no longer being made, and a good prewar model was more valuable than a car. Young women waited impatiently for the chance to join one of the women's services or, less glamorously, to work in a munitions factory; old women knitted or made things out of scraps of material. Hundred-year-old bowling greens were ploughed up for vegetables while noble houses were taken over by the authorities for the duration of the war. Posters appeared on walls to remind Englishmen that 'Careless Talk Costs Lives', and to inquire of them 'Is Your Journey Really Necessary?' Secrecy became a fine art and the story was told of a senior civil servant who received a knighthood for exceptional service, but his wife, who had profited by becoming 'lady', had not the faintest idea what her husband had done.

The Henriques' house was soon deprived of the services of Stubbington, whose mechanical abilities qualified him as foreman in an aircraft factory. The house, which was not large, had to make room for a married couple who came shrouded in secrecy to perform 'work of national importance'. In the village, Mrs. Henriques undertook unpaid war work, and one of her duties was to collect old clothes and household articles and send them for distribution to those who had been bombed in the east end of London. Mr. Justice Henriques continued his duties on the bench, his caseload becoming heavier, but he also dug up his flower garden and planted vegetables. Before leaving, Stubbington had built a hen house that sheltered a dozen Rhode Island Reds. Amy collected the eggs and Mrs. Henriques did the cooking, which was frustrating because the minor ingredients she wanted were never available. Amy, with her rural skills called into service, added to the larder by collecting nuts, berries and mushrooms from round about.

Forming in Paul's mind was the idea that in wartime people tended to show their true colours, there being three basic types. First, those for whom the challenges and difficulties, the minor privations and annoyances were too much to bear. These were the people who were settled in their lives and could not abide disruption. They complained incessantly, recalled the old days with nostalgia and held little hope for the future. "How can she go on complaining," someone would ask of this kind of person, "whining about the food rations, when her neighbour has just lost her son in the western desert?" The worst of them profited from the war in small and contemptible ways. A man who was supposed to be helping Mrs. Henriques to distribute old clothes was in fact selling them on the side.

A second group seemed unmoved by events, accepting what came and changing little. It was not that they didn't care, merely that they were staunch and yeomanly, borne along by the stream of events, not buffeted by the petty swirls and eddies that consumed the attention of weaker individuals. "How can he be so calm?" people asked of Mr. Justice Henriques. "Having to share his house with others, losing his car and driver, and he in the red robes of a judge."

The third group was made up of the young who would inherit the postwar world. They realised, many of them, that the war was an unparalleled experience and that they were seeing farther and learning more than they could have done in peacetime. They found new companionship, wrestled with faith and ideals and were harsh in their condemnation of the older generation whose political negligence had landed the country where it was. Paul was a fully paid-up member of this fraternity, as were his friends in the wardroom of *Badger*. Indeed, the entire ship's company of *Badger* was probably of the same mind. How could the Admiralty, the Parliament in Westminster, the country as a whole, neglect the navy as it had between the wars? The dictators of Europe had given ample warning, Mussolini in 1935 making fools of the United Nations, Franco's war in Spain two years later and Hitler's outrages from then on—behaviour blatant and undisguised. Yet the Admiralty actually scrapped some seaworthy cruisers and allowed itself to become woefully short of destroyers.

"Don't speak about lack of money," said Forsyth-Thompson. "The trouble lay in the weakness of our will, not the weakness of the pound. Money could have been found."

"Do you realise," Laidlaw asked, "that four destroyers cost a million pounds? For twenty million we could have had a fleet of eighty vessels which would have secured the North Atlantic against U-boats. Have we asked ourselves what the North Atlantic is costing in sunken ships and lost cargoes? A single merchant vessel, fully laden with munitions of war, might be worth five million. We're losing ships every month and it's getting worse. There's a story going round that we're going to take over some old American destroyers. They have four funnels and look like something from the turn of the century." He paused. "In honesty, our politicians have a lot to answer for."

Paul rarely spoke on these occasions, but he felt strongly on the subject of the respect that the older generation felt was owed to them by the younger.

"They send us to war with weapons that are not adequate to the task," he said. "How can they expect us to honour them, which is what we've been taught. 'Honour thy father and mother so thy days may be long...' That's what it says, but the people who make the decisions send us off in vessels like *Badger*, which are only half good enough. We all feel affection for our ship, but this is a fishing boat. I think we deserve a bloody good destroyer."

During one of Paul's brief home leaves, or 'boiler-cleaning leaves' as they were called, Mrs. Henriques noticed that her son was spending a lot of time with Rebecca, the vicar's daughter.

"Oh well," she said to her husband, "we can be sure she's well behaved."

It was a statement that did not live up to full expectation. Rebecca, at eighteen, taught some of the younger children at the village school and helped her mother around the rectory. She was mature for her age, read a good deal and compensated for Paul's shyness. She asked if she could accompany him when he went into the fields to snare rabbits and had the foresight to put an old blanket in his knapsack so they could sit and eat a sandwich under the trees. Paul found that her enthusiasm was infectious and noted that she seemed to enjoy his caresses as much as he enjoyed hers. She called him her hero, which he rather liked, and he was soon helping himself to her hospitality.

"I don't think we should go any further," he said, taking some of her brown hair out of his mouth. "I read somewhere that babies can be a bit of a problem."

"I came armed," she replied. "Boots, the chemist, had them in stock. I'll get you set up in no time." She rummaged in the knapsack.

They stood up, undressed each other and embraced for long minutes. Paul had never realised that anything could be as beautiful as the hour that followed. Sadly, the following day he took the train to Liverpool, but his new-found passion was very much the focus of his mind. From Lime Street station he took a taxi and found a quartermaster at the gangway, Able Seaman McLean.

"Sir, Mr. Henriques. Captain wants you."

"Oh, very well. Thank you. I'll pay for the taxi and then perhaps you can get my kit down to my cabin. Uniform box, kit bag and this." He handed him his overnight bag. "Where's the captain?"

"Chart room, sir. And there's others with him."

"Strange," Paul was saying to himself as he ran up the steel ladder, knocked and entered the chart room. There he found the Port Commander, whom he knew, and a lieutenant-commander who was introduced as a security officer, plus Laidlaw, the captain.

"We have a problem," said the Port Commander. "Within the last hour a fishing boat has entered harbour with a mine fouled in its fishing gear. The skipper seems to have taken leave of his senses. He hoisted it clear of the water, anchored in the channel and abandoned his vessel."

"It must be a moored mine," Paul stated the obvious.

"Yes. The Hun was over a couple of nights ago dropping mines from low-flying aircraft. Our minesweepers cleared a channel so we could get the convoy to sea. As you say, it's a moored mine." The commander pulled tobacco and pipe from his pocket. "The only thing is for an officer to go and render it harmless. We don't have any mine experts in Liverpool. Mines," he added, "are usually dealt with by torpedo specialists."

"Well then," said Paul, "I'll volunteer to pull up his anchor, tow him to sea and shoot big holes in it with my four-inch gun. Good practice for the gun crew."

"Unfortunately," said the Port Commander in measured tones, "the Admiralty has informed us that they want this mine intact. It has to be examined."

"Your job," Laidlaw seemed to be mimicking the Commander's measured tones, "is to lower the sea boat, round up a couple of lads and have them take you out to the..." he hesitated, "*Lady Sue*. You must lift out the firing mechanism and then, and only then, do we send a tugboat and bring *Lady Sue* alongside."

"In other words," said the security officer rather piously, "the whole situation can be turned to our advantage if we get the mine in one piece."

Paul was on the verge of asking, "Why me?" but stopped when he realised that he knew what the answer would be. "You're here, and you're as expendable as anyone else."

"Aye aye, sir. Render it harmless," he said and left the chartroom.

Paul went to his cabin, opened his kitbag and pulled out some seagoing clothes. An old pair of blue trousers, jersey and sea boots would do. This whole thing had the stench of NKG about it—No Known Grave. He knew nothing about German sea mines except that they were booby-trapped in every conceivable way with the object of frustrating exactly what he was about to do. The Germans knew their mines would sometimes fall into the hands of the Allies, so they attempted, in their unpleasant Germanic way, to make it impossible to disassemble a mine without exploding it the moment wrench, screwdriver or cutting device was used. Six hundred pounds of high explosive would go up, enough to sink a battleship.

"Render it harmless," he repeated to himself.

He went on deck and found the dinghy alongside. The Leading Seaman was ready with a set of tools to which lanyards had been attached. The loop of a lanyard would go round his neck or, if he preferred, round his wrist, so that tools couldn't fall into the sea. He climbed down to the sternsheets and the Leading Seaman took the tiller and told the bowman to cast off. The water was choppy with the tide moving, but the motorboat covered the distance in a few minutes.

Lady Sue was riding at anchor. She was half the size of *Badger*, built of wood and much past her prime. The mine looked enormous as it hung over the sea from the after davit, which would normally be used to haul in the nets and deposit fish on deck. Paul told the Leading Seaman to go back to *Badger* and return in an hour. Next he rummaged around the galley to find a sharp knife. There was a good deal of motion on the *Lady Sue*, so the mine, having been hoisted clear of the after taffrail, swung wildly. If broken, the horns of the mine would set it off. They pointed downwards, which indicated to Paul that the access plate was on the lower half of the device. He clambered up and began cutting away the tangle of nets. Not too much, he told himself, or the whole thing will drop into the sea, taking me with it. Within a few minutes, the motion of the mine reduced Paul to a state of vertigo. He retched, and tears coursed down his cheeks. His head pounded and his insides felt like water.

"Come on, Henriques," he heard himself saying, "you can do it."

He found the access plate a moment later and cut the net round it. Now what? The cold hand of despair clutched at him and he felt himself passing out as mists of unconsciousness floated before his eyes. Somehow he was able to reach the deck where he collapsed on the wet metal and for a moment was engulfed in silence. He had the sensation of being underwater, then something firm came beneath him—the deck of the *Lady Sue*? Opening his eyes he found himself on hands and knees, but his mind had cleared enough to remind him of his task. When he resumed a few minutes later he felt his strength replenished, but he had the gray, ashen countenance of a man who had exhausted his options. The access plate was attached by six bolts and, with infinite care, he grasped the wrench and went to work. The mine could not have been long in the water, because there was no marine growth and the bolts came away without difficulty. He lifted out the access plate and threw it on deck. Inside there were wires of various colours that were attached to some sort of mechanism. Was that what they call the pistol, he wondered, which makes the bloody thing go off? By this time he really didn't care. He took the cutters and began to work his way through the coloured wires. Finally he loosened the screws that held it in place and lifted out the whole contraption. With the deadly apparatus clutched in his left hand he clambered back to the deck, lurched forward and slumped in the wheelhouse. He felt sicker and dizzier than ever before. Even a childhood bilious attack was not as bad as this.

"You alright, sir? We was worried." It was that very helpful Leading Seaman who threw an arm round him and got him into the motorboat.

A thump from one of the cargo holds jarred Paul back to his present predicament and warned of continuing danger. *Marquess* wallowed in the relentless sea but from his position on the bridge he could do nothing but ride it out, listen to the cargo shifting far below him, pray that the storm would die.

His mind returned to the Leading Seaman in *Badger*. What a first-rate fellow he had been. He had half carried Paul across the deck of *Lady Sue*, lowered him into the motorboat, then steered across a mile of water. He and a couple of others had got Paul aboard *Badger* and down the hatchway to his cabin where they rolled him into his bunk.

"Now, if there's anything more I can do?" had been the Leading Seaman's parting words. Paul remembered nothing more until he awoke many hours later. It was three in the morning; he must have slept for ten hours so he switched on the light and began to unpack. Ross was asleep in the upper bunk. Later that day he learned that a harbour tug had gone alongside the *Lady Sue*, heaved up her anchor and moved her to a berth about two miles distant where a crane had lifted the mine on shore.

A month later, having escorted a large convoy into the Atlantic, *Badger* was back in Liverpool when the captain and Paul were summoned to the Port Commander's office. As he entered, Paul noticed that the Wren secretary was staring at him. He knew her well enough to share a few small confidences.

The Commander waved them to chairs.

"The Admiralty people have looked at your mine and made some interesting discoveries," he began. "It was sabotaged in the factory. It wouldn't have gone off."

"Factory?" Paul asked.

"The Skoda works in German-occupied Czechoslovakia. The workers are slaves, many of them Jews. They screwed up the innards of your mine without altering the colour coding of the wires."

Why 'my mine'? Paul wondered to himself.

"It must have looked all right to the German inspector," continued the Commander. "Our expert said it was too clever to have been a mistake. You can be thankful, Sub-Lieutenant, to some miserable fellow who you will never meet. He saved your life."

Paul was trying to make sense of it all—slave workers, Czechoslovakia. 'In the midst of life we are in death' was all that came to his mind, but the Commander was still speaking.

"The Prime Minister has expressed interest. He observed that the workers in that factory hate Germans sufficiently to risk death if they are caught playing games."

Games, Paul thought. Why do we reduce things like this to the level of games?

"And one other thing. We will say nothing about this to anyone. We don't want the Germans to know we have their mine under examination and we certainly don't want them to realize that the workers are sabotaging their mines. They read our newspapers just as carefully as we read theirs. The whole thing never happened; the fishing trawler got its nets fouled in some wreckage. We're hoping they turn out more mines like this."

"Yessir," Paul mumbled. He was excused and left the room. He paused for a moment beside the secretary's desk and she looked up at him.

"But you didn't know, did you?" she asked. "It must have been awful."

She obviously knew the whole story. She put a signal in his hand and said, "Read it, please."

Paul looked at it and the words came into focus, "Paul Henriques, immediate promotion to lieutenant."

"Thank you," he said. "I wish I could thank the poor...workman who..." But something seemed to have gone wrong with his voice, which sounded broken and far away. He put on his cap and went out into the sunshine.

Even now, years later, Paul's memory returned not so much to the image of the devilishly horned mine swinging in a confusion of rope and nets, nor to the chronic vertigo he had suffered, but to what he imagined might be the circumstances of the mine's sabotage. A poor, ill-nourished slave? A downtrodden captive? Someone, man or woman, had risked everything, as indeed Paul thought he had done but, in doing so, had given Paul his life. How, he asked, can I thank him, whether in this world or the next? The war had three and a half years to run and it seemed impossible that some worker who had so adroitly misplaced the coloured wires would survive to enjoy the summer of

1945, the year of victory, and would walk out of the factory, turn his back on the Skoda works and live to enjoy the pleasures of peace.

Paul was religious in an unorthodox way. He wanted desperately for there to be a God who would set things right, assume His jurisdiction and dispose of the case as justice demanded. He wanted slave owners and Nazis to be visited with the full rigour of the law, be it earthly or heavenly. He would remember that mine for the remainder of his life as the very embodiment of evil, an evil that had been extinguished by the heroic deeds of a slave.

Chapter 4 — Rebecca

Paul thanked God for his scarf; he was sure he would freeze without it on the unheated bridge of *Marquess*. Rebecca had knitted it while he'd been on leave in Broxbourne—a leave that included an incident in the village tobacconist's shop. In his mind it was one of those occurrences, like a bend in the road, where life seemed to move in a new direction. Of course it had been wartime, and war affects everyone. In this case, Rebecca's father had suddenly gained strength and stature.

The two-week leave was welcome and Paul was determined to put his time to advantage by seeing Rebecca every day, helping his mother around the house and garden, and getting his clothes, particularly his seagoing clothes, washed and repaired. He hired a taxi at Broxbourne station for the short drive to his parents' house where the driver helped carry his kit into the hall.

"Thanks," Paul said and then to no one in particular, "Anyone home?"

There was no reply so he went through to the kitchen.

"Amy, where are you? 'Home is the fisherman, home from the sea, and the hunter is home from the hill.' Where is everyone?"

Amy appeared with a basket of leeks and threw her arms up.

"Oh what a nice surprise. We weren't expecting you until tomorrow. How tanned you are, and so much the naval officer."

"It's good to be home. Is everyone well?"

He seated himself at the kitchen table.

"Your mother should be home any minute now. Ever so busy, she's been. She weren't brought up to this kind of work. What I say is, her talents is not appreciated."

"It's kind of you to say so, Amy. And what about my father?"

"He works terrible hard. Scarcely any time to himself. I don't think he's taken a day off since the war started. We've had to dig up the flowers. Food is so difficult. Supper this evening, it's going to be mostly from the garden." She hesitated. "You'll be out after rabbits, won't you?"

"Yes, of course. But tell me, how's my Rebecca? Do you ever see her? I'd call now but the school doesn't have a telephone."

They chatted for several minutes and Paul learned that the two lodgers, who worked for the government, had moved into Stubbington's old quarters. They had it well set up but without cooking facilities. The Bosanquet house, Amy explained, had been turned into a government department with numerous employees, but nobody seemed to know exactly what they did.

"So the war has brought changes," said Paul.

"But life goes on," was Amy's reply.

"And Stubby?"

"From what I hear, he's doing wonders. There's nothing he don't know about mechanical things, and he gets on well with everyone. We do miss him."

Paul jumped to his feet. "I can hear mother coming."

He moved his uniform case out of the way and went outside. His mother had an old-fashioned tricycle which was slow and inefficient, but adequate for the mile of road between their house and the village. He kissed her then took the tricycle, pushing it round to the garage, all the while listening to his mother's chatter. She exaggerated as a matter of course, not realizing that in wartime one did not have to speak loudly to be heard. Of course there were difficulties—it was the same for everyone, and many things one had taken for granted before the war were now only memories.

"Mother," he said finally, "rather than worry about the things we can't change, let's protect what we have. I noticed that some garage tools seem to be missing. Stubby used to keep them in good order, but someone has been in there and, shall I say, 'borrowed' a few things. I'm going to move them to safer ground. People are not as honest as they used to be."

As they sat down to tea the air raid sirens could be heard rising and falling over London.

"I'm glad you're here and not," he waved in the direction of London, "where all that's going on. And Rebecca as well."

"I want to talk to you about Rebecca," his mother said. "Are you serious about her? I mean really serious."

"Yes, of course I am."

"Well, your father and I have discussed it. She's a lovely girl, but remember that she's an only child, and if you were married you might get, what shall I say, too much attention from her parents. If there had been brothers and sisters, all getting married and all with children, then... do you see what I mean?"

"Yes, I suppose so."

"And try to get her parents' permission for your little walks in the countryside. They don't think you should be out alone with her."

"They can't prevent me from seeing her, can they? I've been at sea and I've thought about her. Surely we can go on walks together and talk about the future... supposing there is a future."

"Oh God, don't say that," said his mother. "I don't really know what you're doing but when you come home you must realise that we are all facing hardships."

"Yes, I know that. I see it all around: food shortages, clothes rationing, nothing in the shops, Stubby away, no social life."

"Well please remember to be careful."

In truth, Paul's relationship with Rebecca, whilst continuing to be passionate, had become as much a meeting of minds as of bodies. He had written to her frequently, but following the incident of the sea mine he had become more thoughtful and had wanted someone to whom he could unburden himself and speak with honesty. He could not write about the details of his work and he alluded to the mine in an oblique manner. "I went on a Cook's Tour into the Valley of the Shadow," he wrote, "sufficient to give me a feel for the place, but I'm out of it with no harm done." Talking to his mother was not the same. In a subtle way she would mock him for his seriousness, tell him that he didn't need to think of the awful things that were going on in the world. She had a way of drenching serious conversation with platitude or evasion. Paul's father, on the other hand, was a kind if rather formal man but his duties were so much more than they had been in peacetime, and Paul felt guilty for taking even a few minutes of his time. He wished that Stubbington were still with them because Stubby's ideas would have been welcome. Stubby was not malicious but he was a master of the art of beating the system, of knowing how far you can go and what you can get away with. He had survived the ranks of the British army with humour intact and wits sharpened.

Paul's mind turned to another obstacle—Rebecca's parents. He had known Rebecca's father as long as he'd known her. The Reverend Farqueson was a full-blown local character whose scholarly abilities were superfluous in a country parish. It was said that Major Smith-Bosanquet had "asked for him" under some ancient custom whereby the lord of the manor could exercise influence on the selection of the incumbent. If rumour were to be believed, the Major's preferences hinged on the fact that Farqueson had "seen a bit of the world" and knew a fair amount about wine. In fact, the Reverend was a scholarly man with a reputation for having mastered Old Testament Hebrew and New Testament Greek while still at university, and had subsequently spent five years in the Holy Land "going over the ground", as he put it. His doctorate of divinity had been acquired by way of his publications on lower criticism, that is to say the study of biblical texts, and higher criticism, which included historical research. The word brilliant was often used to describe his work, but many of his superiors—at least those who had taken the trouble to read it—found him dangerously close to the thickets of unorthodoxy, if not the quagmires of heresy. In short, Farqueson thought that the gospel writers were not to be trusted in most of what they said, while Saint Paul was an out-and-out liar when he claimed to have been trained as a pharisee. It was also obvious that Saint Paul was not the author of at least two of the epistles attributed to him. With views like these, it was to be expected that his contemporaries regarded him with a combination of admiration and suspicion.

It was said that divinity was the most difficult subject in which to gain a doctoral degree because it was the only one in which imagination and creativity were not merely discouraged but likely to be harmful. Even the study of tedious bygones like classical Greek or Latin, in which the thin soil of scholarship had been endlessly worked over, would not, however unorthodox, condemn the student to either earthly disapproval or celestial damnation. In divinity, however, the lines were marked out in immoveable detail, the stepping stones of faith established without equivocation, and the student was required to pass unerringly from one dogma to the next. Nor was it a buffet table of beliefs where you picked or chose what you would put on your plate; no, it was all or nothing. There was no room for questioning, no time for hesitation, no space for divergence or, indeed, anything except mental and spiritual compliance. Such is the nature of a long established church. Its adherents take it word-for-word and in the process they become as little children who do not have ideas of their own, nor do they write innovative and thought-provoking doctoral theses.

In appearance Farqueson was a short man with delicate hands and feet. His head was large, his eyebrows unruly and his narrow shoulders seemed scarcely capable of sustaining the burden of his black frock coat. His manner, and indeed his clothes, left an impression of Edwardian propriety. As for promotion within the church, his doctorate must have recommended him as a potential bishop but, when approached, he let it be known that he would be uncomfortable with many aspects of episcopal practice, particularly when it had to do with raising money. In his innermost heart he had no wish to be involved in the ceremonies that would occupy him if he carried the crook and wore the mitre. It would distract him from what he conceived to be his true calling, which was to adduce what really happened in that troublesome corner of the Roman Empire during the reign of Tiberius Caesar. Only once did he ask to be considered for high office and that was when he heard that the throne of the Anglican Archbishop of Jerusalem was up for grabs. The Church of England, not to be outdone by less influential churches that were represented in Jerusalem—Copts, Syrians and the like—maintained a representative at the level of archbishop, although the duties were known to be negligible. Anglicans, it was thought, were not to be over-arched by lesser churches. In the event, a 'political' appointment was made; a political appointment being one of convenience designed to get some nuisance out of the way. With that, Farqueson lowered his gaze from the golden domes of Jerusalem to the slate roofs of Broxbourne. He gathered round him a team of lay assistants to handle the pastoral needs of the parish and relieve him of what he felt were unworthy calls on his time. His sermons were lengthy and erudite, although not much directed to the needs of his listeners, and his public appearances at bazaars and so on were enough to deflect criticism.

Like many others, Paul was rather blinded by his wit. On one occasion, when informed at a parish meeting that a magpie had stolen some coins left on the step to pay for milk, Farqueson gazed heavenwards. "I wish," he exclaimed, "that the blessed Saint Francis of Assisi could make himself available to offer advice and comment." The blessed Saint to whom he referred had been dead for several hundred years but still enjoyed a solid reputation when it came to preaching sermons to the birds. On another occasion, when being shown around an exhibition of village crafts, he hesitated in front of a brightly coloured bed-covering made from scraps of discarded cloth. Looking about him with a well rehearsed air of other-worldliness, he pontificated, "Are we not instructed that the stone that the builder rejected hath now acquired added importance? Scraps of discarded cloth here," he gestured grandly, "to guard against the frigid night air; ends of paper there for children to practice penmanship or budding poets to compose verses in God's honour; carelessly dropped morsels of wood yonder, swept from the shop floor by the apprentice and now used to create useful little... little I-don't-know-whats; strips of leather, perhaps to fashion a dog's collar. I mean, of course, the collar of a faithful canine, not such a one as I am destined by Providence to wear."

It occurred to Paul that his own father was a master of clear thinking and precise language which he employed to lay bare a problem, cut away the tangle of untruth and expose human transactions in incontrovertible simplicity, be they civil or criminal, but Rebecca's father did much the opposite. He would heap word upon word, often leaving his hearers baffled or, as some said, in religious turmoil. Like so many men of modest stature, he overcompensated with words.

Had Paul been more perceptive, he might have realised that Farqueson admired and was jealous of him. He regretted inwardly that as a youth he had not 'lived', nor experienced the world beyond the corridors of learning, and as a graduate student in Jerusalem had even escaped 'the world' and lodged in a monastery. His wild oats, in consequence, or their ecclesiastical equivalent, remained desperately unsown. Here is this young man, as he saw Paul, wearing a handsome uniform, swaggering about the decks of an enormous battleship and doubtless enjoying the companionship of young females in every port. True, he had heard nothing to Paul's detriment, but the idea of him taking Rebecca to the cinema, walking down the country lanes and recounting anecdotes of his rollicking life at sea made Farqueson apprehensive.

Rebecca herself had long ago come to terms with her father's outdated views. She mingled with the other teachers and occasionally with the parents of the school children, she read whatever she enjoyed reading and had her admirers. Her father's holidays in the south of France, which were described as "working holidays", caused her no difficulty because if people were so importunate as to ask what sort of work an Anglican divine would find in such a location she had a ready answer. Her father, she explained, had adduced evidence that in the turbulent years following the crucifixion certain members of the Holy Family had fled to southern France where they formed a community of Christians, and it was of scholarly interest to know what became of them. Her father was accordingly devoted to the task of searching the archives, tracing human lineages and studying the oldest churches. You couldn't argue with that.

Another clue to the character of the Reverend Farqueson was that he was excessively devoted to saint Augustine of Hippo, whose great classic, *The City of God*, formed one of the beacons of early Christian thinking. What attracted him was the fact that Augustine had passed a riotous youth, indulged his appetites, yielded free rein to his passions and allowed the details of his transgressions to become widely known.

In other words, Farqueson seemed more than a little occupied by the delinquency that preceded the sanctity, as indeed he was with the great Anglican divine, John Donne, who was aptly described as "a lily risen from the red earth". He had also spent his youth addicted to the sins of the flesh which were followed by a saintly maturity, although none too quickly, and not before they had been amply set forth and admitted. In other words, Farqueson was something of an ecclesiastic voyeur seeming to apply his mind to the fallen condition of his heroes as much as to their later emergence as champions of the church.

His wife, Mrs. Bessie Farqueson, enjoyed a virtuous reputation, as befitted a woman of her position, but she did not shine socially. She was tedious, shabbily dressed and in the habit of interrupting other people's conversations. Indeed, so far from contributing to a discussion, she managed, by opening her mouth at all, to leave the subject in tatters and other members of the group in a state of irritation. When Judge Henriques found himself seated next to her at the Smith-Bosanquet's table he got through six courses of food without saying anything at all. He was subsequently reproached by his hostess and replied, "Well, yes, but you know what they say about a talkative judge!"

On another occasion, a guest was recounting how he had been fishing in Scotland and had been outwitted by a spectacular trout that was regularly seen in a certain spot but was disdainful of the expensive assortment of flies that were cast in its direction. It would come up, look at what was offered and then swim back under its rock. Finally, a little boy of eight caught it on a bit of egg sandwich. Everybody laughed.

"I simply don't believe it," piped Mrs. Farqueson. "I've never heard such a thing."

Another guest spoke up. "Well, I cannot agree with you, Mrs. Farqueson. I think it's a charming story. Look at it this way: a fable doesn't have to be true in a word-by-word sort of way. Surely you see what I mean?"

"No, really I don't. Am I not correct in thinking that a fable should have a moral?"

"And this one does. It puts the listener in mind of those occasions in human life when a problem attracts complicated and expensive solutions. But then someone turns up with something simple that works perfectly well. The little boy did what was obvious to him. The grownups were trying to be too clever."

"Well, I have never come across such a case…"

This, at any rate, was the lady who shared the vicar's nuptial couch and would presumably be the invigilator of Paul's trysts with Rebecca. How and why the vicar had married her remained one of Broxbourne's more baffling mysteries, although some intriguing suggestions were advanced. Most of them, however, would have been, as the saying went, better translated into Latin.

On the evening of his return, Paul and Rebecca spoke to each other by telephone and tried to make up for the long months of separation. They agreed to meet briefly on the way to Rebecca's school and again later in the day, so Paul was up early and dressed in country clothes so as not to attract attention. He had arranged to wait for her at the tobacconist's shop, which lay between the rectory and school. On arrival, he bought a Morning Post and opened it. The tobacconist, a man called Willis, was a veteran of the First World War who had been shell-shocked in the course of his service, reducing his comprehension and leaving him no more than marginally capable of selling cigarettes and pipe tobacco. The fact that his name was Willis, having a resemblance to Wills & Co.—well known in the tobacco industry—was constantly alluded to by the smoking fraternity. It was the only joke he ever heard and he heard it often.

Willis became immediately suspicious. He did not know Paul, who had been away for almost the whole war and was, in any event, a non-smoker. He was young and fit, and appeared nervous, glancing first at the newspaper and then out the doorway. The wartime Ministry of Information had done its work and in every public place there were notices designed to warn the public against German spies and saboteurs.

"'Ere, why aren't you in the army?" asked Willis. "I don't like yer looks."

Paul looked at him in total astonishment and then laughed.

"So you'd laugh at me, would yer? Very well, you wait 'ere cos I got a little surprise fer you." Willis edged past Paul and out the door. "I don't want spies 'anging around my shop."

"Now really. I am not a spy. I'm known to dozens of people in Broxbourne."

But Willis shuffled off, presumably to summon help. Paul decided to stand his ground and await developments and a few minutes later the tobacconist was back with a burly man who wore the armband of an air raid warden. His gray hair and sagging stomach suggested that he and Willis were contemporaries.

"Now what's going on 'ere?" he enquired.

"I came in here," Paul spoke slowly and deliberately, "to buy a newspaper and wait for my friend. This man thinks I'm a spy."

"Then show me some identity, if yer please. We can't be too careful these days."

"I am a naval officer," Paul replied, digging out his card and handing it to the warden.

"'Enriques," the man read.

"That don't sound like an English name," said Willis.

"And that uniform you've got in this picture," added the warden. "What's them squiggles on yer sleeve?"

"That's because I'm a reservist. Look, it says 'Royal Navy Reserve', and if you don't like my name I suggest you go and talk to my father, Mr. Justice Henriques. He'll be only too pleased to put you straight."

The warden huffed, "I'm not the one who needs putting straight. Not by the look of things. I'm going to ask you to accompany me to the police station."

"Now you're being ridiculous," Paul said. "Give me back my identity card."

"I think not," the man replied, blocking Paul as he reached for the card. "Yer can get it back from the constable if he be willing."

"You ignorant bastard!" shouted Paul, losing his temper. He shoved the man against the counter. "You're half-wits, both of you."

The warden was known in the village and, more significantly, in the Saracen's Head, for having a 'short fuse'. He had been the instigator of more than one fracas, was a failed candidate for council and had been a questionable choice as the village's only air raid warden—an appointment made in deference to his brief and unremarkable army service. As they jostled, his fuse expired and he attacked Paul. Perhaps he believed he had a chance with the help of Willis, who reached immediately for his Irish blackthorn, which he kept behind the counter for occasions such as this.

The fight was short and bitter, and the warden was soon lying face down on the floor. Paul yanked the blackthorn from Willis' grasp and landed one more punch before they were interrupted.

"Good heavens above," boomed Reverend Farqueson from the door. "What on earth is going on?

"I come to purchase a newspaper to inform me of war and destruction elsewhere in the world, and am confronted by a veritable maelstrom of conflict here in my own village. And Mr. Henriques, I would scarcely have expected to find you here. May I have an explanation?"

Paul regarded his bloodstained knuckles. "I came in here, like you, and bought a newspaper. I was standing in the doorway reading it when I was accused of being a spy."

"You was acting suspicious," said Willis, who had regained his feet.

"I showed you my identity card, which the warden here refused to return to me." Paul snatched the card from the hand of the warden, who stirred on the floor.

"Never have I heard such a thing." Farqueson could be quite intimidating when he tried. "I have known this man for years, and I give you my assurance that he is not a spy." He gave Willis a stern look.

"Now help your friend to his feet and get him to lie down somewhere else."

The warden mumbled something, but Farqueson brushed him aside.

"In my judgment, you got what you deserved." Farqueson steered Paul toward the door. "You must excuse the overzealous behaviour of our village officials," he went on. "I suggest, if I may, that you cross the street and walk Rebecca the rest of the way to school, as I was about to." He hesitated. "Perhaps you would care to join us for a simple family meal this evening."

"Of course, I would love to. Thank you."

Paul crossed the street to where Rebecca stood waiting, and for a few brief seconds he held her in his arms.

"Where's father?"

"He said to go ahead while he tends to a couple of lost souls."

Rebecca had something on her mind. "Now that I'm twenty," she began, wiping his knuckles, "I can apply to join the Women's Royal

Naval Service. I want to be trained in signals and be a 'bunting tosser'.[6] Later, you can tell me what happened in the tobacconist's shop, but meantime I want to know exactly what a bunting tosser does and how I can prepare for it."

'The tobacconist's shop' was a milestone in the life of the Reverend Farqueson. Suddenly and without warning he saw the opportunity to be something of the man he had always wanted to be, and he seized on it. There was Paul, whom he secretly admired, being accosted and set upon by two villagers who didn't attend church and spent their idle hours in the public house. There could be no question that he was on Paul's side, and when Willis attempted to strike him with a particularly unpleasant looking stick, Farqueson was delighted to see Rebecca's idol seize the weapon and throw the man to the floor. As for the air raid warden, whose appointment to his post Farqueson had opposed in the village council, he applauded inwardly to see Paul land several blows. Some restrained demon in the heart of Farqueson was released; he had never fought but he was delighted to be on the side of a champion who was clearly more than a match for a couple of beer-soaked villagers. Farqueson's task had merely been to preside over the situation when the conflict was over; in truth, he'd hesitated a moment in the doorway. He had wanted to be in Paul's shoes, tall, strong and confident with a contemptible enemy on the floor in front of him. The next best thing was to pronounce on the event, to be unchristian for a few minutes and revel in the defeat of an evildoer. It was said by those who knew him well—his wife and daughter—that the incident changed Farqueson in small and subtle ways; that he became more outspoken and passionate. From that moment he truly welcomed Paul into his household.

The next few days passed all too swiftly. Paul worked in the house and garden, went out into the fields and shot rabbits, repaired and

---

[6] A signalman when hoisting or lowering flag signals.

strengthened the chicken coop against, as he described it, enemy marauders. For good measure, he also shot one of them—a fox—in the field behind the house.

He and Rebecca spent their evenings together at the rectory or at the Henriques' house, and by day Rebecca taught her class of children. Only once did Paul and Rebecca have a long talk with Paul's father in which he explained how his work had changed in wartime, how the influx of thousands of empire and foreign troops was putting a strain on the legal system. It may have been wishful thinking, but Paul thought that his mother's outlook had also changed in recent months. She reproached him for losing his temper with a couple of village buffoons, but her reproaches were mild and she seemed a little more ready to understand Paul's work in protecting the country's seaborne trade.

"Now that the Americans are on our side," she said, "things are bound to improve."

On their last evening together Paul and Rebecca walked to their favourite place under the trees and she gave him a blue woollen scarf that she had knitted. He used it to wipe away her tears, and he told her that he would think of her whenever he put it around his neck. If he were to die at sea he would be wearing it. The following morning, with a heavy heart, he took the train back to Liverpool. He knew, by this time, that his relationship with Rebecca could end only in death.

The author (right) in his pram, Calcutta, circa 1925. Bazley's father was stationed in India with the exporting firm of Gladstone, Wylie & Co.

Stubbington, in full chauffeur regalia, poses with the Bazley's well-waxed Armstrong Siddeley.

Walter with his father in Bournemouth, 1934. The family made regular trips to the coastal town in an attempt to remain front of mind with an elderly, and very wealthy, spinster aunt who, in the end, left all her money to—of all people—a German.

The author's childhood home, Wormley Hill, Broxbourne, Hertfordshire.

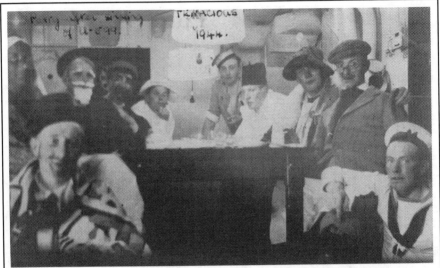

Personal photography was forbidden aboard ship during the Second World War, so photos such as this, showing the wardroom of HMS Tenacious, are rare. The date is May 21, 1943 (not 1944, as written on the image). Sub-Lieutenant Walter Bazley stands centre frame, leaning on the table. It was custom to celebrate following the sinking of an enemy vessel. In this case, the victim was a German submarine, U-599.

First-Lieutenant Walter Bazley working a sun-sight aboard the minesweeper HMS Michael in the Dutch East Indies, 1946.

Walter Bazley in full Royal Naval Volunteer Reserve uniform, 1946. The RNVR was referred to as the 'wavy navy' after the undulating sleeve rings that differentiated its officers' uniforms from those in the Royal Navy and Royal Naval Reserve.

Chapter 5 — The Middle Watch

A roar went up from the three thousand troops who lined the ship's side. It sounded like the cheers that are heard at a soccer final in Wembley stadium when a favoured team had done something praiseworthy. *Badger* had indeed performed a useful deed by rescuing a soldier from the rough water of the North Atlantic and restoring him to his floating barracks, and the soldiers who witnessed the drama, so perfect in its timing and execution, gave vent to their feelings. To Paul, on *Badger's* bridge, it was nothing out of the ordinary. Seamen, in their exposed positions at the guns, were occasionally blown or swept overboard by one kind of mishap or another. Sometimes they could be rescued, at other times they were left while the battle raged on.

The convoy had been steaming southward, two passenger liners converted to troop carriers, plus a heavy cruiser, HMS *Berwick*. Ahead of them was a screen of four destroyers to protect against U-boats. The convoy itself consisted of 16 fast merchant vessels in square formation, a fleet tug and the escort vessels, of which *Badger* was one, forming a screen on the flanks.

Badger was stationed on the landward or eastern side, a thousand yards from the nearest ship in convoy, and Paul, as officer of the watch, was keeping the 'afternoon', midday to 1600 hours. For the first two hours the watch had been uneventful as they steamed southward. The fleet was under the command of a commodore, his broad pennant hoisted in the larger of the two passenger liners, *Homeric*. The fleet was bound from Liverpool to Gibraltar, and the Commodore had kept them well out at sea, two hundred miles from the Portuguese coast. His reasoning was that the danger from U-boats would be reduced if they were far from the shoreline; however, they would soon have to turn eastwards, towards Gibraltar, and Paul assumed that the Commodore would order the turn during daylight hours, when it could be accomplished entirely by flags and no lights would be needed.

Suddenly the Commodore's halyards were festooned, and *Berwick* and many of the larger merchant ships repeated the hoist. This was common practice in wartime because it made doubly sure that all ships had seen the signal and would obey as soon as it was lowered, which was the order to execute.

"Execute!" shouted the signalman on *Badger's* bridge, and Paul leaned to the voicepipe.

"Port twenty," he said. "Steady on oh-nine-five."

"Oh-nine-five," repeated the quartermaster.

But a single flag remained obstinately on the halyards of *Homeric*.

"Flag O, sir. *Homeric* has lost a man overboard," called out the signalman.

"I see it," from Paul. "Answering pennant."

He took a compass bearing on the spot where he presumed the man might be in the water and ordered a turn to starboard. Of one thing he could be sure—the Captain of the troopship had no intention of turning his vessel through 180 degrees and stopping in mid-ocean, which would have been an invitation to a torpedo. In any case, officers aboard *Homeric* must have seen *Badger* turn and drawn their own conclusions. The navy knew when to make signals, and equally, when not to make them.

Paul leaned down to the captain's voicepipe and flipped up the cover. "Come up, sir."

Laidlaw was on the bridge in a minute. He took in the situation and said to Paul, "You carry on," then down the voicepipe to the wheelhouse, "Get the first lieutenant."

"We won't lower a boat," he went on. "Use a Carley raft if you have to, but keep it quick and simple." He turned back to Paul.

"Increase revolutions; you can handle this. I see a smoke flare. Aim for it." He paused, then went on. "I wonder how the hell he fell overboard. Let's hope he didn't bash his head on the way down."

Minutes later the man was sighted; he did not appear injured. Paul ordered "astern" on *Badger's* engines and Percival's men on the main deck threw the man an assortment of lines. In short order, he was pulled, dripping, over *Badger's* side.

Laidlaw turned to the signalman. "To *Homeric*. Man saved."

Next came an order to Ross. "Get his name and rank. Tell him from me how bloody lucky he is."

To no one in particular, Laidlaw went on, "Imagine doing that in darkness, or if he'd been injured and couldn't help himself." Then to Paul, "Well done. Take him back to his ship."

Paul ordered "full ahead" and set *Badger* on course for the troopship. The next manoeuvre would be difficult, because every few minutes there was a pre-arranged change of course. He called the engine room.

"We have some manoeuvring in the next few minutes. If the chief engineer is there, tell him."

How very strange, Paul thought to himself. The last time I was engaged on something like this it was *Artemis* racing to rescue 800 people off the coast of Argentina. Now it's a careless pongo[7] in the North Atlantic. He leaned down to the voicepipe.

"Coxswain, we're going alongside the troopship's starboard side and I want to keep at least ten feet away from her. They'll drop a bosun's chair—I see them getting it ready, and they have a derrick turned out. What we have to do is get our fo'c's'le under the derrick. Remember that the water cast off by a liner's bows will sweep us away from her.

---

[7] A mildly derogatory term that sailors used to describe their counterparts in the army.

"I won't try to give you helm orders," he went on. "You must steer toward her to counteract the effect of her bow wave. My guess is that we'll need ten degrees of port rudder. And we have to do it between zig-zags. Can you see her?"

"Yessir."

In the event, the manoeuvre went off without a hitch and the pongo was restored to his army friends. Soldiers cheered as Paul took *Badger* back to its place on the screen.

"Well done," from Laidlaw. "No dents or scratches."

"All credit to the Coxswain, sir. If you agree, Ross will write something complimentary sin the log."

"Do so," said Laidlaw.

At the end of his watch, Paul went down to the wardroom for a cup of tea. There was a good deal of motion on the ship, so Borges, the officer's steward, gave it to him in a mug. Paul liked Borges, who was Maltese but had joined the navy in Plymouth. He had tried to join as a seaman but failed the physical test and, as *Badger's* officers discovered, he might also have failed the language test if he had been required to say anything. In some instances navy stewards had worked in hotels or restaurants before the war and were well qualified; in other cases, like Borges, they were educated only to the point of understanding English when they wanted to. Borges, however, had one redeeming skill: he seemed able to find fresh fruit or vegetables in the back streets of every seaport, Liverpool in particular. Things that were unobtainable in wartime—oranges, bananas, figs even—appeared in modest quantities on *Badger's* wardroom table. He collected a few shillings from the officers on a monthly basis.

While still two-hundred miles west of Gibraltar, the fleet split up. The larger part of it, the two troopships, twelve fast merchantmen and the cruiser continued south to Cape Town, their final destination being Egypt on the other side of Africa. The four destroyers, meanwhile, would refuel in Gibraltar and with three fast merchantmen make a dash for the beleaguered island of Malta in the central Mediterranean. This was the most dangerous run of all, with German aircraft stationed in Sicily and the Italian fleet in southern Italy. The destroyers, with their speed and firepower, might attempt it, but escort vessels like *Badger* would stand no chance. *Badger* was to refuel and wait in Gibraltar for a homebound convoy.

Laidlaw and Forsyth-Thompson were bent over the chart.

"Do you know Gibraltar?" Laidlaw asked Paul.

Paul nodded. "Yessir. Don't suppose it's changed much since I was there before the war. They'll send us alongside the oiling jetty for starters. It's exposed and a westerly wind drives you away from the jetty. But I seem to remember they have two or three small tugs. After oiling they'll send us to the inner harbour."

"And what about shore leave? Anything for the men to do?"

"Not really. A walk around. I think there's a NAAFI[8] for small things—soap and toothbrushes. The governor lives in an old convent in the middle of town, but it's scarcely worth a visit."

"When were you there, Paul?" Laidlaw asked.

"Let me think. Must have been quite early 1939. I was in a Greek ship. That's when I learned to swear in Greek and eat horsemeat."

As the main part of the fleet parted company and disappeared over the horizon to the south, Forsyth-Thompson calculated their time of arrival in Gibraltar.

"About 28 hours from the point we turned east," he announced. "We should be there by nightfall tomorrow."

This was the most dangerous leg of their journey—a favourite hunting ground for U-boats. The Germans knew the Allies were replenishing their forces in the Middle East, particularly the Eighth

---

[8] Navy, Army and Air Force Institute

Army fighting in North Africa. There was not much they could do about the convoys that circumnavigated the African continent and came to Egypt via the Red Sea, but the Strait of Gibraltar was a trap. As the hot landmass of North Africa converged with the limestone plateau of Spain, U-boats were sure to be prowling the approaches. The fleet now consisted of three merchant vessels, one of them an oil tanker, plus four destroyers and four escort vessels, of which *Badger* was one. Their course was eastward and their commodore, by pre-arrangement, was the senior destroyer captain.

At ten minutes to midnight Ross sent the boatswain's mate to wake Paul and the familiar words, "Ten minutes to your watch, sir," had dragged him reluctantly into a state of wakefulness.

"Thanks, McFadden." He recognised the man's voice.

Paul's mind had become blurred by the unaccustomed division of time into four-hour watches. Mealtimes came and went at all the wrong moments; sleep, light and darkness came and went according to no particular pattern. This is an unnatural way to live, he told himself, and if he felt confused it was because mankind was never meant to live like that. He was now governed by the ten-minute zig-zag imposing a limit on how long he could keep his mind on any one topic, and the four-hour watch that defined his whole working life.

He climbed the two steel ladders, first to the flag deck and then to the bridge where Ross was filling out the midnight observations. The chart table was surrounded by canvas curtains and illuminated by a dim red light that had no effect on night vision.

"Everything quiet," said Ross with finality. "Course 275 degrees, Gibraltar somewhere ahead, speed 12 knots, zig-zag unchanged, our station a thousand yards abeam of the merchant ship. I don't know its name. Oh yes, the captain told me to post two lookouts on the port side because a U-boat attacking from ahead would have to get through the destroyer screen. Tell me when your eyes are ready." Then, as an afterthought, "It's a bloody dark night."

Paul crossed to the asdic compartment and asked the operator, "What are conditions like?"

"Mushy," came the reply. "We're not likely to get an echo over a thousand yards. I'm searching from right ahead to ninety degrees on the port beam."

"Who's on the wheel?" Paul called down the voicepipe.

"Able Seaman McCann."

"Wearing safety harness?"

"Yessir. Got it on, sir."

This was a necessary precaution for the man steering. His hands were on the wheel but it sometimes happened that he'd be caught off balance and flung against the bulkhead. A canvas belt had been devised with stay lines so that he could not be thrown in any direction.

Paul's next routine was to check the armament. The two men on duty by the depth charges wore earphones and were in contact with the bridge. Normally a U-boat would be detected by the asdic while still at a distance, perhaps a thousand yards. On hearing it, the officer of the watch would turn the ship in the direction of the sound and order attack speed, which was fourteen knots. He would then press the alarm so that in minutes the ship would be at battle stations. Next he would go back to the asdic and glean what information he could from the sounds that were bouncing back from the hull of the U-boat, or whatever had caused the alarm. By the time the captain was on the bridge, a picture of the situation should have emerged and the captain would take over from there. In the gun turret were three seamen so that if a U-boat was sighted on the surface a couple of quick shots could be fired. It was notoriously difficult to hit a small target from a ship that was plunging in rough seas, but the attempt was always made.

Badger's bridge was open to the sky with little protection against rain or spray. The lookouts could huddle against the steel bulwark, which offered protection to shoulder level. They would sink down and turn their backs when the bows slammed into a big wave and sheets of spray flew back. Their sou'westers, oilskin coats and seaboots kept them reasonably dry. Paul, in the centre of the bridge, could also avoid the spray by stepping forward into a low depression that ran across the fore part of the bridge. He too wore oilskins over woollen clothing. This particular morning was dark with no moon and only intermittent starlight. Paul used a hand-held rangefinder to keep *Badger* a thousand yards on the beam of the heavily laden merchantman, and his own wristwatch to time the turns of the zig-zag. He preferred his watch over the ship's chronometer, safe in the knowledge that it was accurate to within a second. His father had given it to him when he had first gone to sea and it had proved to be a superlative timekeeper. He wound and checked it daily when the time was broadcast from Greenwich.

Paul had known his father as well as most boys know their fathers, and now his mind went back to his school years when he was allowed to go to the courtroom when his father was sitting. In those days of depression and hardship there had been an increase in theft, particularly foodstuffs, which reflected the desperation of many otherwise decent people. He remembered a young man, charged with theft of food, clothing and a wireless set, to the value of nearly 100 pounds.

"Guilty," the boy said. "I'm sorry, sir."

Paul's father removed his glasses and leaned back in his chair. Behind him, on the wall, hung the royal coat of arms. Paul wondered why the unicorn was not more masculine in its accoutrements.

"I don't want to send you to prison," his father spoke quietly, "but as the law stands, I have little alternative. You did, after all, steal a quantity of valuable items, not all of which consisted of food. Food alone would have been the more excusable." He paused. "So this is what I intend to do. You are a young man. The fact that you were able to carry so much stolen property suggests that you are strong." There was a faint smile. "Ah, I see the naval recruiter, Petty Officer Hargreaves, is present in court. If he will have you, then you will walk out of this court a free man, with no criminal record. It's either the Royal Navy or prison. What do you say?"

For a few seconds there was silence.

"Navy, sir."

"So be it. You are discharged, and I wish you well. Do your best."

Not all who joined the navy, Paul thought, went on their way with the good wishes of a judge and the admonition to do their best.

The middle watch, midnight until 0400, was considered the worst, but Paul had become accustomed to it and, together with the afternoon, which was midday to 1600, had learned to sleep in short snatches at other times of the day or night. The middle watch was usually quiet and he could think his own thoughts while the ship plunged onwards, rising and falling over the great rollers of the Atlantic, jostled and pounded by smaller waves that were blown up by the wind. These winds, he thought, have come from far-away America, the westerlies that blow round the earth. They filled the sails of the galleons that set out from Spain to colonise and conquer South America. These seas had been much travelled in centuries past, but it was not until this war that they had been invaded by a new device, asdic, later called sonar.

The depths of the sea, as everyone knew, could not be penetrated visually, so mankind, if he wanted to explore beneath the surface, had to copy his distant cousins, whales and porpoises, and adopt a system of echo-location. A sound is cast into the water from a device attached to the keel of the ship. Unlike a bell, where the noise goes in all directions, this sound could be made directional and limited to a specific arc. Attached to it is a hearing mechanism so that the operator can not only listen to the sound going out, but also, if the sound strikes an object under water, he can hear the return echo. The result is a 'ping' as it goes into the water and then silence, or just a mushy sound if nothing is encountered. It is this 'ping' that the operator receives in his earphones and which the officer of the watch hears through an amplifier on the bridge. It was the eternal sound of a destroyer or escort vessel in wartime. If the outgoing sound should strike an object it is returned as a 'ping-ding'. It is then that the operator and the officer, a few feet away, experience a sudden heart-stopping excitement. It might be a U-boat or it might be anything else, a dense shoal of fish or a sudden temperature inversion in the water. It could even be a whale, a mass of seaweed or, in shallow water, a wreck lying on the sea floor. Whenever an echo came back, therefore, the operator and the officer on watch were alerted.

"Hold that echo," the officer would call out. "Classify," and the operator would strike again in the same direction. It was like a fly fisherman who feels a touch and then casts his fly several times over the same spot. He'd move right and left and only when sure that the echo was false would he abandon it and resume his search. Other sounds could be identified in the water, the most important being the noise of a torpedo, which sounded like a motorcycle. If the operator called out "torpedo", the officer of the watch would order a hard turn on the assumption that the torpedo was aimed at his ship. He knows it is running at sixty miles an hour so he shouts the helm order, "Port thirty; hard a-port", for instance, and the ship would immediately start swinging to the left. The signalman would then hoist flag 'T' to inform nearby ships that a torpedo was in the water. He would then snatch the captain's voicepipe and shout "Captain, sir. Come up. Torpedoes," and at the same time press the alarm that brings the whole ship to battle stations.

Throughout Paul's watch *Badger* was buffeted by Atlantic waves. *Badger* was a sturdy ship and seemed somehow to be lucky in the sense that sailors use the word. In the two years since commissioning there had been only one serious engagement when a German aircraft had flown out of low cloud and machine-gunned the deck, killing two sailors. Laidlaw, for his part, was a good captain who was liked and trusted, and it seemed strange that he had not been rewarded with the half stripe of a lieutenant-commander. He had been at sea since boyhood and was now thirty-four. Sent on various short courses of instruction before the war, he had not made the mistake of trying to copy the permanent navy too closely, of becoming too 'pusser' as the saying was. He was at heart a workaday skipper whose mission in life was to get the job done by filling the holds with fish, getting the convoy formed up, or whatever task was at hand. He relied on his officers to do their best, felt himself well served and genuinely enjoyed their company. In a word, he had his way without having to brandish his authority.

It was thus that Paul would remember *Badger*. Could it have been the diversity of backgrounds of his brother officers, or the uncomplaining resilience of the young fishermen who made up the crew, and the fact that every one was a volunteer? He didn't really know, but as he kept his watch, gave helm orders to turn the ship in conformity with the zig-zag and listened to the sound of the asdic he knew he was among friends. He was doing what he most wanted to do, was proud of himself and would have wished his parents, his beloved Rebecca, Amy, Stubbington, the lord of the manor and everyone else, to know that he was on the bridge of a ship, however small it may have been, engaged, as they used to say, "on the King's business."

A sudden flash of light lit the eastern horizon and the two lookouts reported in a jumble of words.

"Thank you. I see," Paul said, turning his binoculars on the distant clouds that were momentarily illuminated from within like a light bulb inside a ragged lampshade. It faded in seconds and had obviously been lightning, but why so sudden? Up to that moment the sky had been gross black, but then something like a bomb blast ripped through the darkness. He didn't know how far it was but felt sure that every ship in the fleet had seen it. "Flash of light on western horizon," he wrote in the log.

"Where was I?" he asked himself as *Badger* lifted on a wave, hesitated and then slid into the trough. The motion of the ship, the eternal sameness of the asdic, the darkness and the turbulent sea seemed an appropriate framework for his thoughts, like those lavish Victorian picture frames, gilded and excessive, that enclose a familiar domestic scene. Some frames contained contorted curlicues, mock foliage, serpents, birds and mythic figures designed to embellish and add an aura of importance to the canvas. This is the frame for my thoughts, he mused, the motion of the ship and the asdic probing the depths of the sea. He held the top of the screen so he could see the bows and watch the water shoot up the hawse pipes when the ship struck a wave. He could feel the hum of the engines through the soles of his seaboots, and he leaned his weight against the binnacle to steady himself. I am here, he thought. My duty is in this place on the surface of the sea. There is nowhere else on earth I would rather be.

He studied the hands of his watch and turned *Badger* to the new course. This particular zig-zag had six course alterations to the hour and thereby lost eighteen percent of its forward progress. In the larger ships there would be a midshipman on the bridge whose task was to keep his eye on the chronometer and tell the officer-of-the-watch the exact second when the turn should be made. That was admirable if you had plenty of junior officers, so the officer of the watch, in effect, had an assistant, an extra pair of eyes, but in an escort vessel Paul did it all. He had noted that the two merchantmen in the convoy turned more slowly than the escorts, so he made hesitant turns to reach the new course.

"Port ten," he ordered down the voicepipe.

"Port ten, sir. Ten degrees of port wheel on," came the quartermaster's reply.

"Your new course is going to be 090 degrees," from Paul. "Let her swing slowly and steady on the new course."

"Aye aye, sir. Oh-nine-oh."

In fact she was not steady in that boisterous sea but was thrown from side to side of her intended course. First Lieutenant Percival was due on the bridge at 0400 and Paul sent down to wake him at ten minutes before the hour. The morning watch had been the traditional watch of first lieutenants since the days of sail on the reasoning that they were in charge of the upper deck and could get the men started on their work as soon as it was light. Paul filled out the entries in the logbook—course and speed, zig-zag, wind direction, sea and swell, temperature and barometric pressure—and noted that the flash of light to the eastward had been the only entry under the 'remarks' column. Next his binoculars took a long sweep, first on the westward side where every ship in the convoy was preparing to change the watch, as he was, then eastward toward Spain and Portugal where the horizon was dark and unrelenting.

Spain, he thought, so recently in the grip of civil war—a cruel country, sunlit but austere, a plateau that had prematurely aged, that clung to the accolade of past glories. Islam had gained a foothold but lost it many centuries before; the Catholic Church and a military dictatorship now held an iron grip. From what Paul had seen of Spain before the war he thought of it as an arid society, its king deposed, a country that had not come to terms with loss of empire. The legal system was in chaos; the prisons were the vilest in Europe while the church presumed to control morality, but did little beyond interfering in marriage and family life and spreading its own propaganda. It was a pulpit religion, self-serving, obscurantist and uncaring of the banditry of tax collectors or the deplorable condition of Spain's poor. The national icon told it all, the bedraggled, wispy-bearded knight mounted on his ramshackle horse.

Portugal affected Paul differently, if only because his distant ancestor had been a Portuguese seaman. If Spain was a country of sun and faded colours, then Portugal lay in Spain's shadow. Spain could, at least, dance. It had vitality, but Portugal could do no more than sing of human misery—the sentimental, urgent and ultimately hopeless *fado*, meaning fate. The Spaniard possessed a distant vision of beauty and fulfillment; the Portuguese drank his wine and smashed the glass.

He was yanked from reflection by a star-shell that exploded in the air and began its descent into the sea ahead of the destroyers. Gunfire erupted and flashes appeared.

"Captain, sir. Come up," Paul called down the voicepipe. "It must be a U-boat on the surface."

A minute later there came the crump of a full pattern of ten depth charges.

"That'll make the bastards hold their heads down," from one of the lookouts. "They was set shallow. I saw the explosions."

The man is right, Paul realised. The 'haystack' of water that appeared on the surface indicated the depth charge was set for 50 feet, the shallowest setting. In seconds, Laidlaw was at his side.

"U-boat will have dived, sir."

"Then it won't be able to aim its gun or torpedoes."

The three merchantmen turned south, to starboard, and Paul followed them round and kept his position a thousand yards distant. It was tempting to join in the hunt for the U-boat, abandon the merchantmen and join the destroyers, but that, in the circumstances, would have been wrong. There were four destroyers on the forward screen and three of them would form a hunter-killer team while the fourth remained with the merchant vessels. There might, after all, be another U-boat in the vicinity. *Badger*, therefore, steamed away from the battle. The attacking force continued its depth-charge assaults for two hours and expended more than a hundred charges. Oil appeared on the surface and corpses appeared, which led the destroyers to claim a probable kill. It was known, however, that U-boats would sometimes release oil during an engagement, which would rise to the surface and be seen by attacking ships. They would also, when hunted, discharge corpses from their torpedo tubes. These were the bodies of men who had been killed in air raids, dressed in naval uniforms, and were intended to mislead the attacking ships when seen on the surface. It was said that a ship's medical officer might examine them and determine how long they had been dead, but that depended on whether the captain was prepared to stop his ship and retrieve the bodies.

It was not until after the war, when a procedure called 'postwar analysis' was conducted by the Allied powers, that it could be said for certain that this particular U-boat had been sunk. It did not return to its base in Germany and was never heard from again. It would be another year before Paul himself would be involved in the sinking of a U-boat.

He heard a step behind him. Percival had come up to take over the watch, and Paul's zig-zag thoughts would soon be eased by sleep. But his days in *Badger* were numbered and, in the unfathomable recesses of the Admiralty, someone had decided that it was time for him to move on. When next in Liverpool he received his orders, packed his gear and said his goodbyes. His only comfort was that finally Laidlaw had been promoted lieutenant-commander.

Chapter 6 — HMS *Tarquin*

In later years, as Paul looked back at his wartime service in the Mediterranean, he remembered it as a series of episodes loosely strung together by the ships in which he served. HMS *Tarquin*, a brand new fleet destroyer, was a good ship, efficient and well regarded by the flotilla leader; also a 'happy' ship with few disciplinary problems. It had been built on the Mersey in one of Britain's great shipbuilding yards, was fast and well armed, although the need for haste in its construction had been met at the expense of quality. The navy was launching one destroyer a week from British shipyards, but the fact that four destroyers cost the wartime government no more than a million pounds meant that little time was spent on details. Destroyer losses in the Mediterranean had been grievous and threatened, time and again, to cripple the entire fleet. Destroyers were needed to protect convoys, fight German and Italian U-boats, escort capital ships, bombard enemy coastlines, land commandos on hostile beaches, keep in touch with partisans and rescue the survivors of sinking ships. They were truly the maids of all work.

Destroyers had a complement of eight or nine officers and a crew of two hundred or more. They were crowded and uncomfortable but the numbers were needed to service the armament of guns, torpedoes and depth charges. Added to this were the engine room and boiler room staff, signalmen, telegraphists, sonar and radar operators, cooks, stewards and a medical orderly. In merchant ships it might have been sufficient to have one wireless operator to man the set during certain hours of the day, but in the navy it was manned for twenty-four hours, and the three operators who worked four-hour watches were supervised by a petty officer. It was the same for signalmen, radar and sonar operators—not one man for each specialty but four or five. But it was the gun armament that required the bulk of the manpower. The

4.7-inch guns and anti-aircraft weaponry could fire at a rate that devoured ammunition which, when the ship was in action, had to be moved up to feed the guns from storage in the lowest part of the ship.

The captain of *Tarquin* was a lieutenant-commander of impeccable credentials who had commanded ships since the outbreak of war. He had been at Dunkirk, taken a thousand soldiers off the beaches, and subsequently commanded a so-called 'lend-lease' American destroyer in the North Atlantic. He was in his mid-thirties, and if the war spared him he stood an excellent chance of becoming a full commander in a year or two. His First Lieutenant was a permanent navy officer who had been in the Fleet Air Arm but whose erratic flying had brought him back to the navy for which he had originally been trained. The only other permanent navy representative was the torpedo gunner, a warrant officer whose task was to ensure that the torpedoes, when launched from the tubes, ran straight and at a constant depth. The torpedoes were arguably the main armament of the ship because they had the power to sink an enemy battleship. The guns might be effective against destroyers, but they would do nothing against a capital ship.

Tarquin had been launched without fanfare on a cold day in early 1942. There followed a hasty fitting out, while the crew was assembled over a period of days in a local hotel. The crew consisted of 'hostilities only' ratings, more than half of whom had never previously been to sea. Only the chief petty officers and petty officers and a few of the leading seamen were permanent navy, and while the men under them were volunteers and had chosen the navy ahead of the army, they had much to learn. They came from farms, factories, slums and even, in some cases, well-to-do neighbourhoods, and had been given three months training ashore which, as the First Lieutenant pointed out, was totally irrelevant to their duties aboard a destroyer. Yes, they could march up and down the parade ground, slope arms and order arms, but they had no idea how to sling their hammocks or check away handsomely on a forespring. Unlike the crew of *Badger*, who came from fishermen's families and had been at sea since boyhood, the crew of *Tarquin* had to learn their business from the keel up.

"One thing we can be thankful for," announced Palliser, the First Lieutenant, "they didn't send us any old stripeys.[9] In my experience, they are the worst. They don't teach the young sailors anything except how to avoid work and make nuisances of themselves. Most of them have been in and out of trouble for their entire navy careers."

Palliser had a tendency to take what in fact was a germ of truth and then blow it up.

The officers in *Tarquin's* wardroom, excepting the Captain, First Lieutenant and Paul, were equally lacking in hard experience. The warrant-officer torpedo gunner had spent three years in a Chinese river gunboat. The gunnery officer was a newly promoted lieutenant who had taken the Whale Island course as Paul had done; the anti-submarine officer was on loan from the Australian navy; another reserve officer, who looked after the ship's office in addition to his watch-keeping duties, had been a bank manager and had sailed at weekends. The others had been yachtsmen or just schoolboys before the war. The navy was glad to get them because the Royal Air Force was a strong contender for well-educated and adventurous young men in their late teens or early twenties. There was glamour in flying, plus rapid promotion, and great satisfaction in being a witness to the damage that was being inflicted on the enemy. *Tarquin* also carried a surgeon-lieutenant who had finished his medical training only weeks before the war and had never served a hospital internship. With some justification he complained that he had little work because the ship's company was healthy and aboard ship they never came in contact with disease.

---

[9] An able seaman with long-service stripes.

The month spent 'working up' in the great naval base at Scapa Flow in the Orkneys had, however, gone some way toward preparing officers and men for what lay ahead. They had fired the guns at 'splash' targets towed by fast motorboats, an aircraft had flown over towing a drogue for the anti-aircraft weapons to test their accuracy, and they had hunted a real submarine in the treacherous waters of Pentland Firth. Every conceivable exercise had been carried out, including full speed trials, turning trials, the launching of dummy torpedoes and taking another destroyer in tow. Nothing had gone seriously wrong, although it was noted, time and again, that the standard of workmanship in *Tarquin* was less than perfect. In Paul's cabin was an old-fashioned washbasin but no running water. It took up valuable space so Paul unscrewed it and threw it overboard. The engineer officer also found a lot to complain about, and it was generally agreed that even in wartime there was little excuse for such poor workmanship.

From Scapa Flow, *Tarquin* sailed south to Liverpool and returned to the dockyard for a long list of defects to be corrected. Home leave was granted to all watches and Paul found himself on the unhappiest leave he had ever spent. While in Liverpool, he learned that *Badger* had been lost in the North Atlantic with heavy casualties. There were few details, but apparently they had moved in to pick up survivors of a torpedoed merchant vessel, and had been struck themselves as they lay stopped. In later years, Paul would remember *Badger* as his most perfect ship. Every officer had been a good friend, and every man a comrade. Some ships are like that. They seem to have character of their own, and the crew, all of them, feel an affection for the ship that they cannot explain. But that was not all. Rebecca had been called up and was in training somewhere in Scotland. Her location was secret and a visit impossible, and Paul could do no more than call on her parents at the rectory. In past years, he had found the Reverend F.F. and his rather stuffy wife a little intimidating, not exactly on Paul's good list, but now the old awkwardness had passed and he was able to share with them the disappointment of Rebecca's absence.

At sea once more, Paul's pencil lines on the chart of the North Atlantic, his crisscross chain of morning and evening star sights indicated that it was their turn to join battle in the Mediterranean. His mind went back to *Canopus*, a seagoing beast of burden that in less than two short years had given him some acquaintance with all the ports of any consequence in the great inland sea. They had ventured as far as Odessa on the Black Sea, east to the hot immorality of Alexandria, west to the clean, well ordered outline of Gibraltar. When *Tarquin* was at sea, Paul's duties kept him in the chartroom or on the upper bridge. In harbour he updated his charts with information that was supplied by the office of the Commander-in-Chief, such as detailed locations of minefields and swept passages through the minefields. Wrecks and obstructions were marked and, when time allowed, he instructed the two midshipmen in navigation and signals. He was also an avid reader of whatever he could get his hands on, preferably relevant to the places they visited.

When the Eighth Army liberated central and southern Italy, the south Italian ports were opened to the navy, and Manfredonia, a fishing village on the Adriatic coast, became their forward base. It was a tedious place, with little to recommend it beyond a long wall where a couple of destroyers could lie in safety and then, under cover of darkness, steam up the coast looking for targets of opportunity. The mountains in this part of Italy came down to the seashore, and the railway, bearing German war materiel, was within easy range of a destroyer's guns.

On one occasion *Tarquin* and *Tudor*, flotilla leader, sailed out of Manfredonia and turned northward. The afternoon was misty and their destination, the little seaport of Ancona, lay under the lea of a small hill. Reports from Italian partisans indicated that the German army, which faced the Allies across the full width of Italy, was being supplied by coastal vessels which picked up cargoes in the north Adriatic ports of Venice and Trieste and carried them to Ancona to be unloaded. The dockside facilities in Ancona were thought to be negligible and war materiel was piled up on the wharves. War materiel was a legitimate target, but the first problem was to locate Ancona in darkness, and the Captain of *Tudor*, Captain Cranston, decided the only way to be sure was to close within a mile of the coast and steam northward until Ancona's distinctive hill was sighted. The harbour itself was protected from seaward by a strip of land, and the way in, and indeed, the only way to gain a good view of the wharves, was from the north. The hill itself was defended by gun emplacements.

Ancona was in darkness as *Tudor* and *Tarquin*, in line ahead, reduced speed and circled round to enter from the north. From the bridge Paul could make out the hill, perhaps three hundred feet in height, which dominated the inner harbour. With no more than half a mile to the wharfs, *Tudor* fired star-shell in a great arc of descending light, and both ships followed it up with full salvoes from their 4.7-inch guns. The piles of weapons, vehicles and ammunition boxes were clearly visible. There was little for Paul to do beyond watch the chart closely to make sure they did not run aground. The echo sounding machine, which measures the depth of water under the keel, was kept running and a sailor called out the readings: "Fifty…sixty…eighty feet…" On shore, ammunition exploded and fires blazed, and in the space of a few minutes the bombardment was over. *Tudor* turned with *Tarquin* close astern and made for open water, and it was at this point that the German guns on Ancona hill joined in the action. Splashes appeared round about, but their fire was poorly directed due, in all probability, to the cloud of grey smoke that lay over the bombardment area. To make it even more difficult for the German gunners, *Tarquin's* captain, being astern of *Tudor*, gave the engine room the order "make smoke". A dense cloud of black greasy smoke poured from the funnel and created an impenetrable sight barrier between Ancona hill and the two ships so that *Tudor* and *Tarquin* made a clean getaway, first northwards, then eastward into deeper water. The full extent of the damage to the dockyard, warehouses and equipment piled on the jetties would not be known until a week later when a reconnaissance aircraft flew over and captured the devastation on film.

Tudor hoisted the signal G30, meaning speed 30 knots, and the two ships thundered off into the darkness of the Adriatic. For the first time in his life Paul experienced a phenomenon called 'shallow water effect' in which destroyers operating at high speeds cannot steer effectively if the water is moderately shallow. Water is cast downwards from the ship's bow, strikes the seabed, say forty or fifty feet below, then rises to form a wall that follows the ship. The rudder is in a kind of vacuum and control is lost until deeper water is reached or the ship reduces speed. It came as a surprise to the officers and men who saw it for the first time.

In Manfredonia there were a few small fishing boats, but no shops, taverns or industry of any kind. Mountains rose behind the town, leaving almost no space for agricultural land. An Italy without orchards, without grainfields or stonecutters seemed to Paul to be no Italy at all, and Manfredonia compounded its miseries with an unnatural silence. No music came from doorways, no singing, no laughter, only the blank and hostile stares of people who seemed downcast by their own idle existence.

"I can't pay the ship's company," announced Sub-Lieutenant Humphries, who managed the ship's office. "There's no bank where I could get money, and no shops where they could spend it."

With time on their hands, a group of officers decided to climb the hill that brooded behind the town on the summit of which was perched a monastery.

"We'll get a monk's-eye view," the Australian Lieutenant suggested.

When they reached the summit after a two-hour climb, the view was superb. Manfredonia lay at their feet and the mountainous promontory of Vasto curled around to the north.

"Why is it that sailors," one of them asked, "see a mountain and feel they have to climb it? I mean, what is so special about the Adriatic, or the Mediterranean, for that matter?"

Paul tried to reply. He was hesitant at first, but the places he had seen and the history he had read had found its place somewhere in his mind. He, among his colleagues, was the one who knew the Mediterranean.

"I don't mean to talk like a schoolmaster," he began, "but it means 'middle of the earth', where mankind took his first steps in the direction of civilisation. It seems that very long ago they had flourishing communities round this shoreline, but then came a catastrophe in the form of a warm spell that affected the whole world. The great ice sheets melted—that was about 12,000 years ago, and sea levels went up. The people living around the Mediterranean all have 'flood' stories in their mythologies and, of course, we have ours in the Bible. It seems that sea levels rose twenty feet worldwide. In the Black Sea the Russians have discovered the remains of buildings under water."

Paul hesitated. He didn't mean to show off his knowledge but he was on a subject that he felt quite passionate about.

"For whatever reason, the great civilisations began to emerge after the flood. Not obvious why this was so; at least, not to me."

"Golly," said one of the midshipmen. "School I went to didn't teach that."

The island of Malta, strategically located in the central Mediterranean, was the main operational base of the destroyers. It was a dusty, treeless group of islands of only a hundred thousand people who had lived through bombing and food shortages, had supplied cooks and stewards to the navy for many years and had earned the accolades of another island which had suffered in the war. Malta was admired and many stories told of its bravery. An anecdote widely repeated concerned an English civil servant, a large blustery man responsible for feeding the inhabitants who, for lack of land, were not self-sufficient. During the worst days of the blockade he organised supplies to be brought in by air and submarine, imposed stringent rationing and handed out free packets of vegetable seeds. When things had reached their very worst, a deputation of Maltese elders came to his office and presented him with a portion of bread which was moldy, maggot ridden and altogether unfit for human consumption. They placed it on his desk on a sheet of dirty newspaper and asked him how they were to feed their families on anything so foul. The hunger he shared with the people of Malta had not deprived this functionary of his powers of verbal expression. Although far from his Whitehall office with its carpeted floors, loaded in-trays and leather-bound legal tomes, he nevertheless found words for a speech that was widely quoted. He marshalled the facts, explained the difficulties and expounded his limited options.

"You have eaten the donkeys that used to bear burdens on the narrow streets of Valetta," he intoned. "You have consumed the dogs and cats which used to be your household pets. Now the rats are proliferating, and you know what you must do..."

He glanced out of the shattered, glass-deprived window at the wrecked harbour of Marsaxlokk, a confusion of sunken ships and bombed wharves, and his voice took on a passion that might have been appropriate in formal debate if there had been any but a few desperately hungry Maltese to hear him. Finally, he fell to a whisper and wiped the crumbs from the corner of his mouth. He had been so hungry that he had eaten the filthy bread even as he spoke.

Paul met him much later, Sir Andrew Cohen, and marvelled how his career had been aided by the memory of that single morsel of stale bread. It clung to his record in the way that individual feats of military valour cling to heroes and become reference points that spring to mind when the hero's name is mentioned. Such an event has to be simple because legend must not be beyond the grasp of common man. King Alfred set the tone by burning someone's cakes. Nelson put his telescope to his blind eye. It becomes a sort of decoration worn in perpetuity, its lustre lasting as long as there are people to recall it.

One of many operations that *Tarquin* carried out in the Adriatic took them eastwards one summer night to a Yugoslav fishing village a few miles from Zadar. A rather agitated partisan had come aboard with a British military officer and briefed them on a plan to pick up escaped Allied prisoners behind enemy lines. At that time the Germans were in nominal control of the Dalmatian coastline but were opposed by Tito's partisans who had the reputation of being fierce and determined fighters. However, the partisans were often divided among themselves and not invariably trustworthy when it came to dates, times and places. What worried Paul, who was responsible for getting them to exactly the right place, was that they would carry neither a pilot nor anyone with knowledge of the coast. The partisan and his British army friend were all very well, but with no help in locating the tiny village, no lighthouses or aids to navigation, plus the realisation that the coastal towns were garrisoned with German troops, made the operation seem a dubious venture.

Tarquin's captain could have decided that the risk to his ship was unjustified, that he could be steaming into a trap, that the advantage lay too much in favour of the enemy. But then again he could scarcely argue that he would prefer to wait until there was more moon or that he would only undertake it if there were two destroyers, one to stand off and protect the other when the time came to move in. *Telemachus*, he knew, was in Alexandria and *Tudor* in Malta, and God only knew where the others were—probably on the west coast of Italy supporting the Eighth Army. If the partisans had rounded up a batch of escapees, such a group, however well disciplined, could not be concealed for any length of time in a tiny seaport that was supposedly in German hands. It took little discussion between the captain, Paul and the partisan to decide that it was now or never.

At midday the officers were called to the wardroom and the captain told them as much about the operation as he knew himself. The engineer was ordered to have steam by 1800 hours, and the ship's company was warned to get some rest because they would be at battle stations all night. As the bell struck, *Tarquin* slipped her lines and steamed eastward into the Adriatic. The sea was calm and sailors with excellent eyesight and powerful binoculars scoured the horizon. A month previously they had patrolled this area in daylight to thwart a German landing on the island of Vis, and Paul had drawn freehand silhouettes of the coast every five miles so that if ever they returned, as they did now, he would have an idea of what the outline of the hills looked like in darkness. In the days before radar, this was normal practice and part of a navigator's duty. The village they had to find was on the mainland somewhere between Sibernik and Zadar. It was small, insignificant, surrounded by mountains and reported as having only a few German troops, but its exact whereabouts was not known to either the partisan or the British liaison officer who stood together on the bridge.

This part of the Yugoslav coast is protected by two lines of offshore islands, and both the captain and Paul were agreed that the inner channel was best approached from the northern end at a place marked on the chart as Sestrunj. The gap between the great rocky outcrops was almost certainly indicated to mariners, probably with white painted beacons on shore. The actual gap was thought to be no more than a hundred yards wide but the chance of there being German guns was slight. In the event, the Sestrunj channel was found with remarkable ease and the captain reduced speed. The marks on shore showed them exactly where they were and when the mainland was sighted they turned south. At this point luck was on their side because the little seaport of Zadar was not blacked out and could be seen from miles away. The partisan and his army friend took over from there and by 0200, keeping the shoreline a mile distant to port, the partisan thought they were in the right place.

"Go slow," he said. "Here is entrance." The captain reduced speed and turned toward land.

"You make noise on whistle," said the partisan, but before *Tarquin* had sounded its siren a light appeared briefly and flashed in their direction.

The next few minutes provided an example of seamanship on the part of *Tarquin's* captain, good preparation by Paul, and of superlative co-operation and discipline by the partisans. The tiny harbour had only one wharf but the water inside was deep and the wharf was in line with the harbour entrance. This meant that *Tarquin* could go in astern and out ahead. No manoeuvring was needed inside the harbour.

The captain turned *Tarquin* through 180 degrees and went in dead slow astern. There was no wind and light came only from a waning moon. The partisan seemed confident but Paul, and doubtless the captain also, were inwardly nervous. So much might have gone wrong; they were operating under the very noses of a vigilant and determined enemy. Palliser was on the torpedo deck with a dozen men whose weapons were useless in these circumstances. Fenders were out and the torpedomen cast lines around the bollards on the jetty. No effort was made to secure the ship properly but she lay alongside without movement. It was the silence, the calmness, that Paul remembered. A figure came out of the shadows and Palliser spoke to him.

"I hope this isn't a trap," Paul said to himself.

The man turned, blew a whistle and a mass of humanity appeared and hurried aboard. The jetty was the same height as the torpedo deck so they stepped across and under their weight *Tarquin* listed two or three degrees. It was over in a minute. No gangways had been put out, no orders shouted, and *Tarquin* had its passengers. The partisan raised his hand and Palliser told his men to let go the ropes. He called to the bridge, "We're clear, sir," and the captain leaned down to the voicepipe. A jet of white water shot astern and within minutes they had passed the harbour entrance.

Palliser looked round him in some bewilderment. No one had told him there would be four hundred of them, and it was now his job to make them tolerably comfortable for the passage to Malta. The injured were sent to the sick bay where Dr. Pearce would take over. Palliser's next thought was to get the officers to the wardroom, but this was a hopeless task because none of them wore recognisable uniforms, just the clothes which they had borrowed or stolen in Nazi-occupied

Europe. They found any spot they could on the messdecks, the upper deck and beneath the gun platforms and slept on the bare steel as they had not slept in months. Palliser decided to leave them alone and not attempt the impossible, namely to take their names, ranks and service details, assign them a messdeck and tell them what would be expected if the ship went into action. It worried him that with *Tarquin's* crew at battle stations he couldn't even organise a drink of water, far less a cup of soup. They lay down in their clothes wherever they could find space, the vicinity of *Tarquin's* hot funnel being favoured. The throbbing steel deck and the realisation that they were free men was all they asked.

The captain ordered engine revolutions for 27 knots and *Tarquin* threaded its way between the islands and turned southwards. They thundered over a calm sea and by morning had reached the narrows between the heel of Italy and the mountainous coast of Montenegro, and when Paul calculated that it was time to turn southwest toward Malta, they had only twelve hours steaming on a straight course. He picked his way down the crowded deck toward his cabin, the deck by then warming under the first rays of an August sun. *Tarquin's* white wake stretched back to the horizon. Until that moment he had not realised what it meant to be carrying three times the number of men for which the ship had been designed, although his experience in *Artemis* should have warned him. He tried the door of his cabin but couldn't get in because it was filled with sleeping men. When he returned to the bridge he looked in the logbook to check the entries made during the night and realised it was his birthday. For no good reason he laughed aloud. What did a birthday matter in circumstances such as these?

He would eventually hear some of the stories these men told—stories that would have filled a dozen books. The Polish cavalry officer who had ridden his horse across Europe and, when it dropped dead from exhaustion, he had continued on foot. The British soldiers who had evaded capture at Dunkirk, faded into the countryside and made their way slowly across France. There were French boys who disobeyed their political masters, refused to collaborate with the hated Nazis, wanted nothing more than to fight in the uniform of the Free French. There were airmen—British, American and Commonwealth—who had bailed out of their bombers and parachuted to earth to be scooped up in occupied Europe, passed from country to country and delivered to the Balkan mountains where the partisans directed them to the coast. An American flyer, one of fourteen individuals squeezed into Paul's cabin, said that his plane had been shot to pieces over Germany so he ordered his crew to bail out. The local partisans found him and put him on a 'safe' train to Belgrade. That had been only a week before.

"Now dis is what I call soyvice," he said, tapping the side of Paul's bunk. It was then that Paul learned something he had not even thought about until that moment. A British sergeant, in the clothes of a mountain peasant but with the inescapable accent of a Scot, told him that when he got home he'd not only be entitled to leave but also to his accumulated pay—in his case, two years' worth. Not every belligerent country was as generous toward its soldiers.

"I canna tell ye," he began, gaunt, bearded and dressed in the filthiest clothes Paul had ever seen, "how I long to see my wife and my wee bairns."

A few weeks later, after landing her passengers at Malta, *Tarquin* was ordered to Alexandria. The asdic dome, which was attached to the keel of the ship and housed the anti-submarine equipment, had been swept off, probably by wreckage. A new dome would have to be fitted which could be done only in dry dock. It was a nuisance, because the ship's company would have to be moved to barracks ashore, it being impossible for the dockyard to work with waste-water, effluent and garbage pouring down on them from 200 men above. There was a chance, however, that other defects might be corrected while in dockyard, and there was always the hope that the new asdic would be a better model than the last. Best of all, they might fit one of the new radar sets that were often promised but rarely delivered.

The port city of Alexandria stirred displeasing memories from Paul's visit while he had been in *Canopus*. To his delight, however, the captain suggested that the two of them travel to Cairo by train, spend two or three days in Shepherd's hotel and visit the Cairo museum, among other places. Paul was thrilled at the prospect of immersing his mind and imagination in the arcane mysteries of the pharaohs. For both of them it was their first visit and they found an experienced guide who was glad to offer his services at such a time, the flow of tourists having become much reduced during the war years. Paul had with him a copy of Breasted's great book, *The Splendour That Was Egypt*, and he had assembled some tourist pamphlets.

From the outset, Paul sensed that Egypt was not a completely new experience. As they traveled by train from Alexandria to Cairo he looked over the darkening fields, the smoky evening fires and the clusters of date palms, and was gripped by the conviction that he had, in some obscure way, set his footsteps there in an earlier chapter of his life. When it was too dark to see he turned to his reading and the first name that caught his eye was a pharaoh called Amenhotep. Amen, he thought, 'amen' sounds familiar. He looked out the train window and imagined the people eating their evening meals or bent over some evening task. He himself had never made bricks without straw, nor drawn water from the Nile, nor left his writing on the wall, but a distant race of people had done so, a people who, when you come to think of it, had contributed to his own education. The more he thought about it the more he realised that the connection between himself and this land was not as remote as at first appeared.

The Hebrews of the Old Testament had begun as a band of herdsmen who, in the course of their wanderings, spent several generations, possibly a century or more, in this land where they adopted much of what they found. The Egyptian army had rounded them up in what the authorities of those days must have cancelled off as a skirmish, turning them into slaves who were forced to work on public monuments. This was a situation no more remarkable than it would have been for a landlord to take possession of a few wild goats or a flock of geese that wandered onto his property. The Hebrews, however, were never fully assimilated and clung to their unique tribal character over which they superimposed the myths, the stories and much of the learning of their masters. Theirs was a cultural attachment in which Egyptian fairy tales turned into profound truths, the mythology of their lords was transformed into Holy Writ. Egyptian names were pilfered, identifying beyond doubt their origins. Tutmose the pharaoh, quite obviously Moses—Abraham without the 'A' was Brahmin. Hebrew toil was expended on the sands of Egypt until at last the Pharaoh decided that the Hebrews, always complaining, were more trouble than they were worth. He may have hoped that by expelling them they would form a buffer between himself and the Assyrians. What he could not have anticipated was that they would appropriate so much of the baggage of pharaonic civilisation. They took the mythology and the half-truths of local lore and wrapped it about them like a cloak.

True to character, the Hebrews created a political storm when they took their leave. Nothing about their departure was straightforward, no step factually reported, no event unembellished, and their God, who always put in an appearance on national occasions, was expected to play His part at every stage. Beyond Egypt's borders they wandered aimlessly but finally reached more or less vacant ground, and having taken the precaution of claiming that God had promised them this particular bit of land, they developed an organised society based on what they had learned in Egypt. The pharaoh probably breathed a sigh of relief because his northern border was in good hands.

Paul, steeped in an English classical education where school and church march hand in hand, had learned Old Testament stories from childhood, the King James version with its air of imperturbable authority being the ideal vehicle for this ancient learning. In those days, between the wars, English speech was peppered with quotations from the Old Testament because it imparted a kind of dignity, a sanctity even, to an otherwise flatulent statement. Serious matters might be "inscribed on tablets of stone", they would "cross the Red Sea" when they came to it—might even, when the occasion was appropriate, "rejoice and kill the fatted calf". The New Testament on the other hand, was treated with caution. Victorian strictures remained in place and people would be offended if water were changed into wine with any suggestion of frivolity. It was, therefore, the Old Testament, with its earthiness, rather than the New, which became the source of everyday metaphor and was plundered for all those little sayings that decorated an otherwise tedious conversation. In short, the ancient Hebrews had conveyed ancient Egyptian culture to the Christian church so that English-speaking people, steeped in Shakespeare and the King James Bible, had taken it into their hearts and homes. It was this that had invaded Paul's mind with a sense of familiarity, the feeling that he already knew something of their ancient gods, their prayers and their religious pageantry.

The rooftop restaurant where they dined that evening offered a stunning, almost unearthly view of the pyramids. The ancient stones stood speechless, but not entirely silent, and the two of them, captain and navigator, talked far into the night.

The war in the Mediterranean turned gradually in favour of the Allied forces, and the T-class destroyers were present in many of the major battles. They did not operate together as a flotilla, but individually or in pairs in the landings, bombardments and escort work that characterised the final two years of the conflict at sea. The Italian fleet was no longer a force to be reckoned with, and the Italian ships hiding in Pola, in the north, never left port. *Tarquin* did, however, do battle with an Italian submarine that had been taken over and manned by the German navy. Allied spies knew a good deal about it, including the details of its exceptional size. To become effective, however, it would have to move out of the Adriatic and sail westwards, past Malta, through the strait of Gibraltar and into the Atlantic. Charts were studied, and it appeared that the bottleneck between the heel of Italy and the Albanian coast, the Strait of Otranto, was where it would be most vulnerable.

The T-class destroyers could carry out an anti-submarine search at no more than 22 knots. Faster than that and the water noises reduced the efficiency of the asdic, so with their sister ships *Thane* and *Telemachus*, which were dispatched from Malta to take part in the operation, Paul and the captain worked out a search pattern which, by their calculation, would not allow the enemy to slip through. They would maintain constant speed, steer a crisscross pattern east and west, and remain exactly 10 miles apart. The submarine's best submerged speed was probably seven knots so the chances of locating it seemed good, especially because its captain did not know that spies were reporting his every move.

Tarquin made the first contact. It was early morning and the Albanian mountains rose from the sea a mile ahead of them. Palliser was on watch and even as he gave the order to alter course, the asdic returned an unmistakable echo. Palliser issued a stream of orders.

"Hold that echo. Wheel amidships. Reduce engine revolutions. Call the captain. Sound the anti-submarine alarm." All were meticulously obeyed.

Paul had been sleeping lightly in the chart room, so he and Ken Meyer, the anti-submarine officer, were on the bridge in seconds, the captain just behind.

"Classify," ordered the captain.

Meyer put on his earphones and listened. "Submarine."

Tarquin executed the standard preliminary attack with depth charges set to explode at fifty feet, the presumption being that the enemy had been cruising on the surface or at periscope depth. Six charges were released from the rails and four flung from the throwers to explode with massive booms and stacks of water. The sound echoed from the mountains that rose almost directly from the sea less than a mile away. The Germans had chosen to hug the coastline.

Paul's duty during a submarine hunt was to keep an eye on the chart and mark the location of the enemy. He would also compose a signal to be sent by wireless to the Admiralty in London and the Commander-in-Chief in Malta. He reported to the captain that there were no enemy airfields along that stretch of coast, so air attack could be ruled out. *Telemachus* was contacted by Aldis lamp and the message was passed to *Thane*. Both ships abandoned their search and came at full speed to join *Tarquin*. Within minutes of arrival they had hoisted their 'contact' signals and the three captains spoke together by radiotelephone. The battle plan was to take turns attacking with depth charges, which meant running over the enemy, which had dived to a depth between five hundred and six hundred feet. The other two ships would maintain contact while the third attacked.

It must be hellish in a U-boat, Paul thought. They can hear the asdic on their hull, then would come the roar of depth charges exploding round them. A charge of three hundred pounds had to go off within two feet of the hull to be fatal although within ten feet it might do great damage. Each attack by a destroyer consisted of ten charges at a consistent depth, as ordered by the anti-submarine officer. The depth-setting mechanism, a rubber diaphragm inside each charge, was set by a seaman on the afterdeck, while the charges were released in a pattern determined on the bridge.

Paul had long ago realised that war can take strange turns, but there occurred an event during the U-boat hunt that seemed to carry improbability to new lengths. The captain passed his walkie-talkie to Paul.

"What do you make of this?"

Paul put the device to his ear and heard agitated voices. Like all non-professional wireless users, he simply shook it and listened again.

"Russian, sir," Paul said in amazement.

"What are they saying?"

"I know very little Russian." He tried to catch a few more words. "I think they are tank commanders. There seems to be a battle going on."

The captain looked at him. "How extraordinary."

Paul felt strangely elated that there were others who hated the Germans as much as they did, although it was some time before he learned that the radio phenomenon they had witnessed was not uncommon. The hastily constructed Russian wireless sets were more powerful that they need have been, and when combined, as in this case, with ideal weather conditions, the Russian tank commanders could be heard more than a thousand miles from the plains of Kharkof where they were engaged.

The German U-boat, meanwhile, surfaced after the hundredth depth charge had exploded. It blew its tanks, the sound being unmistakable on the asdic, and suddenly there it was on the surface, ready to be shot to pieces by gunfire. It had a number painted on its upperworks but no name, and all who saw it thought it was the largest submarine they had ever seen.

The German navy, at that time, was armed with torpedoes that could be fired randomly and would 'home' on the engine sounds of the destroyers. To be safe, the three captains stopped their engines and the gunnery officers went to work. Great chunks of the conning tower flew off, the submarine's gun went over the side and in minutes it had sunk. About a dozen members of its crew were in the water.

Tarquin closed in and scrambling nets were lowered so that survivors could save themselves. A few did so, but others swam away into the darkness where they had no hope of rescue. Palliser shouted at them to come back. His German was not up to much although his French was passable, but none of his calls were heeded. He turned to the bridge.

"Sir, I could lower a boat and chase after them."

"Certainly not," replied the captain. "If they choose to die we must let them go."

Hours later, in Malta, when the three ships were being replenished, the three captains met and discussed the battle and the lessons learned. It was mentioned that some of the Germans had refused to be rescued.

"That's understandable," said *Thane's* captain. "One of those men was the U-boat's captain. He must have held other commands before this, almost certainly in the Atlantic. He sank defenceless merchant ships, even hospital ships, and made not the faintest attempt to rescue survivors. In other words, he has flouted the Geneva Convention and made a mockery of a sea captain's duty. If he becomes a prisoner of war, he's shit-scared of what may happen. He prefers death to dishonour. A few of his officers share his preferences."

A huge grey wave rolled across the hatches and *Marquess* recoiled, as though in anger. "Am I to die as those Germans did?" Paul asked himself. He had become light-headed, had reached his lowest ebb yet somehow, vaguely, in his mind, he saw his ancestor, Jaime, standing upon a shore and beckoning him to save himself.

"Where am I?" he asked aloud. "Is this my tomb? Surely to God I am not abandoned..."

Chapter 7 — Looters Will Be Shot

The next step in Paul's career was taken in the port of Naples. The German army did not stand and fight for the city, having suffered defeat at Salerno a few miles to the south and instead, their Commander-in-Chief, Field Marshall Albert Kesselring, retreated northward and established his defensive line—called the Gustav Line —across the mountainous spine of Italy from the Tyrrhenian Sea to the Adriatic. Although closer to Naples than Rome, the line was intended primarily for the defence of the eternal city. Kesselring had begun his military career as an airman but, on Hitler's orders, found himself commanding all German forces in the Italian peninsula. When studying his map, his greatest fear must have been that the Allies would land in northern Italy and isolate his army. It never happened because the Allies were reserving their manpower, their ships, guns and aircraft for the Normandy landings.

In September 1943, with the Allied armies pouring into Naples, the Italians tired of war and concluded a rough and ready peace. There was little rejoicing when the news reached the Allied fighting services and little expectation that the Italian forces would be of any help in the future prosecution of the war. At best, some of the Italian ships might be useful, but not in a belligerent capacity. To the amusement of many, the Prime Minister announced that henceforth Italians would be described as "co-belligerents". Naples was not at war, therefore, and with Germans occupying half the country, not at peace either. Neapolitans were wary of the Allies who, for their part, could find little that was favourable about the Italians. An exception was when Americans of Italian descent, some of them Italian speaking, located members of their extended families. On one point the Allies agreed, however, and that was the high standard of artistry and craftsmanship among ordinary Italians. These people possessed a natural gift for beautifying their work and even a lemonade parlour might be decorated with artistic mosaics.

It was at this time that the Allied services received a special order from their political masters. If the opportunity to kill Hitler should present itself, they were to refrain from doing so. The reasoning behind it was based on Hitler's faulty and amateurish direction of the German war effort and it was to the Allies' advantage to keep him in place and let him continue his military blunders. It would have been a costly mistake to allow the German generals to take over direction of the war.

When Paul looked back on the time he spent in Naples he was at a loss to describe the chaos of war. People to whom he spoke in later years imagined that the war was well organised, clean, tidy and governed by military discipline; but in fact, behind the lines, it was closer to anarchy. The German defences were a few miles to the north and the Italians, many of them, didn't seem to know whose side they were on. The police, *carabiniere*, were on the streets but without much effect, and the Italian army was scarcely to be seen at all. Americans were present in great numbers and controlled the dock area, which was vulnerable to looting. Naples, at that moment, was the greatest port in the world in terms of the tonnage of war materiel being unloaded on a daily basis and passed forward to the front lines. It was claimed that there were sixty 'alongside' berths where ships could unload simultaneously, some with the help of cranes, others by stevedores using simple hoists. It never occurred to Paul that there was any alternative to cargo being carried loosely, or at best in crates in the holds of merchant ships. This was how it had always been done since seaborne commerce began. Tea came in tea chests; gold in wooden boxes; slaves, machinery, cordage, grain and wine jars were all packed into holds as best they would fit. The problems of theft were staggering. It was called 'pilferage', and on nearly all the world's seaways it was estimated that fifteen percent of all goods shipped would be stolen. The solution to pilferage was the steel container, which was, in effect, a 'safe' large enough to hold the items most at risk, and a godsend for small, valuable articles. Containers, however, were still in the future. Naples' dockyard in wartime consisted of hundreds of acres piled high with weapons, equipment and supplies of every kind. It looked like chaos, and notices were posted everywhere in English and Italian: "Looters will be shot." Armed American military police, called 'dewdrops' because of their white helmets, seemed only too ready to comply, and their callous, no-questions-asked, ever-ready justice shocked no one in those desperate times. The genius of the Naples dockyard was British Rear Admiral J.A.V. Morse, and in co-operation with the American army and with a dozen other armies represented in Italy, he kept men and goods in constant movement northward to the front line and reasonably safe from looters.

Paul had often noticed that it was small things that he remembered best. Leading out of the dockyard, with a constant stream of American 10-wheeler trucks passing, was a road sign urging drivers to caution. "Life is so short," it read. A little further on, "Injury is so painful." Time to digest that one, then, "Death is so permanent." Finally, "Drive carefully you silly bastard." No fancy language there.

Then there was the story of a group of American soldiers who didn't much like the reception they were getting in a roadside bar, so they emptied their pockets of money and bought the whole place on the spot. The American town major was widely applauded for establishing not one but five brothels. Prices were fixed and posted on the doors and the women examined by medical personnel. Wine bars were likewise abundant and it was common practice for soldiers to roll a wine barrel into the street, shoot a hole in it and fill up their canteens.

"These were the people who had prohibition until fairly recently," Palliser observed. "They seem to have gone rather far the other way."

Tarquin was overdue for refit and repair. The boilers had to be scoured and the hull scraped clean of barnacles and marine growth. The Mediterranean had a bad reputation for fouling ships' bottoms, reducing speed and wasting fuel. A large dry dock would have accommodated four destroyers, but the first to be brought into working order was small and would take only one vessel of modest size. It happened to be *Tarquin*. The island of Ischia in the Bay of Naples had been taken over by the navy a few days earlier as a rest and recuperation centre and it was planned that *Tarquin's* men would be carried there by ferry the day following their move into dry dock. Leave was granted and a battle-weary crew streamed out of the dockyard and into the littered streets. Paul discovered that the opera house, the San Carlo, had been reopened for the entertainment of Allied servicemen, and that Benjamino Gigli, regarded by music lovers as the greatest operatic tenor in the world at that time, would be on stage. That evening, Paul and Palliser found themselves picking their way through the shattered dockyard toward the San Carlo. Paul's knowledge of opera was exceedingly slight, but his experience of church choirs had left him with some appreciation of the human voice.

The San Carlo was in fairly good condition, except for a hole in the roof. A bomb, Allied or German, had landed in the 'dress circle' where it failed to explode. Its removal had been the responsibility of a team of chain smoking, dubious looking bomb-disposal experts who were paid, so it was said, an extra shilling a day for 'danger money'. Within hours, the opera house was alive and tuning its musical instruments while vocal chords were also given an airing. There seemed to Paul to be irony in the fact that the new military rulers of Naples demanded opera on the one hand, one of the world's more civilised art forms, and on the other, threatened to shoot looters on sight.

"Charmingly unambiguous," Palliser remarked as they entered the hall. "Isn't it rather typical of Naples that Gigli was a fascist, and Germans with swastikas on their uniforms warmed these seats until a few days ago."

Paul did not know how a qualified, knowledgeable opera critic would have judged what he saw and heard that evening, but to him the music was sublime and the audience amazing. Every corner of the theatre was filled with servicemen, many of whom had never heard opera before and had little idea what to expect. They were there because others were there and the performance was free. They filled the seats, crowded at the back, and Paul counted sixteen men in a gilded box. One more, Paul thought, and that box will fall off the wall. In those days the Allies could be identified by their shoulder flashes, and on that occasion the San Carlo was crowded with soldiers from every freedom-loving nation on earth. Americans, British, Canadians and Australians, fierce little Gurkhas, Sikhs in their carefully wound puggarees, Polish soldiers in uniforms and caps that went out of fashion about three wars before this one. There were Free French, Dutch marines, some Norwegians and a few Brazilians who were easy to identify in their dark green battledress. A shoulder flash 'PPA' stood for Popski's Private Army, surely the most improbable unit to find space on a modern battlefield, or indeed, in an opera house. Count Popski, so the story went, raised an army after the fall of Poland. The Polish government in exile was mired in bickering, so the British gave up talking to them and allowed Popski to get on with the job. General Alexander said it was one of the most efficient units under his command.

"That fool Hitler has made enemies throughout the civilised world," Palliser whispered. "I hope that after the war…" He trailed off as a dozen field nurses, for whom chairs had been found, provided a momentary distraction. The curtain went up and the audience fell silent—no, it was more than that, it was unearthly, the silence after battle, and the conductor raised his baton. He wore the tattered and dirty uniform of an Italian infantry officer who must have served in North Africa, and Paul wondered if the audience thought he was intended to look that way. The first violin was some sort of medical orderly with a red cross on his coat; the percussionist, just visible at the rear of the pit, wore what could have been a striped prison uniform. But it was the performers who truly cast a spell. They were outfitted in the castoffs of a bygone era, helped out with street clothes. It looked as though the opera company's wardrobe had been looted somewhere between the German departure and the Allied arrival, the looters having left the more outrageous habiliments which had subsequently been shared by those on stage. Their dress was reminiscent of what might be found in an old trunk in the attic of a country house. One could tell that rehearsals had been hurried because the cast kept bumping into each other and the lighting was perpetual twilight, but nothing else mattered when they sang. The music was moving in its contrast to the shoddy surroundings, and in some way the audience was in sympathy with the hardships of those on stage. These were not highly paid, well rehearsed artists; no, they were ordinary people.

Benjamino Gigli was thought by many to be a worthy successor to the legendary Caruso, who had delighted the musical world in that very opera house fifty years earlier. Paul would remember the serious look, the unbending figure and the high tenor, almost unnaturally high, and his total command of the music. Gigli, the Italian word for 'lily', was friend to Mussolini, the comic-opera dictator, who had been all puff and show, not even as good as Charlie Chaplin, who subsequently mocked him on the silver screen. Unlike Mussolini, Gigli survived the war and the music-loving public forgave him his fascist indiscretions. During the performance he was dressed as a coachman, although there appeared to Paul to be no connection between his clothing and the part he was singing. His leading lady seemed rather in awe of him, but she sang divinely, dressed in a wispy gown that had an Aida, slave-girl, banks-of-the-Nile look about it. Later Paul asked himself whether Gigli could have been affected by his own performance on that occasion, as was his audience, or whether it was just another evening where he could work his magic by the natural magnificence of his voice.

As they returned to their ship Paul and Palliser walked through the bombed and battered dockyard, and quite suddenly Palliser announced with total conviction, "That wasn't a performance; it was the real thing." It seemed as good a way of saying it as any, but Paul was thinking of Rebecca and wishing she had been at his side. How could he tell her, how could he explain? How could he write and say that the audience, by its very quiet, its wonderment, had contributed to a God-given performance?

The island of Ischia lies at the northwest corner of the Bay of Naples, a two-hour ferry ride from the dockyard. It is larger than Capri which is at the southern end of the bay, but not so popular and with fewer hotels and lodging houses. Somehow, on the roulette wheel of wartime affairs, Ischia was allocated to the navy, Capri to the army. It was to Ischia, therefore, that the officers and men of *Tarquin* were taken to receive their share of rest and relaxation. The men, all two hundred of them, were billeted in the largest hotel while the officers found themselves in a boarding house. The twenty non-commissioned officers had a villa to themselves. As they got settled in, Palliser, taking his duties seriously as usual, inspected the accommodations, bathrooms and kitchens to assure himself that no one had cause for complaint. However, to the dismay of *Tarquin's* men, Ischia had no beer, no cinema and no women under sixty, but the food was quite good, wine was available and they could swim in the sea. It was still warm in early autumn and there was no shortage of fish, which the locals caught on a nightly basis, and fruit seemed to hang from every branch. During a long and tiresome war it was not a bad place to spend a few days, perhaps not in quite the same class with Taormina on Sicily's east coast with its view of Mount Aetna, but pleasant enough.

Relaxation was not on Paul's mind, however, when he and Palliser, on the second day of their visit, decided to walk round the island, a distance of about ten nautical miles. There was no traffic on the narrow dirt road, save for the odd donkey cart, because Mussolini had effectively deprived the island, and indeed the whole country, of its petroleum supplies, and there was no way of obtaining more. To remind the poor but peaceful inhabitants of their wartime miseries, there were outdated government posters still on the walls. One read 'The Mediterranean is an Italian Lake', with Mussolini's belligerent face glaring at an empty street.

The day was hot, the road unpaved and, judging themselves to be half way round the island, they entered a forsaken restaurant with its courtyard overgrown with weeds. There were three or four stone tables and no other customers, but a sign said 'Trattoria' so they seated themselves and called for the padrone. "Heil Hitler," he barked as he approached, not being aware, because he had neither radio nor newspaper, that significant changes had occurred during recent days. He didn't have beer either, so they settled for a bottle of wine that was duly brought, together with a couple of tumblers.

At this stage of his life Paul knew even less about wine than he knew about opera. This was because France, which had always supplied England with wine, had been overrun in 1940, Italy had been an enemy until a few days earlier, while Spain exported sherry but not much else. The United States was still recovering from the insanity of prohibition while other wine-producing countries, chief among them

South Africa, had more important cargoes than wine to pack in the holds of their overloaded merchant ships. Wine, therefore, had become something of a rarity and was expensive, even at duty-free prices. Thus, despite the long historic association between wine drinking and the officers messes of the navy, which was exemplified by the fact that an officer's bar bill was still referred to as his 'wine bill', many officers had never tasted it.

Palliser was the exception. He was possessed of 'private means' as they said in those days, and could afford wine. He always drank it when he could, never beer or spirits, and he knew enough about it to take him out of the beginner's class. Paul learned eventually not only to appreciate wine but also to master the language and describe its nuances without bothering to economise with his vocabulary. This wine he might have described as a species of white, a few degrees cooler than the surrounding air. It was cloudy and had probably been trodden out by Heil Hitler's feet. It tasted earthy with stalks and pips predominating and smelled perilously close to a barnyard. As the world measures these things it was a terrible vintage, but the two of them were possessed of an innocent thirst and the sylvan surroundings of fig trees, olives and almonds, with the Tyrrhenian Sea shining in the bright sun, persuaded them to linger and drink a second bottle. This done, they resolutely resumed their journey.

"I don't like this road," Palliser announced after a few faltering steps. "It's trying to throw me in the ditch."

At dinner that evening the captain was at his benign best. "May I suggest, gentlemen, that you leave marching to the army and go fishing instead." His remarks were not directed at anyone in particular. "The best fish in the Mediterranean are gray mullet," he continued. "Why not see if you can catch some for tomorrow evening, and we'll find a white Chianti."

On their return to Naples, the crew of *Tarquin* discovered that the ship was not ready to be refloated and they were to spend a few days in a waterfront hotel. Paul decided to call at the offices of the Flag Officer, Western Italy, code named FOWIT, with the object of finding the officer responsible for charts of the Mediterranean to compare with his own and check for accuracy and completeness. An old friend was, to his pleasure and surprise, sitting behind the desk. They had been apprentices in prewar days, and now they wore the same uniform of reserve lieutenants, entrusted, as was commonly the case with such officers, with navigating duties of one sort or another.

"I have a story to tell," his friend said, "which I think will interest you. Do you remember old Captain Rannach? He had a reputation for being potty, but now there's talk of a court martial." The two of them ate their dinner in the officer's wardroom, and later found a quiet corner. "Yes," he said, "Captain Rannach—five years captain of the *Aquitania*—was said to have been an enormous success with lady passengers on his many transatlantic crossings during the twenties and thirties. He retired at sixty and when the war started in 1939 he presented himself at the Admiralty, by which time he must have been seventy. They asked him what sea experience he'd had so he produced an Extra Master of Sail certificate signed personally by Queen Victoria. And would you believe it, would you honestly believe it, they subjected him to a medical examination which he somehow passed, and sent him here to the Mediterranean to take charge of an information-gathering organisation."

"Information gathering?" Paul asked. "How does a sailing ship man...?"

"The connection," his friend went on, "is this. As you've seen, the Mediterranean is crisscrossed by sailing schooners that do good business between the smaller ports where large ships can't get in. They may be anywhere from fifty to a couple of hundred tons, manned by local fellows, and they carry cargoes of what you'd expect—building stone, barrels of wine, olive oil, dried fish. Of course they are sailing ships, no use to the Germans, who simply ignore them. Most of them don't even have a wireless set. The Greeks have a lot, so do the Turks and Spaniards. They're nearly always owned by the master, who arranges his own cargoes. It's a bit like the sort of fellow in England who owns a lorry and carries goods of every description about the country."

Paul poured another glass of pink wine. "Ravello Rosa," he read on the label.

"I'm beginning to get the idea," he said. "They go ashore, talk with the locals…"

"Well, just a minute. The work of information gathering is done by our own people who are recruited from all walks of life and can speak local languages. They are set to work as crewmen. Some are language scholars from the universities who learn to speak modern Greek, or whatever, with a dockside accent and terrible grammar. They must look inconspicuous, which means that an upstanding man is not what they want. Better to find a short, cross-eyed bloke who wouldn't be noticed in bar or brothel. You get the point—a man who's brave, a good actor and who's prepared to live and work as a deckhand in god-awful conditions, and doesn't look like a film star. One of them was a chap I knew who'd been all over the world with his father, an ambassador. He missed out on the fighting services because of his lousy eyesight, so he signed up as a spy." He paused. "Chris Hyde-Montague. He told me that after he'd been to the tavern and the local brothel in some little seaport he would search out the priest and pretend to confess his sins. He said that priests knew more than anyone about German troop movements, and were particularly good at assessing the mood of the locals."

"If he ever writes a book…" Paul began.

"Yes, but his story, which will have to wait till after the war, would miss the big picture. Look at it this way. The planners in Whitehall, the war cabinet or whoever, are always asking what's going on in the occupied countries like France and Greece, and to a lesser extent the not-so-friendlies like Spain and Turkey. If the Allies were to make a full-scale landing, what sort of help should we expect from the locals? Will partisans frustrate the German defences, blow up their petrol supplies, send their goods trains to all the wrong destinations? Will they knock off individual Germans who get separated from their units, or will they just stand and watch? How committed are they? To get a trustworthy reply to a question like that you need a lot of different viewpoints."

"But what I don't understand," Paul said, "is how Rannach, the Extra Master of Sail, collects the information from his deck hands and puts it together in some way that makes sense in London. In other words, how is the information assembled and sent on?"

"Good question, and I don't know the answer. But what Chris told me was that security is so tight that when two schooners are alongside, our fellows don't even recognise their counterparts. Chris said that the only way he could tell was because their teeth were better. Our fellows don't chew that foul Turkish tobacco."

"So what about the Extra Master? Why not a retired commander or captain of about fifty who had served here and knew the Mediterranean? The job you describe has everything to do with collecting information and nothing to do with sailing ships."

"Exactly, and to make matters worse, Captain Rannach, who is posted here in Naples, is going completely insane. The barracks personnel officer found him a cabin steward—we have Italian civilians for that sort of work—but no, he had his own ideas. A trained steward who had worked for Lloyd Triestino and spoke English wasn't what he wanted. He got himself an Italian girl, about seventeen, no English.

The other day he turned up in the wardroom with lipstick all over his face and shirt. The colonel of Marines... well, never mind."

Paul leaned back in his chair, "Extra Master of Sail! Schooners! I think the fault lies with whoever recruited him."

They were silent for a few moments. A steward approached and asked whether they would be ordering anything more from the bar.

"Not for me," Paul said, and thanked him.

"You know," his friend went on, "if ever I have grandchildren, I shall tell them about Christopher Hyde-Montague who had an honours degree and was the son of an ambassador. He served in the war as a deckhand collecting information under the noses of the Germans and pretended to confess his sins to every priest, and probably picked up all sorts of information. I shan't say a word about an old fool who had been the captain of a great liner and should have been setting an example."

About a month later Paul heard that the Extra Master of Sail had been sent back to England in disgrace.

Before Paul left Naples, his friend in FOWIT made him an offer he could not refuse.

"I was talking to an army type who said he was at school with you. He's on the front line a few miles north. We have a jeep going there in the morning and I thought you might like to renew an old acquaintance."

"Whoever can it be?" Paul asked.

"Do you remember Guy Hannen? He's a lieutenant in some regiment—the Green Howards, is that what they call themselves? Things are quiet at the moment, but you'll have to get some dark clothes. I got involved in all this because our maps are better than theirs. Can you imagine? The navy has better maps of the land than the army."

"Guy Hannen," said Paul. "Yes, I remember him. He played at centre half and his father was something to do with the art world."

Paul asked permission from the captain, was warned against taking unnecessary risks, and the next day found him in an army vehicle traveling north on a dusty road which led them to the outpost where Lieutenant Hannen was dug in with his platoon. They had not seen each other for years but didn't even bother to shake hands.

"I'm lucky," Guy announced. "I have an olive tree to myself."

They chatted for a few minutes and Paul's initial nervousness was eased when he learned that the German outposts could not actually see them.

"Oh, here comes Corporal Armstrong," Guy announced cheerfully. "He's been 'scavenging' for fresh vegetables. You know, farms that have been abandoned."

Armstrong climbed down from the cab and saluted.

"Any luck, Corporal?"

"Yessir. We got plenty veggies." He lifted up the tarpaulin that covered the rear of his vehicle. "Last us a week, this lot. And a bullock what must a' been killed accidental, sir."

"Jolly good. Carry on to the cookhouse."

Paul noticed that the bullock had a bullet hole between its eyes. It was obvious that 'scavenging for food' could mean whatever you wanted it to mean, even in an élite regiment officered by well educated men.

"Good man, that Corporal Armstrong," Guy confided. "Plenty of initiative."

Paul tried to pull his thoughts together on the road back to Naples. "How would I react," he asked himself, "if I was in a hole under an olive tree, half a mile from the German army? What would I think of these Italian peasants who worshipped Mussolini and who were our enemies until the day before yesterday? Would I think it my right to steal their vegetables?" He decided he would draw the line at the chastity of their women.

Paul was not quite finished with his old school friend. When the war ended, Rossellini, the Italian filmmaker, shot a picture using not actors, but just ordinary bystanders whom he recruited on the spot. One of them was Guy Hannen, who appeared briefly in the part of a British officer. Paul recognised him on the screen but never saw him again.

During the final months of war in the Mediterranean, *Tarquin's* role was to be everywhere and do everything. At the Anzio landings they bombarded German positions on shore, firing so many shells that they had to return to Malta to resupply. They were dive-bombed by 87s, the cheaply made German aircraft that caused havoc among the landing craft and on the beaches. In the eastern Mediterranean they sailed through the Greek islands and into the Piraeus where the local freedom fighters, having routed the German forces, celebrated by fighting among themselves. In Dalmatia, when they entered the port of Split, the partisans arranged a spectacle in which they executed collaborators at the dockside, then humiliated women who had been too friendly with German troops. If there was one thing Paul found particularly distressing it was the sight of what women could do to other women. This was how a victorious war against a barbaric enemy ended—behaviour so vile that one was almost afraid to face the peace that was supposed to follow. Paul remembered a schoolmaster, so many years before, who had spoken of the glories of the Mediterranean world.

"They were the first to ascend the steep steps of civilisation," the man had said. "They had written languages and a rich mythology that helped them in their efforts to understand their world. They made laws that punished wickedness and dignified social custom to the point where family life could flourish. They were creative, building houses for the living, tombs for the dead and temples to glorify their gods."

All very well for a schoolmaster who had not seen what Paul had seen.

When the time came to join the Far Eastern fleet they sailed to Alexandria, the city of star-crossed Cleopatra, and continued eastwards to Suez. Through the canal and down the Red Sea there were only six of the original flotilla: *Tudor, Telemachus, Tantamount, Tarquin, Terebon* and *Thane*. Two of their sister ships had been left at the bottom of the Mediterranean. At Aden they refuelled and marvelled at the brown spiky hills, the desert-dried landscape and the furtive, unsmiling Arabs who lived their lives grudgingly according to Koranic law. It seemed they were governed by rules and regulations, like inmates of a prison.

The ship lay alongside the refuelling jetty and Paul pulled out his charts of the Indian Ocean. The captain put his head round the door of the chartroom. "Bombay," he said.

So there it was, Aden to Bombay. Paul's hand searched out ruler, pencil and dividers. Two thousand miles, about four or five days' steaming. The great Arabian peninsula would be away to the north, the heartland of Islam, birthplace of an illiterate camel driver who changed the world with his religious mumblings, nearly all borrowed from somewhere else. He sat at the mouth of a cave, spoke to his followers and left the world a sadder and more divided place. But the captain had more to say. "I'd like Number One and you, Henriques, to give some thought to the problems we'll be facing in this theatre of war. A different enemy, the need to co-operate with an ally."

Yes, in the Mediterranean it had been common talk that allies were more trouble than they were worth, and when the French dropped out and scuttled their ships there was a feeling of relief. Here they found themselves allied uneasily with the Americans whose navy had suffered a humiliating defeat at Pearl Harbour. It was believed that the American President had received prior warning of the Japanese attack, although he didn't know the details of when or where it would be delivered. By doing nothing he would have his "day of infamy" to justify his immediate entry into the war. In other words, his policies were well served by events and he was not despondent at the loss of his out-of-date battleships. He seized the occasion to authorise hostilities against Japan and Germany, although in subsequent naval operations the United States lost heavily, as had the Royal Navy. Indeed, the loss of *Prince of Wales* and *Repulse* had been the result of such chronic stupidity that it appeared nothing had been learned from the first three years of war. In a word, both the United States and Britain had made fools of themselves, which created the wrong conditions for a trusting partnership. The first and most obvious precaution was never to allow shore leave in ports where American sailors might be encountered.

As far as the Japanese enemy was concerned, the chances of falling into their hands were less than the chances would be for their brothers-in-arms in the army or air force. Sailors were not often captured, but if they were, they would have to expect the same inhuman treatment as was routinely meted out to other prisoners. The Germans and Italians had waged war in reasonable compliance with the Geneva Convention. A downed airman would not be shot out of hand, a Red Cross ship or vehicle would not be used for target practice and there was grudging respect for the pathetic remnants of the rules of war. But in the east the Allies were pitted against fanatics and followers of the cult of death. Their god was their emperor, their exemplar a bloodthirsty samurai warrior, their creed to kill without emotion. The Japanese had given the world the suicide aircraft packed with misplaced patriotism, hate and explosives. They were cancelled off as an aberrant branch of the human race, not so much having a few wicked men among them, but as totally evil. When the war was finally won and the gates of the prison camps opened, the fears of the Allies were fully realised.

Paul drew a pencil line on the chart, Aden to Bombay. After that it would be Colombo on the west coast of Ceylon. "Then where?" he asked himself.

Chapter 8 — The Buddha

Jonathan Palliser, First Lieutenant of *Tarquin*, was a long way from being a typical naval officer. Paul did not find him easy to understand until they spent a few days in each other's company, and until they both had small statuettes of the Buddha in their possession. After that, they became good friends.

Palliser had been First Lieutenant since the ship was commissioned in 1942. He had previously served in the Fleet Air Arm and continued to wear the gold wings of a pilot. His flying career, however, had been blemished by a series of mishaps which, had it not been for the war, might have led to early retirement. One of his commanding officers was perhaps being harsh when he wrote in Palliser's annual report, "it is not easy to understand how this officer found his way into the Fleet Air Arm. As a pilot he is no more than adequate, and he has a weak grasp of technical details. He is rigid in his views and not what I would describe as a team player." His brother officers saw him as a relic of an earlier age, a parody, almost, of the days of sail. His brusque manner and decided opinions meant that he had few friends, although he was well respected by subordinates. Perhaps it would be enough to say that he was old-fashioned and out of his time, "a bit of a character."

He had begun his naval career at Dartmouth, like thousands of others over the years, and served his midshipman's training in a cruiser on the East Indies station. There followed a two-year commission as a sub-lieutenant in HMS *Renown*, after which came the necessity of choosing specialist training. He could have chosen gunnery, torpedo, navigation or submarines, but flying, about which he knew nothing, beckoned him because it seemed to embody the naval warfare of the future besides offering room for individualism. As he saw it, he would not have to share his cockpit but would be free to make his own decisions. He duly took his flight training and on receiving his wings was sent to an air station on the south coast of England. At the outbreak of war he was appointed to the aircraft carrier HMS *Glorious*, which was torpedoed by a U-boat in the Bristol channel. He watched as his aircraft slid off the flight deck and joined it by jumping into the sea. A destroyer closed in and rescued him along with hundreds of others.

Another year in the Fleet Air Arm seemed to confirm that he was ill suited to the confined space of a cockpit. He crashed one aircraft on deck and a second missed the flight deck altogether and landed in the sea. He was threatened with court martial and it was noted that his wardroom wine bills, which were read as though they were a barometer of his flying performance, were too high for comfort. He argued that his consumption appeared heavy because he drank wines, not spirits, so it was finally decided that the wings on his uniform would be folded, and he would be posted elsewhere. By some strange logic he would be permitted to wear them as a tribute to his days of flying but meanwhile he would return to the navy of battleships, cruisers and destroyers. He became known as 'the dodo', a dodo being a flightless bird whose wings are decorative and by no means functional.

His next appointment might have been interpreted as a rebuke for squandering aeroplanes and drinking expensive wines, being that of first lieutenant of a rather hastily converted anti-aircraft vessel. The twisted irony implicit in this appointment could scarcely be missed. From his reckless handling of aeroplanes that he was supposed to preserve, it became his duty to shoot at and demolish those operated by the other side. The sailors who serviced the guns saw the connection immediately.

"If he knows how to fly the bloody things, he must k now how to shoot them down."

His new Captain had spent some years trading in the Baltic, and the ship's navigator, like so many navigators in the naval reserve and, for that matter, in the air force's bomber command, had been a teacher of science and mathematics. It was a much-discussed mystery that mathematics was taught at all in schools during the war years. The other Sub-Lieutenant had served as second officer aboard a rich man's yacht, and his most noticeable talent was as barman. Imposing some sort of discipline on the other officers and ship's company was a considerable task, the men having been drawn straight from the seaports of northern England. As was the case in *Badger*, they had received no formal naval training and their induction had been limited to the issue of uniforms and a demonstration of how to salute an officer. To his credit, however, Palliser did a thorough job. He was tireless, imposed a not-too-harsh discipline and explained in great detail the function of their weapons and the art of delivering accurate anti-aircraft fire. Where discipline and good order were concerned, the Captain was not always helpful. On one occasion they came in from sea and the Captain leaned over the bridge and called out, "'Ere Number One, you can let the lads go ashore. There's a good pub yonder. No need for fancy uniforms; they can drink just as they are."

When, after a year, his S.206[10] came to be written by his Captain, it was so laudatory, so full of superlatives that when combined with his mounting seniority as a lieutenant he was appointed without hesitation to *Tarquin*. He had been judged by those responsible for officer appointments to have lived down his inglorious past and the words "varied experience" now appeared on his personal file. That covered it well enough. It also seems likely that the name Palliser had stirred memories somewhere in the reverberating corridors of admiralty, a name that had been known for many years in the navy. He counted an

[10] Confidential Report on Officers

admiral and many other officers among his antecedents. Not all reached high rank, but the name was known and respected.

In *Tarquin* he carried out his duties to the satisfaction of his captain and the bewilderment of his brother officers. Ships routines were performed faultlessly, drills and practices finished on time with Number One, as he was known, supervising every detail. If there was a tablespoon of rum left over from the daily ceremony of distributing the ration, it was cast overboard under his supervision. If the chief boatswain's mate sent two men aloft to perform some task, one had to be right-handed and the other left-handed which, theoretically, would make the task easier. He was a stickler for shipboard protocol and, to get the attention of say, the gunnery officer, he would instruct some seventeen-year-old sailor, "My compliments to Mr. Mitchell and ask him to be good enough to present himself on deck." In his mind, "Tell Sub-Lieutenant Mitchell to see me" was not the right way to do it. Being independently wealthy made him the object of some wonderment and when, early in the war, he ordered and paid for a hundred gallons of high quality paint, enough to paint an entire ship, he established himself as an altogether improbable character. Where paint was concerned he had the sensitivities of an artist, the gangway, ship to shore, being the object of his personal attention. It was only when wartime shortages made such private purchases impossible that the ship reverted to standard gray paint from the purser's store.

There was another side to his character that showed itself in unlikely ways. One of the radio operators acted as ship's barber and plied his trade on the torpedo deck when the ship was in harbour. Number One had told him that he could charge sixpence a haircut for officers, three pence for petty officers and a penny halfpenny for the rest of the ships' company. The quality of his work was dubious but it meant that no sailor could claim that he looked long-haired because he had not been able to get ashore to a barber. When Number One saw sparrows picking up hair that had fallen to the deck and flying off with it, and seemingly touched by the sight, he mentioned it in the wardroom. Humanity had exploited animals and birds so thoroughly that it seemed an aberration of nature that the birds should now avail themselves of human hair to warm their nests. He thought the course of nature had been dangerously reversed. The conversation got round to evolution and he was adamant that while the concept was irrefutable and might apply to others, his family was exempt from its every provision. The very suggestion that his forbears were descended, however distantly, from ape-like creatures was unthinkable, and any officer with less than five years' seniority would do well not to express views on the subject.

Like so many other conversations in the wardroom of *Tarquin*, this one fell victim to his ill-considered opinions. He was, after all, the president of the mess and it was only when the captain was present, which was rarely, that a level exchange of views was possible. In earlier times naval officers were, as likely as not, a boisterous collection, and captains often preferred to keep to themselves. In *Tarquin's* wardroom, therefore, the First Lieutenant's word was law among the junior officers. When they went into dry dock, however, for what in the language of cars would have been called 'six-month servicing and checkup', which included boiler cleaning, Paul found himself accepting the suggestion that he and Palliser spend their ten-day leave together. The haven where they found themselves was Ceylon, considered to be one of the foremost jewels in the imperial crown.

"I have relatives who live somewhere here," Palliser announced casually. "It might be proper to drop in. The old boy was an admiral and he'll want to know whether standards in the navy have slipped since his day."

"How did he come to settle in Ceylon?" Paul asked.

"Every one of my relatives will answer that question differently. At some time during his service on the East India station he came here and fell in love with the place, so he decided it was where he would retire. There's a story about him being offered a governorship, and another about a beautiful woman who was dying and refused to go back to England. No two Pallisers tell the same story. It's characteristic of our family."

That evening the two of them boarded the train at Trincomalee on the northeast side of the island and reached Kandi, the old capital of Ceylon, early the following morning. As they stood on the platform waiting for their baggage, Paul was approached by an elderly, white-clad Sinhalese and behind him a boy carrying a chair.

"Clean your ears, sahib?" intoned the man. "Expertly performed. Much comfort restored and recommendations from distinguished personages," all in a singsong voice. He produced a handful of notes from inside his off-white robes and invited Paul to read the remarks made earlier, presumably by clean-eared customers.

"My ears aren't dirty," was all that Paul could say. "I heard you perfectly. You speak excellent English."

"But sahib," came the pleading reply, "wax build-up of many years."

"Well, thank you, but no. I'll come back to Kandi if I find..." He turned to Palliser. "I say, old chap, do your ears need a spell in drydock? There's a fellow here who recalibrates them to the satisfaction of a large and distinguished clientele, and you can take the whole thing sitting down."

They walked to their hotel, which was within sight of the Temple of the Tooth. "The tooth of the Lord Buddha," he was assured by the clerk who registered them. "They bring it out every few years and the people venerate it," but Paul was scarcely listening. He was staring through the open doors at the red stone building, like a fort, which reminded him of the castle that stands in the city of Carlisle, surrounded by the bleak gray houses of northern England. How strange, he thought, a temple in the form of a fortress, housing a holy relic. Paul had heard Reverend Farqueson preach on the subject of relics from the Middle Ages, the part they played in the life of the church. A splinter of wood from the true cross, the charred bones of some local saint, a Roman coin—one of those fateful 30 pieces of silver—that bridge the gap between the worshipers and their God. Yes, relics were big business in the medieval church; likewise this tooth, of questionable provenance, as Paul discovered later, was kept in a huge castle and guarded by yellow-robed monks. Western scientists had declared it not to be of human origin, which made it a myth in the sense of conveying a truth without being literally true itself. It served to remind the worshipers that Buddha had walked the earth and chewed his food like an ordinary mortal.

There are times in people's lives when exultation, vividness and joy come to replace the more sombre moods of human existence. Impressions that last a lifetime come into focus and, for Paul, those few days in Ceylon were one such episode in his life. Perhaps he had become tired of endless seas and gray ships, the sameness of the horizons, the hard, artificial life of wartime, the long, tedious watches and the unceasing motion of the ship. To him, the island of Ceylon, as he always called it, was one such flash of memory. He would remember it not as a paradise but as an explosion of colour, a wealth of unexpected discoveries and the strange intrusion of an Oriental faith. When he arrived he knew nothing about the island, had no expectations, had not read a guidebook nor spoken with people who had left their footprints there. Nor did he come as an explorer who presumes to know what he will discover, like the enthusiastic Frenchman who was so determined to find China that when he stepped ashore on the banks of a Canadian river he named it La Chine.

Paul had read that Samuel Baker, the bearded African explorer, had been in Ceylon at the end of the last century with a mandate to subdue the herds of elephants that ran wild in the interior. Elephants were classed as vermin because they made it impossible to clear the jungle and introduce tea cultivation. Hunting them was dangerous because of the dense jungle and poor visibility. Elephants could handle the steep slopes; the Bakers with their heavy, black-powder firearms could not. Nevertheless, the land was eventually cleared of its jungle and nearly all its elephants. This was the same Samuel Baker who became celebrated for another exploit. He bought a slave in an Arab slave market, an Englishwoman, and did the right thing by marrying her. She accompanied him on many of his subsequent journeys and no one could accuse him of failing to turn her life around. Yes, he had heard of Baker the explorer, elephant hunter and husband of the slave girl who became Lady Baker but, beyond that, Ceylon was no more than a name.

An unlikely side of Palliser's character emerged when the two of them had done their sightseeing for the day, returned to the hotel and taken their seats in the dining room. He called for the dinner menu but found it incomprehensible, being written in a combination of languages, so he demanded to be shown to the kitchen and then to the cellar. He was polite but wasted little time, and his demands met with only mild confusion among the kitchen staff. "A satisfactory meal," was how he described it in the end, "with three bottles of wine. What a stroke of luck to find a white Burgundy." In such circumstances he displayed the aplomb of a French nobleman.

The following day they traveled by bus to Newa Eliya, the centre of the tea-growing district. They made their way to the Planters' Club, met Admiral Palliser and were supplied with a jeep that had been purchased from an American officer for six bottles of whisky. Paul had served in the war for long enough and was well enough acquainted with his American allies not to be surprised by this transaction. Americans were inordinately fond of Scotch whisky. Their military accounting system was somewhere between sloppy and nonexistent and they could always get another jeep just by asking for it.

The Admiral, when they met him, red-faced and white-haired, was a superlative host. First he arranged for them to visit Worlds' End Drop, a spectacular cleft in the mountains, after which there were ancient ruins and abandoned temples to be seen, villages with their bazaars, and everywhere yellow robed monks. But it was the tea gardens that appealed to Paul. They clung to the hillsides, a brilliant shade of green, with a few trees left standing from the primordial forest. A 'garden', as it was called, was usually about a thousand acres and employed the same number of people to pick the tea. From a distance they looked like brightly coloured birds, industrious and ever moving, as they filled the sacks on their backs with the three uppermost leaves from every twig. There was something gentle and biblical about it, an occupation for women that could not be rushed, and which depended on the rain for a 'flush' or growth of leaves. Only three leaves were harvested at each pluck, one full grown, one half grown, and the bud. Of all the world's major crops it was tea that seemed to Paul to be the most Eden-like. Coffee growing in South America looked dark and uninviting, sisal was spiky like weapons of war, rice a confusion of endless puddles, wheat and corn in the American Midwest a horizon-filling patchwork.

The Planters' Club at Newa Eliya became their headquarters for the next few days and the two of them were the centre of attention.

How was the war going? What was morale like among our servicemen? How and when would it end?

"Of one thing we can be sure," Paul replied. "The prewar world will never come back. We will defeat the Japanese, but the people of Southeast Asia don't want the colonial powers to return. In many places the locals have fought against the Japanese. When the Allies win and Japan is finished, they'll go their way and we'll go ours. India is talking openly of an end to British rule."

Conversation turned to other subjects and the two of them were persuaded to climb Adam's Peak that night and watch the sun rise over the Indian Ocean.

"Adam's Peak, in the centre of the island," someone said. "You don't have to be a Buddhist to be affected by it. It's the mountain of the transfiguration where Buddha left the shadow of his soul. It occupies the same place that Mount Hebron does for us."

"And the view from the top is terrific," from the Admiral. "All of us have climbed it. By standing on the summit and watching sunrise you will gain membership in the society of those of us who love this island and wish it well." He paused. "But I warn you. There's a belief that when you reach the top you will be compelled to speak the truth as you have never spoken it before. The plain, unvarnished truth. You will be protected by the Lord Buddha."

"If wives go up, they climb separately," someone added.

The two of them drove to the foot of the mountain, arriving a little after midnight. A faint moon illuminated the path and the climb itself was no more than a steep walk that delivered them to the summit some four hours later. Their progress had been slowed by other pilgrims, many of whom carried torches. They pulled on their sweaters and sat down under the canopy of stars, the same stars that had shone on the lenses of Paul's sextant and enabled him to determine *Tarquin's* position on the surface of the earth. The night was so clear that Paul could see the lighthouses round the coast and identify them by the periodicity of their flashes. There was Colombo, Galle, Batticola and Trincomalee, all as bright as Mars, shining out their messages to mariners and offering the welcome of a bountiful land.

They were silent for what seemed like a long time, then Palliser spoke, his voice sounding weary and far away.

"I almost murdered my commanding officer."

Paul turned in the darkness, scarcely believing what he heard.

"I keep asking myself what the war has done to me. Sometimes I think of going into the church, but I'm not religious; they probably wouldn't have me. Trouble is I don't believe in Christianity any more than I believe in the Buddha's footprint over there. Or his tooth."

"Or his presence?" Paul asked.

"I don't know. This is their holy mountain. Perhaps the pilgrims have given it an aura of godliness."

For several minutes they were silent, then Palliser resumed. "We were flying off a carrier against land targets. Trouble was that our flight leader was a bastard of unspeakable proportions. He cursed and he swore, insulted us, imposed restrictions and penalties that made our lives miserable. He wanted to be awarded the Distinguished Service Order and it was we who were to earn it for him."

He shivered in the cool air.

"There were twenty of us and without any real discussion we decided that the war effort and the Fleet Air Arm would be better off without him. It was the obvious thing—just get rid of him and make it look like an accident. Sooner or later one of us would be flying behind him over enemy territory. We weren't equipped with gun cameras; it would have been the easiest thing to shoot him down and tell a story about anti-aircraft fire. The others were all in favour.

"A week later it fell to me. The leader saw a target and called me on the radio to follow him down. He attacked something that was hidden in trees, but I held my fire. I simply couldn't see anything. It just looked like forest. Then at some point I realised his radio had gone dead. Without it he didn't stand a chance. Visibility was poor and he'd never find the carrier. There was anti-aircraft fire and I never saw him again. My aircraft was last to land and my guns hadn't been fired. At the debriefing I explained how I followed him, saw him attack but couldn't identify any target. The anti-aircraft fire persuaded me to turn. What I didn't say was that I could have come round, found him and led him back. I killed him by what I failed to do."

He fell silent and Paul tried to find words of wisdom or comfort, but as he did so there came the first streaks of morning. While the fates of great nations are being arbitrated on the battlefields of the world, Paul thought, petty differences are settled in sordid and ignoble ways. How fragile is the balance between honesty and falsehood, and now that I am privy to his secret, how am I affected? Am I co-conspirator to a dishonest and cowardly act committed in someone else's war, someone else's mind?

The sun rose from the sea in its eternal majesty. "Sol invicta" they had called it before Christian times, the sun victorious, an imperishable light without which mankind could not exist. It chased the darkness from the valleys below them, turned them from shadows into men. The two of them rose stiffly from the grass and were shown the footprint of the Lord Buddha, after which they took their way silently down the mountain. And then, as they descended, Paul was suddenly assailed by the memory of a shameful incident that he himself had been involved in many years before. It flooded him with memories. He had been a mere boy then, an apprentice in *Canopus*, his last posting before his navy career began with appointment to *Artemis*. With shame he recalled the details of an event that had occurred in the Mediterranean, off the North African coast. The ship had taken on cargo in Tripoli—a few tons of 'miscellaneous'—and by nightfall they were at sea steaming westwards. Paul remembered it as a warm, dark night with no moon and the distinctive odours of sand and village life wafting up from the south. He was keeping the first watch, 1600 to midnight. Paul was eighteen and very conscious of his responsibility to keep the ship on course and safe from all hazards. He was assisted by two seamen, the quartermaster who steered the ship, and a lookout.

"Mr. Henriques, sir," came a voice from behind him. "We found stowaways." It was the ship's boatswain. Paul had been leaning against the binnacle, his eyes searching the dark sea. He turned, "Oh God," he said, "What a damn nuisance." But there was worse to come, and the boatswain went on, "They knew about ships, they was hidden with real cunning. Something else. They're all sick. Sayeed thinks its leprosy. He's talking to them in Arabic."

"How do you know, boatswain? I thought leprosy didn't look like much..."

"Sayeed says they knew as how they had leprosy. They planned this caper months ago. They was hoping to reach a country where they'd get treatment." The boatswain paused. "Sooner we get rid of them..."

Paul knew what he meant. It was common practice in ships that carried no doctor, had no facilities for the sick, where food was rationed and accommodation crowded, for stowaways to disappear into a watery grave, and there were other considerations. The shipping companies, whose policies were formulated in offices ashore, were in the habit of applying a charge against the salaries of ship's officers when stowaways were landed. Local authorities, backed by national governments, would present the shipping companies with outrageous bills for every illegal immigrant who was brought ashore. The shipping companies took the view that the officers should have prevented unauthorised persons from getting aboard in the first place, so they passed the expenses to the ship. A final thought crossed Paul's mind. His captain was, even by the standards of those days, "a proper bastard." He would blame Paul and almost certainly stain his career with a very unsatisfactory report.

Paul's mind was made up. "Do what you usually do," he said to the boatswain. "How many?"

"Five."

In the months and years that followed, Paul's war, which had been dominated by service in *Artemis*, *Badger* and *Tarquin*, had forced the five lepers of Tripoli into the background. He knew that he had been complicit in the murder of his fellow men but excused himself with the words "in all the circumstances." Perhaps his worst sin was that he had never told his father to whom, in Paul's disciplined world, he owed so much. As he and Palliser climbed into their jeep at the foot of the mountain he remembered the Admiral's words, "You will feel compelled toward the truth." He wanted to tell Palliser but could not bring himself to do so.

Later that day, washed, restored and very hungry, lieutenants Palliser and Henriques were at the Planters' Club rejoicing in their newly acquired acceptance as full members of a fraternity of those who truly loved Ceylon. The Admiral raised his glass and the room fell silent. His words were intoned like a judgment. "It is said that those who have climbed to the summit of Adam's Peak and watched the sunrise will be relieved of their anxieties by the Lord Buddha. To remind us of the time we stood upon his mountain, we keep a small statue in our private apartments."

He reached into a bag and drew out two statuettes, offering one each to Palliser and Paul.

The room was very quiet.

"Thank you," they both said. "Thank you."

A week later they were back aboard *Tarquin* preparing for sea. A signalman entered the wardroom and handed Palliser a message from Admiralty. "I am instructed to inform you," it read, "that in the course of the action in which your squadron leader failed to return he is now known to have been brought down by anti-aircraft fire. You may rest assured that no blame attaches to yourself. It was unfortunate that he flew over an enemy battery and did not turn westwards as you did."

"The Lord Buddha," Palliser said to Paul, "has lived up to all expectation, and the Church of England is better off without me."

When, in later years, Paul remembered the destroyer *Tarquin*, Jonathan Palliser was the one officer who remained fixed in his mind. He had been out of the ordinary, a little unbalanced in his views, the relic of another age. His duties as First Lieutenant were well performed, he ran the ship to perfection, and while he caused bewilderment he did not provoke rancour. It was apparent to his brother officers that he was wealthy—his perfect uniforms, hand-made footwear, the way his cabin was arranged with a small curtain across the scuttle and matching bedspread—all spoke of care, attention to detail and money besides. How his family came by its wealth was answered by nothing more than speculation. Without a scrap of evidence to support him, the First Lieutenant of *Tudor* lowered his voice and confided that it was something to do with the slave trade.

Paul, however, having himself experienced a small shaft of enlightenment on the mountaintop in Ceylon, now remembered Palliser only as a man of contradictions, beset by doubts yet nourished by antiquated certainties. As they sat on the mountain, sacred to the Lord Buddha, he had exposed a dark side of his character, a blemish in which he confessed to having been part of a plot to kill an unpopular commanding officer. Palliser, nevertheless, was strange and distant in never having spoken about his family, his home or his friends. Surely he must have a girlfriend, Paul mused, although it was difficult to imagine any young woman who would share the extremities of his views. To Paul, therefore, Palliser had been no more nor less than an efficient officer, easy to work with but difficult to know personally, who happened to be independently wealthy.

The possession of independent wealth carried certain overtones in the navy of that period because there was widespread belief that wealthy officers, who cared little if they were court-martialled and dismissed from the service, were the only ones who would stand up to their superiors in cases of injustice, incompetence or sheer blind folly. It was undisputed that many past improvements in the navy had been achieved by officers who had spoken loudly and critically and had, in all probability, lost their commissions in consequence. Every wardroom in the navy could quote examples, and most of the messdecks as well. The navy had been afraid of criticism and reluctant to change, and the conversion of ships from coal to oil-fired furnaces came immediately to mind. Some coal-fired ships, which should have been out of service during the First World War, were still at sea during the Second. Another disgrace was the slow pace by which the Fleet Air Arm was accepted, the procrastination in the construction of carriers, the failure to build air bases in strategic locations like Scapa Flow, Malta and Singapore. But if there was a single event that rankled most within the messdecks of the navy, it was the sinking of the old battleship *Royal Oak* by a German U-boat. The navy had basked in twenty years of peace in which to secure Scapa Flow, its great northern base, against intimidation by air or sea, but within weeks of the outbreak of war in 1939 a U-boat had sailed in on the surface, using an undefended channel. Any old wreck of a ship could have been scuttled in that channel and made it impassable, but no, 700 lives were lost aboard *Royal Oak* as it lay at anchor, supposedly safe.

Wealthy officers, therefore, were thought to have a special part to play because it was they who would confront the doddering old fools who ran the navy's affairs, who had been responsible for the loss of *Prince of Wales* and *Repulse* and the fall of Singapore. If, as individuals, they were few and their views unorthodox—ahead of their times, perhaps—it was the price that had to be paid for any hope of improvement. Palliser, therefore, was excused his more outrageous moments. In the long focus of history, with the country at war, the Pallisers of the navy were cherished rather than condemned because they dared to speak. What did it matter if Darwin's discoveries on evolution did not apply to them?

Chapter 9 — The Long Journey Home

As the year 1944 passed into history, the enemy in the Pacific was in retreat toward the sprawling islands of Japan. The Allied war machine, led by Americans, had become a massive and overwhelming combination of land, sea and air power; islands and their surrounding seas were captured; a glance at the map showed that Japan would soon be deprived of its outer defences. It would stand alone in a sea of menace, and it was at this stage that Japan, in desperation, introduced the suicide bomber—the *kamikaze*. Typically, these aircraft were armed with a single bomb weighing five-hundred pounds, the task of the pilot being to fly deliberately and mischievously into an Allied ship, so that a successful attack would inevitably claim his life and possibly sink the ship. It was the weapon of last resort, the product of mentalities distraught by the concept of defeat. The kamikaze was used increasingly as the Allies closed in but, at worst, did little more than delay their advance. The antidote was for the Allies to sustain a ring of fighter aircraft in defence of their ships, combined with effective anti-aircraft weaponry. The third solution, which seems not to have been available to the Japanese mind, would have been an outright surrender, but it was not until they had suffered a final humiliation that the word defeat was heard in Japan.

For much of this period the T-class destroyers operated with the United States navy and often under their command, a situation that was strained because the Allies were suspicious of each other and uneasy in each other's company. Indeed, the Americans seemed to desire nothing more than to embarrass and make life intolerable for their British friends while the British were baffled by matters that seemed to consume American minds. The phrase "not during an election year" was heard incessantly and reminded Paul of the phrase so frequently heard in Moslem countries: "not during Ramadan". The holy month of fasting seemed to affect every activity so that nothing was done on time, nothing worked properly and mundane requests were met with the mantra that they could not be undertaken during Ramadan. Likewise in the Pacific, the war seemed to be governed by the fact that it was an election year and co-operation was made more difficult by the mindset, "we don't know who the next president will be". To the British, an election year was no different from any other, you simply got on with your job as though politics was none of your business.

Something else that surprised and dismayed the British was the flow of derogatory comments made by their allies on the subject of ships and armaments generally. It was true that certain aspects of their weaponry were disgraceful. American torpedoes, for instance, that failed to run straight or explode once they had hit a target. One torpedo was on record as having run in a circle and sunk the American submarine that launched it. But this kind of failure did not warrant the epithet "tin can" which was how destroyers were described, or "flat-tops" for aircraft carriers, which made the British feel they were being drawn into a way of thinking that was foolish and derogatory. Perhaps it was no more than a complaint against the war in general, but to the British a ship was 'she', and referred to with some respect. In a word, the British were glad to leave Japan to their American cousins and accustom themselves to the idea that their Far Eastern empire was lost and would return to its original owners in a few short months.

It was in August 1945 that the war stumbled to a standstill and there was much uninformed speculation about 'the bomb' that had decided the issue. Technically it had been a well kept secret, its workings a mystery to the vast majority. Phrases like 'nuclear fission' were bandied about, but nobody seemed able to explain what they meant. Before 'the bomb' the Japanese were a boastful, strutting horde of self-styled warriors; after it they were crawling on the ground and pleading that none of it was their fault. Few Japanese spoke English in those days, which was as well because in the task of conveying naval prisoners to mainland Japan there was no desire to hear what they had to say. The phrase commonly heard in the messdecks was that the atomic bomb had saved a million Allied lives.

Tarquin and the other T-class destroyers had been operating as a six-ship flotilla in preparation for the American landings planned for Kyushu and Honshu. In the Mediterranean, the ships had worked singly or in pairs, as *Tarquin* had done in the Adriatic; but this was not how destroyers were designed to be used. Indeed, in the prewar years, a rear-admiral commanded all destroyers in the Mediterranean fleet so that manoeuvres, mock attacks on an enemy fleet, gunnery and torpedo exercises could be practiced with as many as forty destroyers operating in concert.

The T-class destroyers had been under the command of Captain Cranston in *Tudor* since commissioning in 1942. He carried the rank of full captain, with four stripes on his sleeve, and was always known as 'Captain (D)'. In *Terebon* was a commander, second in command of the flotilla, while the other four captains, including *Tarquin's*, were lieutenant commanders. It took them little time to re-learn the work of a flotilla. From having acted independently, or in twos and threes as when bombarding enemy positions on shore, or hunting enemy submarines, to the perfect station-keeping required when combined, it came almost as second nature to their captains, navigators and signals staff to operate as a unit. In the Pacific war, therefore, they merely resumed what they felt was normal practice.

When the end came, Paul and his shipmates counted themselves lucky to have witnessed the signing of the peace treaty on September 2, 1945. Tokyo Bay held more than 250 Allied ships on that fateful occasion, the American battleship *Missouri* being the stage on which the formal surrender was signed. Whole fleets lay in trotts[11] and their crews in the thousands manned the upperworks. With his binoculars, Paul could see at least a part of the ceremony which encompassed the formal humiliation of Japan. The Japanese signatories, he noticed, wore morning dress, complete with top hats, which made them appear pompous and ridiculous. Why, he wondered, do they choose to pose in garments long abandoned as practical workaday clothes in the countries where they had originated—his particularly. Their conquerors stood around them in military dress that looked well worn and, in MacArthur's case, almost shabby. Paul heard his words, which echoed from loudspeakers across the bay, and were brief and to the point: "It is my earnest hope—indeed the hope of all mankind—that from this solemn occasion a better world shall emerge…"

Not as good, not as memorable, Paul thought, as Nelson's words before Trafalgar.

In later years, Paul would remember the signing of the Japanese surrender not so much as a great event in history, but in terms of the disgraceful wartime conduct of the Japanese and their well-deserved humiliation. The war against Japan had lasted 1,364 days according to one American broadcaster, and it was widely considered by servicemen in America and Britain that the Japanese deserved more atomic bombs than they received. In Paul's mind a single detail predominated. Two Allied generals had been captured by the Japanese, one American, Jonathan Wainright, the other British, Arthur Percival. They had both been signatories to the surrender and had been paraded on *Missouri*'s deck, starved and emaciated, for all to see. The vileness of the Japanese and their inhuman treatment of captives was exemplified in these two tortured men. What if one of them had been my father or my future father-in-law, Paul kept asking himself. How would I have felt?

---

[11] When several ships, usually of the same class, are secured alongside each other.

Following the surrender, thoughts turned to the voyage home. Battle weary but proud, *Tudor*, *Tantamount*, *Telemachus*, *Tarquin*, *Terebon* and *Thane* would sail in company, 14,000 miles, under the command of Captain (D). On reaching home, the crews—all those who were designated 'HO' or hostilities only—would walk out of the dockyard gates in their uniforms, receive their pay and be supplied with civilian clothes. They would cast a final glance at their ships and thereafter turn to the drab realities of civil life. The ships would pass into dockyard hands and only when ready for sea again would their two red funnel bands be painted out and replaced by whatever distinguishing marks were chosen by the new flotilla. The crews loved those red bands [12] for the colour they added, the jaunty style.

The crews, Paul remembered, had joined at the outbreak of war when still in their teens and had little to offer besides rudimentary schooling. Their boyhood had been spent in a world struggling with economic depression. For many of them, prewar memories were outlined in hardship. When first issued with their navy kit, which consisted of two sets of blue uniforms, two sets of tropical whites and various other necessities, many found themselves in possession of a wardrobe more extensive than they had ever owned. Even their rations were more nourishing and plentiful than the food that had been on their plates in peacetime. They had learned much in four years, some good things and some bad, but they could scarcely have anticipated the bombed and battered country that they were now to call their own.

---

[12] Two red bands had been chosen arbitrarily to distinguish the flotilla according to regulations established by the Commander-in-Chief in the Far East. In fact, funnel bands had been adopted by all destroyer flotillas. There had to be two bands, two feet in width, two feet apart, the uppermost two feet from the top of the funnel. A flotilla could make its own choice from red, dark blue, light blue, yellow, green or any combination. Smaller vessels, such as minesweepers, had one band only. It was observed that morale was improved by this simple distinguishing feature, although it was never copied by the US Navy.

Before they reached their promised land, such as it was, they had to sail half way around the world. The Indian Ocean produced storms and calms, westerly winds one day and glassy tranquility the next. Whales rolled and plunged; there were flying fish and schools of porpoises. It was the ocean of perpetual variety, and sailors homeward bound from the war, no longer attentive to their wartime duties, had time on their hands to watch and marvel. *Tarquin's* bridge became suddenly quiet. No longer was the sonar probing the depths.

Westwards they steamed in the perfect formation of well-practiced ships. When the coast of Africa appeared, a deputation of seabirds came to greet them as though to ask what offerings they brought from the mysterious east. A dusty smell came off the land as they left Socotra away to port and shaped course for Aden. After that it was the Red Sea and Suez Canal, and soon they found themselves in the choppy waters of the Mediterranean. Within sight of the Pharos light and with fuel replenished, they took station on *Tudor*, the flotilla leader, and again steamed westwards; but, in one respect, the Mediterranean differed from the way it had been a year before. It was now dotted with fishing craft, some of them mere rowing boats, plus a few substantial vessels under sail or powered by every imaginable sort of engine. A few rested alone on the sea, others gathered like flocks of seabirds. One could guess that they were plundering shoals of fish that the war had protected.

Awaiting them in Malta were bags of mail that some authority, in its wisdom, had diverted from Japan. There was a letter from Paul's mother that surprised and delighted him, saying that his father had been awarded a postwar knighthood and would receive it from the King. He longed to write them a letter and address it to Sir Frederick and Lady Henriques, but quickly realised that his letter would arrive no sooner than he. His congratulations could await his return. In the meantime he would go to the ship's office, ask for his personal file and make a correction where it detailed 'Names of parents or next-of-kin'. The Sub-Lieutenant who ran the ship's office would satisfy his curiosity as to what Paul had written and the news would be round the ship by sundown. There were no secrets aboard a destroyer.

From his mother's flowery handwriting Paul turned to another letter, this time from Stubbington. The writing was square and punctilious and he seemed not to have heard about his former employer's sudden elevation in rank. "There's something I feel should be passed on," he wrote. "It's being said in Broxbourne that the Reverend F.F. is leaving the parish and moving to the Holy Land. It may be, of course, you already know this seeing as you write regular to Miss Rebecca and she to you. What I must add is that it was not being spoken of kindly, rather as though his services was no longer needed. He is still respected by many within the parish and I hope this is all a mistake, but I thought best let you know."

Paul put down the letter and looked round him at the small cabin that he shared with 'Guns' Lawson. How was it possible, he asked himself, for the war to have affected others but left him unscathed? An earlier letter from Stubbington had informed him that his father was ill but continued to work. The doctor said it was something picked up in India—histolitica, was that the name? Paul was told to prepare for the worst. If his father had spared himself, asked for a reduced caseload and eased himself into semi-retirement he might have slowed the progress of whatever ailed him, but his determination to see the day when the war would end and his son return spurred him to efforts of mind and will. Like many others of his generation, the war carried him to the day of victory but not beyond. It was as though the effort and courage needed to fight had left nothing for the subsequent labour of rebuilding. Yes, the promised land had been reached, but the problems of making it habitable were too much to contemplate.

In his heart Paul knew that his father would care little for the accolade of knighthood. He was respected within his profession and would continue to work if he was Mr. Justice Henriques or Sir Frederick. His mother, however, would be delighted. Henceforth she was Lady Henriques, a step above the ordinary, the recipient of more respect than if she had been just plain Mrs. Henriques. Not even Smith-Bosanquet, owner of a huge property and master of foxhounds, had been knighted.

The situation regarding F.F., the astoundingly Reverend Fortescue Farqueson, was another thing again. Why was he leaving, what had happened? All during Paul's schooldays he had been the very rock of the Church of England in Broxbourne, a parody of correctness, an exemplar of ecclesiastical propriety. When travelling about his parish he affected the dress of a nineteenth century divine in black breeches, gaiters and a frock coat. His mastery of theology was said to be profound and at his own expense he had prepared and published dissertations on the Old Testament prophets with whom it was thought he shared many characteristics. The very idea that he had fallen into theological disrepute, or any other kind of disrepute, was unthinkable.

Suddenly Paul realised that he himself had changed during the war years. It washed over him that he had grown older, gained experience and maturity. He had heard his friends announce with finality that they would go home and get on with their lives and never talk about the war again, that they would excise it from their consciousness as a surgeon might cut out a piece of decaying flesh. But to Paul the war had been a course of higher learning. It was multi-sided, had compressed, in a few short years, enough instruction to inform a lifetime of peaceful existence. If Paul had been a father at that stage, he would not have wished on his son what he himself had gone through; but at the same time he would not have wanted to avoid the experience himself. This he could not explain.

Five years earlier Paul had regarded F.F. with misgiving, as an unadventurous man, too clever, the relic of an earlier time; but now he saw Rebecca's father as being a warrior within the confines of his own profession. The war had sent men like Paul to sea in ships that were slow, ill-armed and out of date. The coal-fired minesweepers in Gibraltar came immediately to mind, the hopeless lack of anti-aircraft weapons in the early part of the war, the sheer bungling and lack of air cover for *Prince of Wales* and *Repulse*. But the Reverend F.F. had found himself in comparable circumstances because he was called upon to preach a religion that few modern and educated parishioners could accept. In one of his letters, Stubby had said that walking on water, virgin birth and rising from the dead were not merely out of the church curriculum, but had been well and truly laid aside. He went on to say that scholarship had loosened every handhold of the church's teaching and, in consequence, the people of Broxbourne had reduced their church attendance to accommodate only those three most moving elements of life: birth, marriage and death.

Thus it was that Paul felt a sense of brotherhood with the man whom he hoped would soon be his father-in-law. He could now respect the wisdom and sympathise with the struggle of Rebecca's father, even as he did towards his own. In doing so, Paul was reminded of something F.F. had uttered in one of his more florid moods: "You are the sum of all those whom you have known." Yes, in war, character is writ large whether good or bad. The First Lieutenant of *Artemis* came to mind, the officers and the leading seamen in *Badger*, the unspeakable former Captain of a great ocean liner in Naples, Palliser on the summit of Adam's peak. How could one avoid being affected? These were the men who had shaped Paul's character, had given him the first shreds of wisdom.

That he, Paul, would be claimed by an angry sea had not been his greatest fear. Bombs, mines, torpedoes, shellfire—such were the devils with the sharpest claws in the war in which he'd served. There was one other fear, however, which added poison to the chalice of any officer charged with navigating duties in wartime—miscalculation, "The stars in the wrong places," they used to say. Charts that were all wrong or out of date; undersea hazards that in wartime were not properly marked; wrecks shifted or misreported—these were the horrors of daily existence for a navigator. Paul remembered with gratitude the night when *Tarquin* had gone stern-first into the tiny Dalmatian fishing port to rescue Allied soldiers. All had gone well, but in the annals of the navy it had not always been so. Few navigators had not read of the frigate *Birkenhead*, which struck an unmarked rock and sank with huge loss of life in February 1852. The great trade routes of the modern world, well charted and oft-sailed, were safe enough, but the hazards in wartime were of another order. Paul had been lucky and he knew it. He was also keenly aware, but never would have admitted, that he had his icon, a turtle, to thank for guiding his observations, his calculations and his pencil lines for five long years.

Oh well, Paul said to himself, these perils are surely over, and now there's no reason to think that Rebecca's demobilisation will be delayed. He put the letters in his pocket and as he turned to go a sailor saluted and told him he was wanted in the captain's cabin.

"A slight diversion," he was told. "Naples via the straits of Messina. D'you happen to know if the lighthouses are working?"

"I'll find out, sir. There's a pile of mail for me on the chart table."

"My guess," the captain went on, "is that we'll get passengers. The Commander-in-Chief probably has a staff that he doesn't need any more."

The captain was right. When they reached Naples they were told that each destroyer would get sixty passengers, twenty of them officers, which placed a strain on the wardroom facilities. Palliser was in charge and let it be known that he thought destroyers totally unsuitable for people who were inexperienced and would probably fall overboard when being seasick. He had a way of coming right out with it. A 24-hour lifebelt watch was ordered, and a midshipman was told to go ashore and find brown paper bags to be handed out, two per passenger.

"Steal them if you have to," shouted Palliser. "Your promotion depends on it."

The passengers were waiting on the jetty and were helped aboard together with their luggage. Paul was to accommodate four officers in his cabin, which had two bunks, one above the other.

"I'll sleep on the settee in the chartroom," he said. "That frees the lower bunk, but Lawson will be keeping regular watches and must have his ration of sleep. Somehow you fellows will have to make yourselves comfortable any way you can. I'm sorry this isn't what you're accustomed to, but we'll have you home in no time."

"Good God, is this the best you people can do?" one of them demanded. "I'm a paymaster and for my entire time on the staff of the Commander-in-Chief I had a room to myself."

Paul looked at the man in disbelief. "This isn't a luxury liner. We'll fit you in where we can."

"I don't think it's proper to expect officers to sleep... I'm going to speak to someone about it."

"Speak to who you like," Paul replied, "but before you do, I want to tell you about the last time we carried passengers. There were four hundred of them—escaped prisoners. We picked them up behind enemy lines. Fourteen were in this cabin. Fourteen! And they thought they were bloody lucky. A Polish colonel was stuffed into that corner and when I managed to get the door open about six inches he handed me my coat and asked me to convey his heartfelt thanks to the captain."

The other three were fascinated by the thought that *Tarquin* had ferried escaped servicemen from a dozen different countries. One of them, when his turn came, spoke about the palace of Caserta, a few miles from Naples, where they had been quartered. Each bedroom had a gilded chamber pot, which they actually used because the heads[13] were so far away.

"One other thing," Paul told his new friends. "There are no dress regulations aboard a destroyer at sea. You can wear what you like. Officers on duty wear their caps. That's about it."

'Hands to stations for leaving harbour' was piped and Paul went up to the bridge and assured himself that the midshipman had placed the correct chart on the table. Next he tested the masthead and navigation lights and noted the wind direction and force. The captain came up and in minutes *Tarquin* had slipped, was turning and making for the harbour entrance. *Tudor* and *Terebon* were ahead, *Telemachus* astern, while the other two, *Tantamount* and *Thane*, were still alongside the jetty and would join when refuelling had been completed.

Tudor signalled, "Act independently: Proceed at slow speed and you may barter fresh fish from fishing vessels. Bear in mind we are due to pay off and old rope may be disposed of."

This was an established tradition in destroyers, but one that the passengers from Caserta had probably never heard about. The chief boatswain's mate would hoard items that were beyond use in a warship but acceptable in a fishing vessel. The seaboat's 'falls' for instance, which hoisted and lowered the boats, were, by regulation, used for only six months after which they were discarded and replaced by new cordage. Their size, that is to say their circumference, made them of little use for any other purpose in a ship of two thousand tons, nowhere nearly strong enough for securing the ship alongside, yet a

---

[13] The naval term for a toilet.

fishing vessel, because of its size, could use them for years. Likewise empty one-gallon paint pots, when scoured and cleaned, would serve as cooking vessels and were worth fifty decent-sized fish. After some haggling in bad English and worse Italian, *Tarquin* took station in the flotilla with half a ton of fish on the steel torpedo deck and men from each messdeck gutting and cleaning them. To the passengers aboard *Tarquin* it must have seemed a long way from the gilded chamber pots of Caserta. The misty outline of mount Vesuvius sank into the sea astern.

In HMS *Tudor*, Captain Cranston was unsympathetic toward the miseries of his passengers. The Mediterranean had been good to them and he maintained a speed of 22 knots, entered Gibraltar to refuel but slowed to 12 knots as they were confronted by the rollers of the Atlantic. A gale was blowing from the west—not a full gale, but something like six and six as recorded in the sea-and-swell scale. The waves were like rows of bungalows breaking off at the crests but fairly short between one row and the next. The forward part of the ship would rear up as she struck a wave with her sharp bows and sheets of spray would be flung over the forward guns, bridge and flag deck. In a ship of twenty thousand tons such weather would hardly be noticed, but in a ship of two thousand it was heavy going.

Captain Cranston was leading the port column with *Tantamount* and *Telemachus* astern. He had been in the navy for thirty-three years, nearly all of his time having been spent in destroyers. This, he knew, would be the last time that he would command a flotilla or a ship. He had been told there would be no more promotion, but if promotion meant sitting in an office with a staff of paper pushers, then perhaps it was best to get out while memories were still fresh with salt spray. A swell, seemingly greater than the others, swept under *Tudor*, lifted her for a few moments then allowed her to plunge into the trough. I will go home and sit with my wife, he said to himself. She will insist I meet her friends and I shall do so to please her. In all probability I shall then find a job. What about secretary of the golf club? Similar thoughts, geared to their station in life, must have occupied the minds of hundreds of crew members.

The shattered country to which Paul returned in the dying days of 1945, supposedly the year of victory, was emerging slowly and painfully from its wartime ordeal. The lights were on again and the blackout curtains had been torn down, but shops were empty and food rationing still in force. It seemed as though the country was still at war, still surveying its desolation and mourning its dead. To those who had returned from overseas, like Paul and his shipmates, the mood seemed excessively gloomy and they soon tired of hearing, "things will never be the same again." It seemed perverse that in victory the predominant emotion should be defeat. It might have been described as bloody-mindedness, a cry of "look-what-we've-been-through-and-what-do-we-get-for-it."

Tarquin's men had scarcely set foot ashore when it became clear that some of those who had preceded them through the customs barrier had been bloody-minded. The building had been wrecked beyond recognition by men who thought they deserved a better welcome than being made to stand in lines while their kit was searched. After absences of as much as three years, this wasn't good enough, so telephones had been ripped out, furniture overturned and papers burned. Customs officers had been maltreated but without serious injury. The authorities, realising the hopelessness of their position, made no effort to bring those hundreds of soldiers and sailors to justice, or what they conceived of as justice. Similar incidents took place all over the country and were hushed up as far as possible by the new Labour government. The customs inspectors, on their side, had been attempting to uncover firearms, particularly revolvers taken from enemy officers. An unfaithful wife, an angry serviceman, a small and easily hidden weapon—with such combinations, the national murder rate had nowhere to go but up.

On the other side of the customs barrier, the feelings among men who had served away from their homes and families were complex and varied. They had received no gesture of welcome, no thanks, but something in the nature of 'what-took-you-so-long' on the part of many civilians. In fact, the men knew exactly what had taken them so long—the incompetence of the country's leadership between the wars. They had set out with the wrong weapons and insufficient training, and had suffered terrible and unnecessary losses. At one point in the war, the island of Malta, Britain's vital bastion in the central Mediterranean, had three antiquated biplanes for its defence. For minesweeping at the western end of the Mediterranean, the navy had four coal-burning vessels which might have been scrapped at the start of the First World War, never mind this one. These ships were put up for sale between the wars, but no one wanted a four-hundred-ton, single-screw, coal-fired vessel which would have been marginal as a fishing trawler. The asking price was one hundred and fifty pounds, the sort of sum that a successful poker player might have in his trouser pocket; but no, that was too high a price. Instead, they were re-commissioned at the outbreak of the Second World War, and forty men in each ship risked their lives daily in vessels that were inefficient, dangerous and barely seaworthy. It was said in the navy that the further you found yourself from home waters, the more foolish the wartime decisions that affected you. The utter failure of the defence of Singapore was a case in point.

If the bomb damage and heaps of rubble were the conspicuous consequence of the war, it was the shortage of food that touched the rawest nerve. Rationing was as bad as it had ever been because England had insufficient land to grow the food it needed. France had always been a prime agricultural country, less industrialised than Britain and better able to sustain itself without imports. What was equally important was that France had not used up thousands of hectares of the best land for building airfields. Indeed, from 1940 to the end of the war its agricultural land was spared. In England, only sixty percent of its food could be produced at home, even when every flower garden, every border and every spare plot of land had been planted with vegetables. The airfields made it worse, so the balance had to come from overseas, primarily Australia and Canada. However, three thousand merchant ships had been sunk and it would take years to replace them. Even Germany, increasingly detested as the evidence of its barbaric practices mounted, could rely on its farmers for the necessities of life. To hungry Englishmen and women, who by their endurance had won the war, it all seemed cruelly unjust.

It was, therefore, the shelves of England's grocery shops that measured the recovery of the country. Food was the yardstick of well-being, the indicator of a decent living standard, and its shortage was the prime subject of complaint. Besides food there were other exasperating shortages. When Paul arrived home he discovered that for the past year the household had managed on three light bulbs. New ones were unobtainable because the factories were tooled for war production, so his father, mother and the housekeeper were reduced to carrying a light bulb with great care from one room to the next. He was told that it had been common practice that when the sirens sounded the light bulbs would be removed, leaving the house in darkness. The concussion from bombs or anti-aircraft fire could shatter them, even at a distance.

When Paul arrived at Broxbourne's normally quiet railway station, there occurred an incident that should have warned him of what lay ahead. He unloaded his kit from the luggage compartment with the help of a soldier who had been his travelling companion on the short run from central London, then stood looking around. There was no taxi, but a horse and cart was available for hire.

"Where yer from?" the driver asked.

"Far East. Japan," Paul replied.

"Don't I know yer?"

"Henriques. I've been away the whole war. You have a good memory."

"Oh yes, son of Justice. He's done well for himself as I hear it. Well, let me tell yer you'll not find things the way yer left em. I'll 'ave to charge yer ten bob, and just you remember we have a Labour government."

Paul looked at the man. Ten shillings. Before the war it would have been two shillings and better manners. The distance was just over a mile. He had a metal uniform box, kitbag and a piece of hand luggage.

"Very well."

The man made no attempt to help him so Paul struggled to get his uniform box on the cart, then the kitbag and hand luggage.

"You can sit up 'ere beside me."

"I prefer to walk."

A telephone call early that morning from Paul had informed Lady Violet Henriques that he would be leaving Portsmouth at midday and expected to reach London an hour or two later. He would cross the city and take the first train to Broxbourne.

Home, she thought, he's coming home. She went upstairs and contemplated the remains of what had once been her lavish wardrobe.

"I must dress up a bit." She still had one or two outfits, a remnant of what she had possessed at the outbreak of war. She had used her wartime ration cards for one purpose only: to buy handmade shoes, one pair a year, beautifully stitched by a local craftsman. Without a sewing machine and with little chance of finding one, she had spent countless hours working with needle and thread and had become skilled at converting the forlorn and shapeless dresses of the 1930s into more practical and austere clothes that were acceptable in wartime. She had no wish to be seen, even in the village of Broxbourne, appearing frivolous or juvenile. At least, she thought, I am better off than those poor souls who lost everything in the bombing. She would make do for another year until sanity and reasonableness returned to what people were now calling, with biting sarcasm, "this sceptered isle". Yes, she could dress becomingly, and the work she did in the vegetable garden had kept her in good physical condition. Many people's health had actually improved during the war years and she knew enough to be thankful for the garden that kept her supplied. Her mind ranged over her other assets: a very dear husband who was failing but might keep going for a few more years, a son who was on his way home and would marry a sensible girl. Rebecca was prettier than Violet had been and would make up for the daughter she never had. Lady Violet wanted grandchildren and could not imagine that Paul and Rebecca would let her down. Then there was her house, which so well reflected her exotic tastes. Friends, companions, people of her social level—of these, however, there were few who had survived the war. The young had gone away, as Paul and Rebecca had done. The middle-aged, like Stubbington, had gone to work in factories and offices. Even the elderly had found war-related employment. One of her distant cousins, a woman in her sixties, had taken a job as teacher and astonished colleagues and students alike with her knowledge of the gems of English poetry. Another friend, secretary of a local club, by then into his eighties, had refused to resign when the club restaurant closed for lack of food, and had stubbornly hung on even when the ministry of agriculture ploughed up the fairways for growing potatoes. He was left with a car park that was used only once a week when the Home Guard turned it into a parade ground. As secretary, he was left with a small office, no salary and a bunch of keys. Merely to 'carry on' was esteemed a virtue during those painful years.

Early in the war Violet had volunteered for work in the parish hall with Bessie Farqueson. Old garments donated locally had been washed, ironed and sorted into piles, dark blue for the navy, socks and underwear for the Home Guard and everything else for dockworkers and their families. She was relieved when only a single coat hanger remained bearing the red coat and white breeches of a huntsman. After a short discussion it was placed on the dock labourers pile. Bessie had not intended humour when she proposed that it be worn by a crane operator. Thereafter, the only clothing that came to the rectory for distribution was from elderly parishioners who had departed this life. These generally consisted of women's long dresses, bodices and aprons of a bygone era, breeches and waistcoats for men. The phrase "someone will get use out of it," was much heard. Deprived finally of her volunteer work, Violet turned increasingly to her sewing and her garden. She also read, painstakingly at first, the classics which had lain untouched on the library shelf for the whole of her married life.

But there was something more. She had not, in her youth, been a model of virtue, and had borne a child while still in her teens. Without confiding her secret to her parents, she had gone to France for the birth and had spent nearly four months "learning French." The baby had been adopted by a young childless couple. She had no idea how the war and German occupation of France had affected the couple who had so desperately wanted a baby that they accepted hers without formality. Not even her own mother knew of it, and when the war broke out in 1939, Violet had been secretly grateful that a curtain had fallen between England and the event that she most feared, namely the appearance of the foster parents. Her daughter, whose name she did not know, would be grown up now, married in all probability. Paul would never know that he had a half sister.

Sir Frederick Henriques shuffled to the front hall when he heard a knock on the door and a cry from his wife.

"Paul, it's wonderful to see you!" The embraces took almost a minute. Violet wept for joy, as did Amy who had appeared from the kitchen.

"I must get my luggage," Paul said finally. "It's on a cart outside," then he saw the familiar navy letter form on the hall table and reached for it. His parents stood close to each other as he began to read. "I'll be on my way home in a troopship in a few days with two other girls. Please meet me in Southampton."

There was more, but it could wait.

"I have a bottle of something," his father said, "but, if you agree, we'll keep it for Rebecca."

Paul carried his luggage into the house and read the remainder of Rebecca's letter. "It's been such a long time and so much has happened. Let me say that our parents, yours and mine, have suffered greatly and endured much. When daddy stands in front of us in his vestments—you in uniform, I in mum's wedding dress—and asks me whether I take this man, Paul Henriques, I shall probably break down. I love you as I always did but I'm older and a little wiser and I have seen things I could not have dreamed about. I shall probably speak of it for the remainder of my life. Oh, by the way, the Admiral has invited us..." the letter went on.

So there it is, Paul said to himself. Rebecca.

Next day he took his bicycle down from the garage rafters, cleaned it, and searched for oil or grease to make the chain run smoothly; but, like everything else in those deprived times, a can of oil was unobtainable and he had to use a spoonful of lard from the kitchen. Next he rode up and down the driveway to make sure, as he told his mother, that it worked properly and he hadn't forgotten how to ride it.

"We could have sold it for fifty pounds," his father said. "Prewar it cost nine or ten, but with petrol rationing, which meant no petrol at all, bicycles became more valuable than cars. The factories that made them, Stubby told us, were producing Spitfires. Sports cars went first because they use a lot of petrol and don't carry a useful load." He paused. "This is a foretaste of things to come. One day the world will run out of oil, and bicycles will be back."

"But meanwhile," Paul added, "we don't have enough tankers to carry oil from the Gulf. I've seen them go down..." he trailed off.

Paul tapped lightly on the door of the rectory and stood waiting. The year 1945 was fading but there were roses in the garden, a few birds busied themselves at the fountain, and the church tower, which had borne witness to a millennium of village life, brooded between trees and sky.

"Oh it's you, Paul. How good to see you. Your parents must be overjoyed. For my part I thank God for your safe return."

Paul hesitated, then put out his hand. Before him was not the opinionated scholar whom he remembered from the early days of the war, but a man whose fifty years seemed supported precariously on a withered frame. The white hair appeared venerable, but not the weariness in his voice nor the defeat that was etched on his face. Is this the loquacious encyclopedia of learning who taught me from an early age, Paul wondered, the voluble cleric who preached Christian humility yet spoke with the assurance of a medieval pope drumming up support for his pet crusade? Is this the man who could mumble like a chastised monk and drink wine like a Frenchman? Where is the dagger sharpness, the wit of the man who, requiring a Latin maxim to support some unprovable contention would invent one on the spot? It was said of him that if he had worn a toga in ancient Rome he could have out-debated Marcus Aurelius. He was credited with being the first scholar to observe that one of the so-called psalms of David was an exact copy of a hymn attributed to a king of Egypt a thousand years earlier. When Egyptian hieroglyphics had been matched against Old Testament Hebrew he saw an exact similarity of meaning that no one else had noticed. Years earlier he had accepted a challenge to debate against a renowned Jewish scholar, but only with the provision that the language of debate be New Testament Greek. This was the Astoundingly Reverend F.F., as he was variously called, a man of many parts who, if he had lived in an earlier age, would have found his place on the list of Anglican divines in company with John Donne and William Tyndale.

"Come in, come in, my dear fellow. You can leave your velocipede by the door but do remember to chain it to a lamppost when you are in the village. I fear that the level of honesty exhibited by the poor people who were bombed out of their homes, and who have wrapped themselves in the garments of our mercy, is quite deplorable. A chain and padlock is not a Christian symbol. No, it is a symbol of slavery, but I am at a loss to suggest an alternative."

"I shall be careful," Paul replied.

"Let me say that I anticipate the purpose of your visit. I think you have come here to ask for my daughter's hand. I hear from her regularly, as I am sure you do, and she has matured as you have."

"We shall, of course, ask you to marry us." There was finality in Paul's voice.

"Yes, but I warn you that I may not be here in Broxbourne for much longer. I am planning to resign my living. Come inside..."

A few moments later, seated in the study, Paul came out with it. "I can't believe what I am hearing. People like you don't give up. You're like my father."

"What a magnificent rebuke. I say this with shame but my faith in Christian doctrine, or certain parts of it, has been undermined. My research has revealed... I shall call them 'aggravations', which I cannot ignore."

"What will become of your congregation? For a thousand years they have gathered in that church," Paul waved toward the window, "in good times and bad, their spiritual life has been served, there has been a man of God to administer the sacraments." Paul hesitated then struggled on. "You, or someone carrying your cross, was here when the Church of England was established, and again when King Philip of Spain sent his armada and tried to wipe it out. You were here when Shakespeare bent over his manuscripts, when Napoleon strutted about the continent of Europe and laid the groundwork for modern war. You saw the bombs falling on London. You are the captain of your ship, joined to this place by blood and tears. How can you just go?"

Then, as an afterthought, "and if you leave, where?"

"Paul, you speak with the voice of angels. For myself I shall hope to obtain a teaching post in the Middle East. Universities specialising in theology maintain what they call 'campus' in the Holy Land. They undertake archaeological work and study the original languages, and of course make translations of documents that come their way. The Americans are the acknowledged masters. They have excellent scholars and almost unlimited funds. I think I could make a useful contribution by teaching and translating, and by supervising excavations."

"Excavations? I would have thought there was nothing left to dig up. Surely they've gone over all the ancient—"

"Oh, heavens, no! Every time someone puts a spade in the ground they find something new; that is to say, old. In one place—Greece, as I recall—some fellow was digging foundations for his garage and came across an amphitheatre. How can an amphitheatre get lost?" He gestured but went on, "I've heard through my friends that some scrolls have been found in a cave near the Dead Sea. None of our people have seen them; in fact, ownership is not yet established."

"But surely," Paul searched for words, "it's not the same as being in charge of your own parish, of having a church. The church music, the goodwill of a congregation. Here, you are captain of your ship, master of ten thousand souls. You have the affection of all. And let me remind you that you invited me—yes, asked me in all sincerity—to abandon what I had planned, give up thoughts of the sea and train for the church. That was when I was a choir boy."

"Yes, Paul, you're right. Before I discovered what was amiss with traditional faith, before I realised that the ship, as you call it, is made with partly rotten timbers, founded on exaggerations and wishful thinking. I have lost the gift of faith in dogma which, in the cold light of science, is demonstrably absurd. The fact that people have believed them all these years no longer counts. Listen to this, Paul: We think we have found evidence of the earthly father of Jesus. Yes, that's right, the man who got his mother pregnant out of wedlock. And we think we know roughly where Christ's body was interred, where he lay, together with other family members—mother, brothers and wife."

Paul looked at him in disbelief. "Wife?"

"There isn't a shred of evidence that Mary of Magdalene was a fallen woman, but there is much to suggest that she and Jesus were in love. The early fathers of the church, so-called, who were trying to give Christianity the gloss they wanted, turned her into a harlot, which is the oldest and meanest trick that men can play on women."

"This is a bit beyond me," Paul said. "I always believed pretty much what I was told to believe. It was put to me by yourself and others that the things I was taught came from the very top and had never been seriously doubted. It all seemed so clear and definite, but now, you of all people, are having second thoughts.

"Yes, but only in light of fresh evidence."

"Is anything left?" Paul asked, "or are our churches to become curiosities, like the temples that line the banks of Nile."

F. F. spread his hands. "A great deal is untouched, but now we have a family man, a teacher who, when he was put to death by the Romans, was laid to rest in the family tomb by his grieving mother, and may still be there. The next few years should provide answers."

There was silence for a moment.

"You know, I expected to find changes when I got home," Paul finally said. "Like many others, I felt that changes were overdue. But from what I can see, the changes have come in those places where I expected it to be the same. Religious belief, ordinary good manners, complaining. What has happened to our optimism, our hope for a better future? I am beginning to wonder whether we won the war or lost it."

Chapter 10 — RMS *Orion*

The Royal Mail Steamship *Orion* steamed eastwards over the vastness of the southern ocean. The Cape of Good Hope, southernmost point of Africa, lay three thousand miles astern, Australia two thousand ahead. Great rollers, a mile or more separating one whitened crest from the last, moved eastward in splendid phalanx, the persistent wind that created them being impeded on the surface of the globe only by the rocky spine of South America, the awkwardly shaped islands of New Zealand and the dry tableland of Australia. The wind blew almost round the earth, but *Orion* took the long swells in stride, her speed only a little less than that of the waves themselves. Her motion was corkscrew with her counter first being lifted by a wave that would surge forward along her length and slowly deposit her in the trough with a roll to starboard. The passengers had accustomed themselves to the motion of the ship and stood watching at the ship's rail, marvelling at the sheer magnificence of sea, sky and vessel.

In bygone days this ocean was feared less for its turbulence than for its vastness. Most sailing vessels could take these long swells, their sails steadied them so there was less to be feared than in other seas that were hemmed in by land. At its worst, the Mediterranean was spiteful and acrimonious, as the apostle Paul discovered to his peril. The southern ocean, however, was unknown to the ancients, whether Egyptian, Phoenician, Roman or Greek, and had only appeared recently in Western history books. It had not borne the cargoes of grain or the wine jars of ancient commerce, nor the slaves whose labours would have built ancient civilisations; no, this ocean had carried only the forlorn cargoes of outcast humanity which were deposited on a dismal shore.

Paul stirred himself at seven bells. Rebecca was still sleeping in the other bunk so he stood for a moment, his eyes caressing her, then quickly dressed. He took his binoculars from a drawer where he kept them wrapped in a sweater and went down the deserted passageways to the ship's galley for tea and an oatmeal biscuit. Next he climbed to the bridge deck and stood for a few minutes until his eyes had become accustomed to the dark.

"How's she steering?" he asked the man on the wheel.

"Well, sir. Due east."

An experienced quartermaster. He didn't keep making silly little corrections but allowed the ship to steer itself.

He turned to the third officer who was sweeping the horizon one last time before going below.

"Anything?" Paul asked.

"No, sir. Very quiet. I've written up the log. If you're ready..."

"Away you go!"

Nice boy that third officer, Paul said to himself. He had missed the war and lacked the unforgettable experiences of wartime: the huge convoys of merchant ships spread over miles of sea, the air armadas, the submarine hunts, Japanese suicide attacks, the roar of guns. He would fault his parents for the remainder of his life because his sister was two years older than he. If only they could have arranged for him to be born first he would not be suffering the indignity of a uniform that bore not a shred of coloured ribbon.

Paul made his way to the port wing of the bridge where a solitary lookout stood somewhere between sea and sky. "Them waves is so big a small ship could be lost behind any one of them."

Paul smiled. "Not many small ships in this ocean." He put out a hand to steady himself then turned his eyes from the sea to the great curtain of stars which plunged and reared in the canopy above. The Magellanic cloud seemed as though torn from the Milky Way, dominated by the bright and beautiful star Canopus. Ah yes, Canopus. That name brought memories. The southern heavens, he thought, emptier of stars than the north, perhaps because they are less familiar. His mind turned to Rebecca, his Rebecca, his passion, his soul's companion. We are now in the same ship, he thought, after five long years. We are borne on the same ocean, we see the same stars. He remembered that his father had used his influence to intercede with the directors of the steamship company to include Rebecca as assistant purser, bearing in mind her three years of service in the Women's Royal Naval Service. He pointed out that young immigrants would be at ease with her and would be impressed if she were called to the bridge when signal traffic became heavy—entering or leaving harbour for instance—to help with flags and signal lamp.

Rebecca had been an instant success. She was friendly and sympathetic, she had a glorious sense of humour, and the young passengers crowded round her on deck or in the lounge. They had passed a huge merchantman off the Cape of Good Hope four or five miles distant and the Captain, wishing to impress a group of passengers whom he had invited to the bridge, ordered Rebecca to signal "What ship and where bound?" She switched on the six-inch Aldis, aimed it and tapped out the message, then turned to the group of passengers and asked if anyone was writing it down. "Later," she said, "it must be copied into the ship's log together with the exact time." The other ship began to signal and Rebecca read it with confident ease. "*Southern Cross* Sydney to L-I-V... Liverpool, via A-D-E... Adelaide, F-R-E, Fremantle, S-I-N-G, Singapore and C-A-P, Cape Town with cargo of wheat, frozen lamb, wine and other M-I-S-S—" Rebecca laughed. "He doesn't know how to spell 'miscellaneous'."

"There, you see," the Captain said to the awestruck little group. "Now they'll make the same signal to us: 'What ship and where bound?' and Rebecca will reply, '*Orion*, London to Sydney carrying the British government's solution to the population shortage in Australia'."

They all laughed. "Goodbye and good luck," were the final words from *Southern Cross*.

A few minutes before eight bells the Captain came on the bridge.

"Morning, Paul," he said. "Did you get stars?"

"Yessir, five, first magnitude. Horizon's a bit thick. My triangle isn't perfect but I think we're slightly north. Probably a current coming up from the Antarctic. I didn't make any course correction."

"Fuel consumption?" The captain asked.

"Standard. No worries there."

"Have you anything planned for the forenoon?"

"I want to see inside number two hold. Boatswain says he can hear some thumping. A bit of loose cargo. I'll get down there and see it myself."

"What's on top?"

"Settlers' effects. Furniture and luggage."

"Below?"

"Machinery."

"Very well. I want you to take a telephone so you can tell me what's going on. How many men will you need?"

"Ten, to be safe."

Paul gave instructions to the boatswain for the covers to be partly removed from the hatch—not an easy operation when the ship is at sea, but far worse would be for the cargo to break loose and crash about the hold. He found Rebecca in the purser's office and together they went to the dining room for breakfast.

"I'm a bit worried," she said. "This help-yourself buffet is all very well and reduces the need for stewards, but some of these passengers have never seen food like this in the whole of their lives. They grew up in underprivileged households and when the war came with its food rationing, things got worse. Now they're over their seasickness and putting more food on their plates than they can eat."

"There's a way of dealing with that," Paul suggested. "No serving spoons on the buffet table and the food out of reach. Someone comes with his plate and says to the steward, "I want some of that, and the steward ladles out a reasonable quantity."

"I'll try it on the purser," Rebecca nodded.

Paul spent a long forenoon in number-two hold and found, as he suspected, that some machinery had been packed insecurely, the crate not being up to maritime requirements.

"Sloppy wartime job," in the boatswain's words.

Twenty tons of other cargo, mainly settlers' effects, had to be moved before the problem could be corrected, the work made difficult by the motion of the ship. They all breathed a sigh of relief when the hatch covers were back in place and the cargo secured.

Paul didn't want to be seen by the passengers in stained overalls so, after reporting to the Captain, he went to his cabin to get cleaned up and back into proper uniform. It was his custom to go around the decks and lounges before lunch. Rebecca entered a moment later.

"How did it go, darling? You were down there a long time."

"We found the problem," Paul replied, "and the Captain didn't have to stop or reduce speed. Opening up a hold when the ship is at sea is something no captain likes to do. It's alright in the tropics when there's a dead calm..."

"This could hardly be called a dead calm."

Rebecca sat down and looked at herself in a small mirror. "I'm going to get some of this cut off," she said, shaking her head, "back to where it was when I was a Wren." She hesitated for a few seconds. "Paul," she asked suddenly, "do you like being married?"

He looked at her. "Being married, yes I do. There's so much hope and promise. It's all I ever wanted. But the business of actually getting married. That was rather heavy going." They looked at each other and laughed.

For five years they had something very private and beautiful until the engagement was announced and, as Paul observed, "all the hatches were opened." There were letters, telephone calls, questions, busybodies on all sides, people with advice and silly suggestions.

"It was as though we had offered ourselves for public scrutiny," said Paul. "That was the part I didn't enjoy."

And the big day didn't go off smoothly.

"Could we say it was a fiasco?" asked Rebecca.

"I suppose it was the best that could be done so soon after the war."

"From a woman's point of view—I mean, as seen by your mother and mine—it was one disaster following another." Late trains from London meant late guests, food was just about non-existent because of rationing, flowers were scarce in a country where gardens grew only vegetables, cider had to play the role of Champagne, the boy sopranos had seen fit to acquire their manhood the week before, and the cake arrived after everyone had gone home.

They laughed and embraced, one hand to hold each other, the other to brace against the roll of the ship.

"But look at it like this," Paul continued. "The people who counted were there, your parents and mine. Does anything else matter?"

"No, of course not. You're right. Your father's speech was perfect, and your mother, well, she really held the whole thing together. What I liked was that she didn't keep apologising. She simply gestured and said it in French."

"You've reminded me of your father," said Paul. "I have the idea that his wounds are self-inflicted. When I was a boy I really didn't know what to make of him. He was too complicated, too difficult. He wasn't quite of this world."

"He'll be packing the vicarage by now. Oh God, I lived there most of my life. You know, mum and dad didn't want me to see them leave.

They thought it best I be here with you—spare me the sadness of going away. What will my mother be thinking?"

Rebecca stood up and looked out of the brass-bound scuttle at the gray sea. "Your best man, Jonathan Palliser. He told me how the two of you went on a sightseeing tour in Ceylon. I do hope we shall be friends for many years to come."

After lunch, Paul returned to his cabin and lay down for a light sleep. Indeed, he was not even sure whether he was awake or asleep when he saw the shadow of his father coming toward him across the water. In later years he would remember that moment for its purity and strangeness; its overwhelming spirituality. "I am going on my way," his father seemed to be saying. "Do not grieve for me. Go where your duty lies and be protected by the ancient sea turtle. Raise your children to the Glory of God. Care for your dear mother and for your Rebecca..."

Paul sighed and lay very still. His father had come to this barren and unforgiving ocean to bid him goodbye. He had seen and heard him, not in the flesh but in spirit and in truth.

An hour later a telegraphist approached him as he bent over the chart with the Captain.

"I'm sorry, sir," the boy said as he handed the message to Paul. It began, "Deeply regret to inform you..."

Paul handed it to the Captain. They had just discussed Sir Frederick's appearance in Paul's cabin.

"Uncanny," said the Captain, shaking his head. "From your mother, obviously. I'm afraid there can be no possibility of getting home for the funeral. Another week to Fremantle and six weeks from there. They are planning regular air flights but we're nowhere near that yet."

"I do understand, sir. Anyway, my father seemed to want me to continue what I'm doing now."

"Your wife know him well?" the captain asked.

"Yes, very well." There were tears in Paul's eyes.

"And you were in the naval reserve for the entire war and your wife a Wren, she was saying."

"Yessir. I'm still in the reserve. I got my half stripe a few weeks ago."

"Lieutenant-Commander. Twenty-eight, aren't you? That's damn good. You have my heartfelt condolences on your loss and congratulations on a well-deserved promotion."

Paul excused himself to tell Rebecca. At the purser's office two decks below he found the master-at-arms, two individuals handcuffed together, the purser and Rebecca close behind.

"What's going on?" Paul asked.

"We found two stowaways," replied the master-at-arms. "Purser is attempting to get their names so he can communicate with the authorities back in London. Trouble is, they have no identification and they don't speak English; at least, they pretend they don't."

"I see," from Paul. "The first thing to be done is to take them to the sick bay. They must be examined for communicable diseases. After that, it's up to the Captain."

"Must they be handcuffed?" asked Rebecca. "We have a lot of young people on board. I shall be asked about it."

"If these two are not handcuffed, the young people might have even more to be alarmed about," the master-at-arms replied. "They don't have tickets and they don't have luggage. They're on board illegally and if they tried to escape we'd be held for negligence."

The purser stepped in. "These two are not passengers, Rebecca. I have reason to suspect they are Nazi war criminals. We have a duty to protect our passengers, not just entertain them. I can remember the time when stowaways were thrown overboard."

Oh God, thought Paul. It's all fun and games on the upper deck. Sumptuous meals and comfortable beds at night, and now comes this unwelcome reminder of the past. Criminals, death just around the corner—that's a side of life that Rebecca has not experienced. She's a modern woman with a mind of her own, but her time as a Wren, passing signals from a secure signal tower to ships in Portsmouth harbour, didn't expose her to the harsh realities. Paul often thought of his brush with stowaways in *Canopus*. Time and experience had eased the pain, and while he knew that what he had done was wrong, he still felt no need to condemn himself. Five men, lepers—yes, he had consented to their deaths. It was still law in many parts of the world that if lepers stray beyond the boundaries designated for them, behind which they must live their lives, then clean people may, and indeed should, stone them to death.

The two stowaways looked inoffensive enough. They were probably in their twenties, but to the trained eye of the master-at-arms they had been in some sort of military or disciplined service. If they had been citizens of the United Kingdom they would have identity cards, speak English, and would have received the government's assisted passage. The purser's guess that they were Nazi's on the run was probably not far off the mark. To Paul's orderly mind, there was a procedure to be followed. First, get them medically examined and then, if they can't offer any explanation for their presence, assume the worst and put them in the lockup. Paul recorded the incident in the ship's log and called it to the Captain's attention. "Very well," was all the Captain had said.

But a piece of loose cargo had been another thing altogether. It could be truly dangerous and had to be corrected immediately, hence Paul had given it his personal attention that morning.

Was he presaging the future? He would never know, but here he was in *Marquess*, in immediate danger of sinking, all because of an item of cargo that had been carelessly, indeed, dangerously loaded. Aboard *Orion* the hazard was manmade; but in *Marquess* it was a huge stone, taken with infinite care from a South African mountain, which now lay at the bottom of the Atlantic. The beauty of its markings had been made by a billion years of geological activity. Now it would lie undisturbed on the seabed for another billion. It had torn loose from its chains like some ancient god that had been restrained and had sought freedom by plunging through the side of the ship.

Orion's Captain, who had commanded ships throughout the war, instructed Paul to muster the younger officers and senior crewmembers and tell them exactly what he had done in *Orion's* hold, and what the dangers were. Rebecca made sure to be among the listeners.

"This was not as bad as it might have been," Paul began. "I don't think we were in any danger. But sometimes a cargo can shift, as they say. Bales of wool may not matter, but machinery—aircraft engines, turbines—that's when it becomes a nightmare. Look at it this way. We may have loaded a hundred tons of mixed cargo into a hold. We put the heavy stuff at the bottom, the lighter, more perishable items on top. It is probably going to be loaded right up to deck level, then covered. But the ship will roll and pitch, and after weeks of movement, our best efforts to secure it with chains, ropes, baulks of timber, wedges, have loosened. Imagine the weight of a turbine destined for a hydroelectric plant—and don't think other items of cargo will wedge it in place. That's not how it works. Each bit of machinery is housed in its own crate, so when the crate is smashed, you have a loose cannon. Now let's add another dimension. If all the cargo is to be unloaded at Fremantle, our first port of call, that's fine, because the sequence of loading hardly matters. But if there are turbines for Fremantle, lumber for Adelaide and finished goods for Sydney, then you have loaded in reverse order of unloading. And one thing you absolutely can't do is spread them all over the jetty while you are digging for some piece of machinery at the very bottom. Theft, pilfering and a day wasted.

"Another thing I'd like to mention," Paul went on. "Did you notice how the stewards refused to allow passengers to keep large trunks in their cabins? People were asked to unpack, put their things in drawers, and their trunks were taken to a special storage. Why? Because more legs have been broken by heavy cabin trunks sliding across the floor than by falling down companionways. My steel uniform box, which I had all my naval service, could be a lethal weapon.

"So let me finish by saying again that a loose cargo can mean disaster. I want to thank our boatswain for being alert to the problem and knowing how to correct it."

That evening, Paul finally had the chance to tell Rebecca about his father's unearthly visit and the telegram that confirmed his death.

"I wish your father were here to answer my questions," Paul said. "He could explain to me how I knew of my father's death before the telegram was even sent. He could tell me how I understood his words without hearing them, how I saw him although my eyes were closed. Your father would know. I hope he's able to give some comfort to my mother."

A week later, on the way into Fremantle harbour, *Orion* was in collision with an outward-bound Chinese vessel. *Orion* was under the command of a harbour pilot so the Captain was legally absolved from blame. Twenty feet in length above the waterline, however, was a gash that could be repaired without going into dry dock. The dockyard announced that the ship could be seaworthy in twelve to fourteen days, and it was agreed that the insurers of the Chinese vessel would pay the bill.

"I don't want to feed six hundred passengers for two weeks if I don't have to," said the purser. "Best put them ashore and let them see Australia from the train windows." There followed meetings with the passengers and with representatives of the Australian railways. Special trains were arranged and the passengers accepted an offer to cross the continent by rail. Most of them were bound for Adelaide, Melbourne and Sydney. The train journey east would cost them nothing. They watched their luggage being loaded from *Orion's* hold into wagons on the jetty while Paul and Rebecca checked every item to ensure that each passenger and his luggage stayed together. In England the emigrants had been told to paint their names on everything they possessed, but there were a few who had not done so, which made for delays. When repairs were completed, *Orion* would sail to Adelaide to pick up fresh passengers and cargo.

With six hundred noisy, excited passengers landed, cleaning crews aboard and the Australian police in charge of the stowaways, *Orion* was suddenly and unnaturally quiet.

Paul searched a gray horizon from the bridge of *Marquess*. His thoughts were of his family. His mother, now well-cared for, had a comfortable place to live, her daughter-in-law was nearby and there were two grandchildren in the nursery. If Paul had not been her ideal son—if, like his father, he had failed to recognise her needs and had sailed off to the ends of the earth in pursuit of his own dreams, her life had surely been rewarded in other ways.

Paul thought of Rebecca and wondered what would become of her if he went down with his ship. There was something gracious and straightforward about her. Her patron saint, if she had one, was Theresa, who told her novices: "However slight the task on which you are engaged, put your heart in it and perform it well." Rebecca had another faculty that Paul admired. Unlike many women, she could play with her children and teach them without reducing herself to their level.

And his father, well learned in the law, judge of all men's affairs, who had long been the custodian of the Henriques heirlooms and family secrets—goblets, spoon and inkwell, handed down through many generations from Jaime himself—had his father known the truth, the strange influence of the turtle, the shape of which was engraved on each piece of silver? Had his father been borne across the wastes of the great southern ocean to bid goodbye to Paul and bestow upon him a paternal blessing? Had he the power to see what others could not see, a vision frayed by gray seas, of Jaime on a distant shore and a long-suffering, humble creature ready and willing to save a human life? Did Jaime stand and beckon to all mankind? Was this ugly but long-lived creature the last best hope of earth? Paul did not know; he saw only Jaime, his distant ancestor, who seemed to offer help in his distress.

Chapter 11 — The Outback

Stubbington had become the proprietor of a roadside filling station and repair shop. His establishment was on the outskirts of Broxbourne on the London road and he prospered not just from the sale of petrol, which increased as wartime restrictions were eased, but also because the vehicles of that era were shoddy and forever breaking down. Before the war there were many car manufacturers in England, a high proportion of them producing finely engineered vehicles, but few survived the standardisation of the postwar period. The call was for cheapness, so that all sorts of rattletraps took to the roads, giving Stubbington, and others like him, a lucrative business keeping them roadworthy. It was said that all the best carmakers had gone out of business, while the worst, which were mass-produced, had become household names. In those days the expression 'prewar' implied something well made and dependable, 'postwar' indicated poor workmanship.

Stubbington, then in his fifties, had stepped confidently into the management of his new business. He enjoyed the work of repairing things and at the same time meeting and conversing with his customers. In those early postwar years there was one topic of conversation that seemed to unite the country; namely how the war had altered people's outlook and changed their lives. Stubbington's mind was full of ideas and viewpoints that were not quite his own, but which he had gained by conversing with car owners. He also kept up a correspondence with Paul that was courteous and well informed. He wrote of the affairs of the village, the changes and loss of innocence that had afflicted many neighbourhoods bordering London. In one of his letters he recalled the story of the Crismaru children who had lived a mile down the laneway from the Henriques house and been selected, before the war, for transportation to Australia. They were to have been adopted by a farm family "far from the crowded conditions and squalor" which was thought to afflict their parental home.

"Dear Mr. Paul," wrote Stubbington, "you will remember, I am sure, the two children, Tim and Annie, who were sent away like little criminals to the western part of Australia. They were to have been adopted, it was said, by a childless couple who would treat them as their own. After some adventures they were found at the roadside by the Tollands, who already had children and found these two outside a tavern in a place called Kondinin, a hundred miles from Perth. The people that were supposed to get them were childless, for sure, and had gone to do their shopping, then stopped for a few beers, leaving Tim and Annie in the street. Well, Arthur Tolland came across them, asked some questions of the driver who had brought them from Perth, and decided that the couple in the tavern were unfit to be parents. Imagine, if you will, two tired and hungry little ones who had travelled half way round the world to be welcomed to their new country by a mum and dad who leave them outside a tavern. Anyway, the Tollands took them and added them to their own family. Arthur had been an army sergeant and football player, not a man to be trifled with. His wife, Betty, an absolute winner. They live twenty miles from Kondinin and raise wheat and sheep on a big property. From then on, the fortunes of Tim and Annie soared. They didn't miss a day of school and ten years later were admitted to the University of Western Australia in Perth, Tim to study land surveying and Annie to get her degree in business and accounting. How, you may ask, could they afford expenses such as accommodation, tuition and books? I'll tell you. It was because Tim was a water diviner, a skill which he inherited, it was said, from his Romany ancestors. The country being dry, he earned good money locating water, and his services were always in demand. Weekends would find him and Annie doing the country properties—the outback they call it—driving an old vehicle that had seen service as a hearse.

Oh yes, Philippa, the eldest of the Tolland children, went through to become a qualified nurse. She visited us in Broxbourne when she was on an exchange program and said that Annie had become a beautiful young woman, like a Romany princess. On her travels about the country with Tim she met Peter Carrington, who runs a huge property somewhere beyond Meekathara. His dad is Brigadier-General Carrington, DSO, one-time Lieutenant Governor of the province. It is said that his land carries a million sheep. Peter Carrington joined the Australian Air Force when he was 20 but the war ended and he went back to civvy life. So our little Annie has become Mrs. Peter Carrington of Carrington Springs, West Australia. Philippa told us that if all the wool sheared from their sheep were knitted into a neck scarf it would stretch clear across Australia. Annie is learning to fly their plane so that when she wants to go shopping she doesn't have to bother her husband for a lift."

The letter went on, "Annie's brother Tim works at Elders GM, the biggest land and stock company in Australia, with offices in every town and village. Their business is what affects farmers and graziers; Philippa called it a "super" company to work for because their reputation is beyond reproach and they care for their employees. I do hope, Mr. Paul, that you will visit them if ever you find yourself in those parts. You must write their story, and what a story it is, all because a man called Tolland came upon two little strangers in the street."

On an impulse, and with the Captain's permission to take five or six days leave, Paul and Rebecca hired a car for the drive to Meekathara. The ship was empty of passengers, the dockyard had assumed control and they both felt strangely lightheaded as they drove north along the coast between Perth and Geraldton. At Carrington Springs, Paul called Annie who, of course, remembered them. At first she had simply not known what to say, but she soon collected herself and invited them to visit.

When Paul put down the telephone he stood contemplating for a full minute. Annie's voice had changed from that of a child into a confident young woman. She had acquired the typical accent of Australia, but there was more to it than that. She had, in a word, reached maturity in her new surroundings. He remembered her bright eyes when she was a child—eyes that were downcast for so much of the time in his presence. For her part she had noticed his shoes, well shined by the strong hands of Stubbington, and his woollen stockings, darned and washed by Amy. There was, she knew, a chasm, a deep social divide between her world and his, between the crowded cottage where she lived and the comforts and cleanliness of his parental house. She had nursed a secret passion for him nonetheless. To her he was a god, aloft and unattainable. Her heaven was a pool in the river, shaded by weeping willows, with shiny pebbles underfoot. She had wanted to go there on a warm summer evening, to sit on the grass with Paul and reveal her innermost secrets. That was a dozen years ago, and now she was thrilled at the thought of meeting him again.

Paul held the car door for Rebecca and they took the road northward. Never far from the sea, the road was paved but narrow, its bitumen surface appearing strangely blue in colour. The coastal strip had enough rain for a few farms and fruit orchards, cattle grazed and eucalyptus trees broke the rounded outlines of the hills. If this were the northern hemisphere we'd be somewhere about the latitude of Cairo, he said to himself. But here the westerly winds are cooled by the southern ocean giving Australia its famous white light. An artist among the passengers had told him that when he arrived in Australia he had thrown out his darker, northern paints and found white, clean colours that were truthful to the pure air of the southern hemisphere.

Geraldton was a seaside village consisting of a few rather rundown shops, but there was also a restaurant decorated with old notices which had been posted in the church halls and meeting rooms of southern England a hundred years earlier to attract "young females of good character" to a new life in Australia. In those early days, when Australia was still shaking off the bad jokes and coarse reputation of a penal colony, there had been a chronic shortage of women and the simplistic remedy had been to ship them out from England by the windjammerful. It was spelled out that they were to be of "sound health and good character" and carry with them a letter from their parish. They were to supply themselves with blankets, ample clothing and personal items. They could expect to find "immediate employment" in Australia with the option of marriage in due course. One hoped, Paul said to himself, that whoever wrote these dubious phrases was not aware of the conditions at this end, nor the destiny that awaited the females in question. They were seized at the dockside, the pretty ones fought over and marched off without ceremony to a life of isolation and loneliness on the farms or cottages where chance placed them. The men wanted women to share their loneliness, cook for them, provide them with children and give their lives the gloss of dignity. A few did reasonably well, but the majority endured a hard life and bore many children; some were utterly devastated. In the benign light of history they were crusaders to be applauded for the part they played in the early history of the continent. They were poor and uneducated and, if they had remained in England, their lives, in all probability, would have been spent in dreary and unfulfilling ways—as domestic servants in large tyrannical houses or, perhaps, as seamstresses in sweat shops, all the way down to prostitution and petty crime. In whichever hemisphere they found themselves, a rewarding and happy life was not likely to have been theirs.

Paul and Rebecca made their way round the dining room and read the unctuous phrases, "Captain Hawke, master... keeps a fatherly eye on his passengers"; "Divine Service on Sundays unless weather is inclement; fresh provisions when possible." Yet despite the lies, the hardship and the death that must have overtaken many of them on the high seas, and kept Captain Hawke's book of common Prayer well thumbed on those pages where was set out "Burial of the Dead at Sea", those who survived gave new life to Australia. The one document lacking on the wall of the restaurant, Rebecca thought, was a sample of a clergyman's letter attesting to a young woman's virtue. A few days, or hours, in their new homes, and both the letter and the virtue to which it referred would have been mislaid.

Paul and Rebecca made an early start the following day and took the road eastward toward Meekathara. The landscape changed from green to brown, from farmland to desert, and for mile after mile there was nothing but low scrub and parched grass. How, Paul wondered, do sheep find sustenance in such a harsh land? Kangaroos were adapted to it and there was a wealth of bird life, but merino sheep had come from Spain where conditions could scarcely be as stark as this. Meekathara, when they reached it, seemed to have grown out of the surrounding desert. It was hot, dusty and treeless with a propensity for everything to be built of corrugated iron.

"I read somewhere that Australia has to import nearly all the wood it uses for house building, fences and even furniture," said Rebecca. "I can understand that now—I mean, they have so few trees."

Paul nodded. "The early sailing ships must have been in difficulties when they had to make repairs, or when they needed a new mast. If I have the story right, they had to go to Norfolk Island, somewhere in the Pacific, to find a straight, strong tree. The eucalyptus that grows here is useless because the wood cracks and isn't watertight. This must be the only continent... whoops, that looks like the post office."

He got out of the car and called Peter Carrington on a very ancient telephone.

"Our plans are a bit changed," Peter said. "I was flying over one of the small stations this morning and saw no sign of Jim. The dogs were in the yard but there wasn't any smoke from the chimney. I can't land there, so I flew back. I'll take a jeep this afternoon."

"Can I meet you there?" Paul asked.

"Yes of course. It's about two hours from where you are. Road's a bit rough and you'll have to take it easy. But yes, sounds like a good idea—just follow the track." There was a pause. "Annie wants to come. She's getting ready."

Paul filled the petrol tank and studied the map. The postmaster gave them a box of supplies and some mail for Carrington Springs and in half an hour they were driving on a track through the bush. In one place they crossed a flat plain that looked like an old lakebed and tried to imagine what it must have been like at some time in the past when water had been abundant.

Jim's house was no more than a shack with a rough door and a single window. There was a windmill outside, the sails scarcely turning in the light breeze. A flock of pink and gray parrots rose screaming from the water trough. Paul parked and looked round while three dogs greeted him noisily. He tried the door of the shack and was momentarily overcome by flies and stench. "Oh God," he said. The poor fellow must have known what was coming because he lay on his bunk with one hand across his chest and the other, Paul thought, in the act of brushing away the flies. He covered the dead man's face with a sheet. The dogs were whimpering outside.

Paul walked slowly back to the car and put out his arms as though to protect Rebecca.

"I'm sorry," he said. "The Lord giveth, and the Lord taketh away."

They stood looking at each other and Rebecca said very quietly, "Blessed be the Name of the Lord."

A minute later they saw the dust of an approaching car.

"I'm afraid he's dead," were his first words. "Don't go in, Annie."

There were no introductions, no formalities. "I'll look after the dogs," Annie said. "You boys must decide what to do." She turned to Rebecca. "Perhaps you'll help me."

"So we take matters into our own hands," Peter announced when he had seen the body. "We dig a grave or we make a fire. In this ground it's going to take a week to dig and I don't even know if there's a pick and shovel. Best we start collecting wood right away. I hope you understand, Paul." The two worked for an hour, first collecting firewood that was stacked behind the cabin then, to augment the pile, they used old fence posts and other timber. Finally they took the wooden door off its hinges and laid the body on it, having first examined it.

"I'm bound to be asked questions," Peter said. "Just so long as I can say that we saw nothing suspicious. No blood, no bullet holes, no knife wounds."

Annie had found food for the dogs and made sure the horses had hay and water. She seemed to gain comfort from the animals. Finally the two men carried Jim's body on his crude wooden door and laid it on the funeral pyre. It was covered by a blanket to conceal the indignity of death. A match was applied and the four of them stood back. The sun was plunging earthward as the fire took hold.

"Please, Paul," said Annie, holding one of the dogs. "There must be a prayer. I'm sure you know what to say."

"Yes," he said, "I'll try." In wartime he had performed this duty, committing a sailor's body to the deep. The words would surely be the same. He took off his hat and looked down at the ground. Rebecca stood beside him.

"The life of man is short and full of sorrows. He brings nothing into the world and takes nothing out." He paused. "The Lord is my shepherd, I shall not want. He makes me lie down in a green pasture. He leads me beside the waters of comfort."

The fire crackled and Paul hesitated, searching his memory. Annie, he thought, you are as beautiful as they said. She was looking at him trustingly. Rebecca, brought up in a rectory, had been closer to the realities of life and death and had heard these words many times.

"Yes, even if I must walk through the valley of the shadow of death, I need fear no evil because… because you Sir, are with me all my life. You have given me…" he extemporised, "sheepdogs and horses to help me." There was a catch in his voice. "You have anointed my head with oil, like a king or a queen, and my cup shall be full of beautiful clear water."

He paused, then struggled on. "God's mercy and kindness will follow me all the days of my life and I shall dwell in the house of the Lord forever." He extemporised again. "This is the house of the Lord. We are in it now." One of the horses thrust its head upwards and let out an almost human sound. Paul finished with the words, "It has pleased Almighty God to take the soul of his servant, Jim, Jim who? Do you happen to know?"

"Jim Shankland," Peter answered.

"Thank you. We do therefore commit his body to the fire. Ashes to ashes, dust to dust, in sure and certain hope of life to come…"

"That's beautiful," Annie said. "'Sure and certain hope'."

Paul turned to the others. "That's the best I can do."

Tears were on Annie's cheeks. "Jim did a lot of good things," she said, "despite his being so lonely. He sheared his sheep and the fleece was made into blankets and sweaters for people in cold places. I hope he knew what it was to be in love. There must have been poor people in the world who were warmed at night. Perhaps they prayed for him and thanked God and thanked Jim. He was the shepherd of his flock."

That was the best speech, Paul thought to himself, that I have ever heard.

For a few moments no one spoke. The only sounds were from the fire, the occasional swish of the horses' tails, the gentle questioning sounds made by the dogs, and the distant chatter of wild parrots.

"We must decide what to do," Peter said finally. "I was thinking that tomorrow I could ride the stronger of the two horses back to the Springs and lead the other. Annie can drive the jeep. Paul and Rebecca, perhaps you'll take the chickens with their legs tied. I saw a metal box in the corner, one of those wartime ammunition boxes. I'll give it to the police at Meekathara."

"There may be relatives in England," Rebecca suggested. "If there are, they may ask for the ashes. Perhaps we can put them in something..."

"Yes, and where the sheep are concerned," Peter announced, "the best we can do is to find out how many he sheared last year, and report that they're in good condition as far as we can see. A property like this should carry three to five thousand. The water mills seem to be working. I can fly over and keep an eye on things until the lawyers get themselves sorted out."

The four of them spent the night under the eucalyptus trees. They had water from the pump, a supply of food and some blankets Peter kept in his jeep, and they had each other and the dogs for company. Peter explained that if they had been seriously in need of food they could have taken a young sheep—a wether—slaughtered it and cooked the meat. To comply with unwritten law they would hang the skin on the fence to inform the authorities that needy travellers had passed that way.

In the morning Paul roused himself before dawn. He began by lighting a small fire for boiling water and cooking the eggs that Jim's chickens had laid during the night. Next he swept the warm ashes from the cremation pyre and placed them in a dark green tin that bore the familiar name of Harrods. A long way, he thought, from the bustle of Knightsbridge in the heart of London.

As the sun came up he woke the others and made tea with leaves that he found in the cabin. In an hour, the four of them had packed Jim's belongings and set out for Carrington Springs, fifty miles distant. Peter led the way, riding one horse and leading the other, followed by the dogs. Annie drove the jeep and Paul came a few minutes behind in his rented car. Jim's possessions, pathetic by Western standards, consisted of a few tools, a couple of saucepans, some provisions and personal articles. We bring nothing into the world, Paul thought, and we take nothing out.

Whatever impressions had been left on Paul's mind from the evening before, he was unprepared for what they encountered after they had travelled for an hour. A small, twelve-seater bus, advertising itself as 'Holiday Tours', was parked at the roadside. Its passengers, dressed unsuitably in dark clothes, were gathered round Peter, who seemed to tower above them astride the larger of Jim's horses. It occurred to Paul that these white-faced, expressionless Orientals had probably never seen a horse before. A few moments' conversation revealed that they were to become tour guides and were being instructed in their craft. Soon they would be bringing busloads of tourists to witness the emptiness and backwardness of Australia. The leader of the group had seen Peter approach and seized the opportunity to reveal to his students what the outback was really like—men on horses, dogs resentful at having their space invaded, the dust and the flies. Paul stopped the car and got out. If they had wanted the old Australia, he thought, they could have done worse than to have been present the night before. They would have witnessed Jim in his little hut, the windmill, the gray and pink parrots. Now here was Peter presenting the new Australia, articulate and knowledgeable, speaking of the fragility of the environment, the lack of underground water and the fact that wildflowers were protected by law and were not to be picked by tourists. He told of how some horses brought from Mexico for an equestrian event had carried their native grass seeds with them, whether in their hairs or their digestive systems, and shortly thereafter distinctively Mexican flora began to appear in the paddocks where they had grazed. Kangaroos, he explained, the original fauna of Australia, were soft-padded, but horses, cattle, sheep, even pigs, were hoofed animals which did damage to the grass and hence to the soil.

"We say that Australia has prospered on the backs of the sheep, but a more realistic assessment is that the sheep are in process of destroying the land. So now we look at what is under the surface, the minerals. We have iron mines in the Kimberleys that have no equal in the world."

Paul didn't hear the rest of it. Peter was inviting his new-found friends to Carrington Springs, an off-the-cuff, spur-of-the-moment invitation which Paul realised was standard in the outback. Until then, Peter had probably thought of Asians as inward-looking, consumed by their own problems, but now he was persuading them to cover themselves with Australian blankets and eat mutton. The Far East was an obvious market for Australian produce, if only they'd learn to dress warmly and give up bean sprouts in favour of lamb chops.

Carrington Springs was all that Paul and Rebecca could have imagined. Eucalyptus trees, planted years before, surrounded the low buildings. The main house stood by itself amid gardens of tropical flowers, a water tank dominated the shearing sheds and workshops. Horses stood quietly in a paddock, which was enclosed by a white fence. There was a small shop with a post office, a rest house where travellers could find a bed, bath and basic food. The aircraft, a six-seater, stood at the end of the landing field at one end of which a familiar sausage-shaped windsock stirred in the light breeze. There were birds everywhere, sheep dogs and a pet camel. All this, Paul realised, in the hands of the young couple who had slept under the stars the night before.

Paul took the dark-green Harrods tin and carried it into the house. For a long moment he stood at attention, thinking of Jim, whom he had never known, then placed it on the hall table.

"I'm sorry I had to meet you the way I did," Paul said. "But, my wife and I and these good people who are your neighbours, we did what we could for your earthly body. You also had our tears. Beyond that we could give you no more."

Later in their lives, Paul and Rebecca invented a dinner game, the object of which was to recall those occasions which had been most memorable and, if possible, repeat exactly what had been said. The dinner they shared that evening with Peter and Annie was the one they best remembered. It was not so much the food or the Australian wine, but the memories of childhood, the harsh experience of wartime, the strange events that had brought them together round that well-used table.

"As a child," Annie said to Paul, "you were so punctilious, so serious and difficult to talk to. As though the responsibilities of the world were yours to carry alone.

"It was said that Judge Henriques was a great man," Annie continued, "and that your mother had been to every country in the world. I knew that a deep gulf lay between us because we were poor, the object of mockery, and we did not go to church because my parents could scarcely speak English. I could not imagine what it would be like to live in a big house and not have to share my bedroom and my bed. I wanted to go swimming with you, perhaps to wash myself. I was in love with you in a childish way." She paused and the others were silent. Paul's father had once told him, "Truly great conversationalists know when to say nothing."

"So, I had my wish. My brother and I were taken from our family and brought here to Australia. It was called a 'dismal shore' because it had hurt so many people in the past. But we were lucky, and we shall be eternally grateful to those who helped us."

"You speak so beautifully," Rebecca said. "But tell me, do you think my husband has changed over the years? Has the war served him well or badly?"

Annie eyed Paul across the table. "He clings to his secrets. You will not be truly married until you find out what they are."

Peter waved a hand. "Annie sees things," he said. "She is a true Romany. I think she lives in a world different from ours."

"I can't help it. My grandmother was said to have been the same." Annie looked again at Paul. "He also sees things that are hidden from others. Rebecca must pray for the day when he abandons the sea."

Late that night, after they had retired, Rebecca whispered, "Nothing could have prepared me for these past few days. On the very day that your father was to have been buried in a country churchyard at the other side of the world, you gave Christian burial to a man you had never met. A few days earlier, your father appeared to you on the waters of the great Southern Ocean. He bade you goodbye and gave you courage for the present and hope for the future. Then you thanked God for sheepdogs and horses. Even God Himself must have been surprised.

"And here we are, half a world away from the English village of our childhood, and a young woman who has not seen you in years seems to be telling you that all is not plain sailing. I don't think I understand. You, abandon the sea? What did she mean by 'seeing'? Seeing what?"

There, in the outback of Australia, Paul was at a loss to respond.

Epilogue

For five days *Marquess* struggled to remain afloat but finally two ocean tugs appeared from the west. They were businesslike, noisy, and festooned with fenders a yard thick. They rose and fell on the swell and went about picking up the tow with practiced efficiency. The first tug grappled the anchor on the starboard side and Paul controlled the brake, letting out the anchor cable link by link, while the tug hauled it in with its huge midships capstan. The tug attached it to its own towing line, which was a steel wire rope twelve inches in circumference. The port anchor was more difficult, but eventually it too was secured and ready for the tugs to edge forward. Paul eased out the cables on their brakes until *Marquess* was connected on its own anchor cables with the addition of the towing cables supplied by the tugs. It was a superlative piece of seamanship by the tug skippers, and now it fell to them to increase their speed with infinite caution so as not to make a sudden jerk or bring the tow to the surface 'bar taut'. Paul described the operation at length in the log, and drew diagrams. Even the navy, he thought, with hundreds of men on the upper decks, could not have taken a battleship in tow as efficiently as that.

Once under tow, there was little more Paul could do. He went to his cabin and stood looking at his picture of Rebecca taken in Broxbourne. She had been younger then. In these past few days he had wondered if he would see her again. Even under tow, things could go devastatingly wrong. But he was determined to stay aboard *Marquess* until she sank or was secured alongside in Boston. At 8:00 pm, 2000 hours, he switched on the radiotelephone and spoke with Boston. He learned that *Marquess* would be met by a salvage vessel somewhere off Cape Cod and the water could then be pumped out before the harbour tugs took over. The important thing was not to let her sink in the harbour itself.

Later that day a coastguard helicopter flew over and dropped supplies on the after deck. There was food, drinking water and a spare battery for the radiotelephone. It was generous and typically American and he unwrapped the food carefully. There was something called Boston clam chowder and there was apple pie. He had no means of heating them, so he ate them cold.

Finally, on a dark autumn evening, *Marquess*, having had hundreds of tons of sea water pumped from her hold and engine room, was nudged alongside the jetty in Boston from where she would be taken into dry dock the following day. Her holds would be cleared of cargo and the damage assessed. Experts would examine the ship, notebooks in hand, and when the unloading process had finished, *Marquess* would be an empty shell.

Paul was on the starboard wing of the bridge as they came alongside. The pungent odours of the great city took him almost by surprise. He watched the men secure the ship with head and stern ropes, breast ropes and a forespring against the current of the river. Suddenly he realised that he was tired, bearded and in need of a bath. There were groups of people on the jetty only a few yards away. He saw photographers and among them he recognised the tall figure of Sir James Currie, the shipping company's managing director; next to him a woman in a dark blue coat and hat. He looked again in the half darkness of the September evening and for a moment he couldn't speak, couldn't move. It was Rebecca. She must have flown out from England on the invitation of Sir James. She ran up the gangway and then three more decks to the bridge, and was beside him in moments.

"Oh God," she said, "I thought the day would never come. You're wearing your scarf," she added, trying to remain composed.

"I've had it on for a week."

Having waited a few minutes, Sir James joined them on the bridge.

"Well done, Paul. Thank you for bringing my ship safely home."

"The tugs did an excellent job, sir," Paul replied. "Perhaps tomorrow I can locate them and thank the skippers. Even better if you could say something yourself."

"Very well, but in the meantime I want you to fill out the ship's log to the moment you came alongside, then turn it over to me. Oh yes, by the way, I have two harbour police who'll be here overnight. My suggestion is that your wife helps you to pack, then we'll go to the hotel together. That sound alright?"

"One thing," Paul said. "Our passengers and crew left all their kit in their cabins. In effect, they abandoned ship. I was wondering how we get their belongings back to them."

"If there's anything I can do," said Rebecca, "specially where women passengers are concerned."

"That's very kind of you, but I'm flying out some of our employees from the London office. I think we'll be alright. It's a big job to strip a ship before going into dry dock.

"But I must warn you," Sir James went on, turning to Paul, "you are a bit of a celebrity. A newspaper correspondent snapped a photograph from a helicopter a few days ago and created a sensation. Your photograph was on the front page of every newspaper in the country. You'll see the pictures and read what they say. 'The lone Captain, not forty years of age, who had refused to abandon the ship that had been entrusted to his care, keeping a lonely watch on his windswept bridge.' A former admiral spoke of it in the House of Commons, his words applauded by all sides."

Later that evening, Sir James joined Rebecca and Paul for a quiet meal in the hotel's main dining room. The media commotion had subsided and Paul had handled their questions as best he could.

"I feel as though I am intruding on a very private occasion," said Sir James after the first toast of the evening, "but I wanted you to hear what I have to say. I'm offering Paul an office next to mine with the title of deputy director."

Rebecca caught her breath and clasped her hands.

"In effect you will be Senior Captain of the fleet," he went on, "and it takes effect as soon as you're ready." He turned to Rebecca. "We are building two cruise liners and a lot of details have yet to be decided." Then to both of them, "This is going to be an important job, and I know you can do it. I offer you my hearty congratulations."

"Thank you," replied Paul without hesitation, "and of course, I accept."

"Darling," said Rebecca with obvious relief, reaching out to Paul.

"There is one more thing," Sir James went on. "I realised only this afternoon that *Marquess* has one of those old fashioned mahogany binnacles to house the magnetic compass. Well, I want it taken out and installed in the main foyer of our London office. There's something solid and comforting about it. And you must have leaned on that binnacle many times during your ordeal."

"I did; I think that's an excellent idea. It would send a message to visitors: we know where we're going."

"On a sea turtle's back, perhaps?" said Rebecca with a mischievous smile. Then she realised that Sir James might not understand. "There were some silver heirlooms passed down to Paul when his father died. Paul was at sea, so I packed them away. They bore the mark of a turtle and I only recently learned its significance." She looked at Paul. "Will you tell Sir James?"

"It is a strange story," Paul said quietly.

"Let's hear it," said Sir James.

"When I was a child, my father told me about a seafaring ancestor who was wrecked in the Indian Ocean; it must have been four hundred years ago. My best guess it was near Goa. Jaime Henriques. He was the sole survivor; probably in the spice trade. Legend has it that he was rescued by a giant sea turtle. He climbed on its back and was carried to a sandy beach where he was found. He subsequently adopted the sea turtle as his family emblem."

"Was that the secret Annie referred to?" Rebecca asked.

"It must have been. Yes. Of course," he added, "sea turtles have been credited with other rescues."

"Indeed they have," said Sir James, "and you should know that there is one well-documented story at the heart of our own company. I often wonder whether it's believable in the modern world."

"Oh, do tell us more," said Rebecca.

"It happened shortly before the First World War, long before I joined the firm. One of our ships was outbound to Calcutta. A passenger, rather too well refreshed, made his way out of the bar and somehow managed to fall into the Indian Ocean. He regurgitated a lot of seawater and whisky and watched the ship's transom disappearing toward the horizon. It seems he was not a devout man as the world judges these things, but he felt that the occasion demanded that he address his hitherto somewhat neglected Creator. 'Sir', he said, 'as you know I am a betting man, and I am prepared to offer You a thousand pounds if You will get me out of this damn mess.' In those days a thousand pounds would have bought a very decent house. But it was at this point," continued Sir James, "that a huge sea turtle came up from the depths and the man clambered on its back. He was picked up half an hour later by the ship, which had turned back to find him. He was duly hauled on deck by sailors who confessed they had never seen anything quite like it, or words to that effect. Nearby, a young woman passenger watched from the ship's rail and was touched by the sight of the lumbering sea turtle, its duty done, swimming down into the clear water of the Indian Ocean. She was an artist.

"God cannot have been displeased with His wager. As soon as the passenger was back aboard he ordered a cheque to be brought from the purser's office and at the purser's suggestion he made it out in the amount of one-thousand pounds, payable to the 'Distressed Seaman's Benevolent Society', and in brackets, 'God'. At this point the young lady took the pen from his fingers and drew a sketch on the face of the cheque showing the turtle with the man on its back. In course of time it was honoured by Barclays Bank and subsequently claimed by head office, which arranged for it to be enlarged and touched up a bit. It hung in the entrance hall of the old London office and caught the eye of every visitor. As a piece of art it was not remarkable, but visitors, when told the story, always looked at it for long moments. Americans wanted to know what the man had been drinking in the bar; devout Catholics crossed themselves; ladies enquired whether the marital status of the two persons had been affected by the events described; visitors from India commented favourably and at length on the beneficial karma of the sea turtle."

Sir James paused for a sip of wine. "When people go into the head office of one of the world's great steamship companies, they expect to see magnificent pictures of ships—the conquest of the sea, that's what they think, and indeed the conquest of the whole world by the perseverance and skill of mankind. Yes, sun shining, calm seas—in those days people spoke of an empire over which the sun never set, and it was our ships that held it all together. And then people would come to our head office and see a picture—crudely drawn on a cancelled cheque—of a forlorn drunkard on the back of a sea turtle. It made them hesitate and ask questions.

"After we were bombed in the war, the picture was found in the rubble. I still have it and I'll get it cleaned up and put in a new frame."

"Do you suppose I could have it in my office?" Paul asked.

"Why not? I remember Jonathan Palliser telling me you were the luckiest man he'd ever met. I believe he was right. You seem to have lived your entire life on the sea turtle's back."

Rebecca reached over and took Paul's hand. "But now it has brought him ashore," she said, "I shall do my best to keep him here."

fin